# Spinning Jenny

Dale Smith

Obverse Books
info@obversebooks.co.uk
www.obversebooks.co.uk
Cover Art by Lawrence Burton
Cover Design by Cody Schell
First published November 2017

Copyright © 2017 Dale Smith
Faction Paradox © Lawrence Miles

The moral rights of the authors have been asserted.

All characters in this book are fictional. Any resemblance to persons, living or dead, is wholly co-incidental.

All rights reserved. No part of this publication may be reproduced, stored in a retrieval system, or in any form or by any means, without the prior permission in writing of the publisher, nor be otherwise circulated in any form of binding, cover or e-book other than which it is published and without a similar condition including this condition being imposed on the subsequent publisher.

Printed in Great Britain by TJ International Ltd, Padstow, Cornwall

For Charlie and Zac

Number _40_ of One Hundred
Anniversary Edition Copies

# 1. January 1854, Strines

The world was barely there anymore. With a squint, James could just read the sign on the other side of the tracks, but moments later it too had vanished. Even as he stamped his feet to warm them, his footprints disappeared beneath him. The snow was inches thick on the ground, and the air choked with it. He couldn't see more than a few feet down the track in either direction, but in this weather it was almost certain there would be nothing coming. One by one, the lines into and out of Manchester had closed. The Sheffield line was apparently still running, but only a fool would risk it tonight.

He didn't want to take his hands out of his pockets to look at his watch.

He would give it another five minutes.

The station had no lights, and the waiting room was closed and locked.

But what little James could see was ghostlit by echoes of light colliding with the blizzard. Everything seemed cold and blue-tinged. His feet had stopped tingling some moments previously, and only now did he consider that this might not be a blessing.

He wondered briefly about the horse and trap he had left at the foot of the hill. Hopefully if one or the other looked close to freezing solid, Joe at Whitecroft Farm would take them in to thaw. He wondered if there was even anything left of the world save the few scant feet of snow and station he could just make it. If it wasn't for the money, he would have gladly gone to find out.

It was a few moments before he noticed. It was only the echo of the whistle that made him realise the engine noise had been steadily building for some time. In a burst of heat and steam, the train was in front of him. The brakes screeched a little as friction ate into the ice forming on the rails, and the train slid a little further than was comfortable into the station. James could just make out the fireman peering back to check that the carriages had kept their grip, and then he disappeared again. James envied him the heat of the furnace.

James wondered if he should indicate somehow that he wasn't boarding the train, and then he wondered if anybody would alight at all. What would he do if the steam billowed again and the train moved away with him still alone at the station? Money or not, surely he would have the good sense to go home? Perhaps he would wait just a few moments more.

"Mr Braddock?"

He hardly heard the voice over the grumbling of the engine. But a carriage door swung open, and through a final blast of steam he saw an elderly lady looking down at him. James took a couple of steps forwards to offer a hand, but found that his legs had frozen as he waited. She didn't notice his discomfort, stepping easily down from the carriage and moving steadily towards the path down to the village. James ended up steadying himself on the door, his muscles cracking and creaking like ice slowly melting.

"My bags are in the carriage, if you don't mind?" the lady said.

And they were: three large cases that he would have struggled to carry on a temperate afternoon when the path down to his trap wasn't slick with ice and snow. He turned to say something, but the lady in black had already disappeared into the snow. James had an aunt who was seventy and seemed to be made from vinegar and brown paper: the old woman from the train looked even older than dear Aunt Sarah, but she moved with a speed and a poise that many a young lady would be envious of. He only hope he could keep pace without losing his dignity on the icy slope.

James heard the fireman tut loudly, and did his best to quickly pull the heavy bags down onto the platform. He thought again of the money, and dragged them over to the gate as best he could.

Behind him, the train hissed and spat and disappeared into the snow again.

James negotiated down the cobbles, using the suitcases as ballast to stop him slipping over when he needed. Even if it hadn't been blowing a blizzard in his eyes, it would have been all but impossible to see his charge: the old woman was dressed in a black-lace evening dress that suggested she might be in mourning for the passing of the last century, and her skin barely had enough colour in to distinguish it from her hair. The road to the village doubled back under the railway line, and as soon as the old woman passed under the archway she might as well have been invisible.

James rolled his shoulders and hefted her cases back under his arms.

The moment the darkness had him, she hissed in his ear:

"Did anybody else leave the train?"

He gave a little cry and dropped her bags: he could hear them skittle and slide down the cobbles. He made to follow them, but she grabbed his arm and tugged him close to her lips.

"Quickly," she hissed sharply.

James tried to think.

"I don't think ...' but the woman frowned, and he corrected himself. "No, no-one."

She didn't look back, but gave a slight sigh, disappointed by his lack of certainty. She moved into the light and down the icy slope with a sure-footedness that surprised him, and again James found himself hurrying to catch up, rescuing her bags from the frozen ground as he stumbled.

"Mrs Howkins —" he called after her.

He wanted to sound bright and capable, but he could hear the ragged edge as the cold and the pace took his breath. She was already at the foot of the cobbled hill, absently fussing the waiting horse. Her eyes followed the road as it curved around the number one reservoir, over the gas bridge and then faded into a flurry of snow and ice. She turned to the iron gate in the shadow of the trees beside her. James saw that she was pulling at the collar of her dress. Buttons and hooks popped and pulled, and even before he had reached the foot of the hill her black dress was hanging open.

"Your room is only a moment away," James said hurriedly. "You can have privacy there."

Mrs Howkins ignored him. With a dismissive shrug, her dress slid to the ground, the hard black against the cold white earth quickly fading away. Underneath, she wore what looked like a military uniform, but one that was dyed black. He could see with the dress gone that her frame was lithe and stocky, a million miles from the dry-stick gauntness of his Aunt Sarah. It suited her clothes: it was a soldier's body.

"Put the bags on the trap as quick as you can," she ordered, already striding towards the gate. "You can keep them and their contents: I won't be joining you. And don't worry: I hired you only as a distraction. The people following won't shoot once they realise I am not with you."

"Shoot?"

"Leave," Mrs Howkins ordered softly. "Now, and at speed."

James decided not to argue.

James pushed Mrs Howkins' bags roughly onto the back of the trap before hauling himself up into the seat. The horse was a little skittish, perhaps feeling his nerves through the reins, and her hooves slipped a little as he moved her off. He looked at the trees that lined the curving road and tried to spy the assassins with rifles hidden within. But all he could see was snow. As he glanced back, he thought that perhaps he saw a dark figure float gracefully over the works' iron gate, but then it was lost in a swirl of white. He turned his eyes to the road and urged the horse on.

He knew that the moment he was back in front of the fire, the patrons of his pub would be badgering him. They wouldn't be happy with half a story. But that was their lookout – James would be quite happy to be ignorant and warm, and to live his life never knowing what happened to Mrs Howkins. And on top of the extra money she had promised if he came to collect her, he also wouldn't have any of the trouble of having a guest under his roof. No breakfasts to cook, no sheets to clean, no …

The room had not been paid for yet.

As the horse trotted on, James quickly went through the suitcases next to him – she had said he could keep them, so there was no crime there. There was nothing in them that would cover the price Mrs Howkins had promised for the room and the inconvenience. James had been tricked. Worse, James had been cheated. He couldn't swear that all his toes would survive the night, and he had not a shilling to show for it.

The horse crossed over the gas bridge and stopped, the river raging beneath it. The road ahead forked up out of the valley and home to the pub, or to the right and into the Print Works. The gate that Mrs Howkins had scaled led to the path between reservoirs numbers one and two, but she must have been intending to creep through to the works unnoticed. If he left the trap here, James could probably catch her before the horse even started to notice the chill.

Probably …

James cursed quietly under his breath, and tied the reins to his seat. He slipped and fell hard on his knees as he jumped down, but that only made him more determined to collect what he was owed. He pulled himself back up, and sank his feet ankle deep into the snow. The works buildings were all whitewashed angles, hiding amongst the heaviest flakes. They lined up against the shore of the lake, but faded in and out as the storm raged: he thought he could recognise the squat shape of the gasometer, and then rising up from it one of the two great chimneys, still pumping out smoke since it would cost too much to let them go cold. He took a few tentative steps through the snow, and when he glanced back, he could already see nothing of the horse.

He hesitated, but decided to press on.

As he turned to move, he found a rifle in his belly.

The gun pinned him frozen for an age. He couldn't take his eyes from it, couldn't even look up to see who had it pressed against his gut. It didn't waver, didn't shake so much as a hair's breadth.

"She with the horse?" the gunman hissed.

James looked. The gunman was a moon-faced girl, dressed in the uniform of a British Army sergeant. Her hair was so black as to be invisible, save for the flecks of melting snow, and James would have guessed that she was his age, or maybe a touch younger. She was looking over his shoulder expectantly, and then tutted softly to herself when she realised she couldn't be heard over the wind.

"Is she with the horse, Thompson?" she shouted again.

When she shouted, the air stayed clear. Not a breath of steam left her mouth.

"No," came a distant reply.

The girl clicked her tongue in annoyance.

"Where did she go?" she snapped, the rifle pressing just a touch harder into James' stomach. "How long?"

"She changed her mind," James heard himself answer. "She sent me away as soon as she got off the train."

"So where are you going?"

"She didn't pay me," he admitted reluctantly.

Her eyes squinted as she considered him. A second passed, and then she swore softly under her breath.

"Where's the Captain?" she shouted.

James heard a barely disguised moan.

"Come on, Sarge!" somebody complained in the darkness. "How about this once we do something spontaneous?"

"Where's the Captain?" the girl snapped sharply. It wasn't just annoyance in her voice: there was an edge of real panic there, too. "We need new orders. We –"

The recoil of a pistol echoed through the air.

All heads turned to the print works.

It came from inside.

## 2. January 1854, Strines

Elizabeth jumped down from the gate and landed with little more noise than a leaf on the path between reservoirs numbers one and two, the tip of her nose just brushing the snow. There were trees at this end of the path, and under their branches she was just another shadow in the snow. She closed her eyes for a moment. She could feel the pressure in the air. Her head ached with it, her stomach shrivelled. It had started. They were coming … they were close. She clicked her tongue impatiently, and raised her head to look around her.

So far, so good. The wind was starting to pick up, and the ice covering the two reservoirs was beginning to creak and strain. Other than that, it was quiet. Bill stood on the path ahead, looking down at her with a look of wry amusement on his face. He was wearing his mustard blazer, from that summer at Alderley Edge. There were no soldiers in the trees, and no sign of any hiding in the old weaving sheds either. Perhaps the Major didn't have the numbers he'd had when he'd chased her to ground in Musselburgh, or perhaps her charms were working and her luck was holding.

Elizabeth eased up into a crouch, a good quarter inch of snow falling from her back as she shifted. Soon the whole world would be nothing but snow, and her just a solitary black dot slowly fading in it. And Bill, of course, a streak of hot mustard in the cold. She had always loved that blazer. They had eaten an impromptu picnic perched on the Edge, and as the evening had turned chill he had quietly slipped it over her shoulders to keep her warm. Now he didn't even offer a hand to help her up. He stood maddeningly out of reach, his bad eye gazing west as the other twinkled at her. She wanted to speak to him, but couldn't be certain the Major didn't have men within earshot.

She took a breath and felt the chill in her lungs.

There was something there in the darkness, just close to Bill's foot. A bump in the snow, a dark stain, a buried feather. She moved over, her eyes still searching out redcoats in the darkness. Brushing the snow aside, she found the corpse of a small blackbird. There was a wound on its shoulder that suggested a desperate raptor had taken a swipe at it, but from the condition Elizabeth guessed that it was actually the cold that had killed it.

The wings were still firmly attached, and its two dead eyes glistened with jelly. It would do: Elizabeth pulled a pouch of herbs from her overcoat pocket and stuffed them into a pouch she tore in the bird's belly. With her thumbnail, she popped one of the eyes from its socket and let it roll into the palm of her hand. She glanced up at Bill, but he gave no indication of looking away.

"Stubborn old goat," she whispered.

It was an empty insult: he wasn't a day over twenty-seven and a half, whereas Elizabeth was only a few weeks shy of sixty-four. But it made her feel better about what she was about to do: she tossed the severed eye into her mouth and swallowed it whole. She didn't look at Bill. Then she whispered a prayer as quietly as she could, and threw the bird up into the air. Its feathers quivered in the growing wind, and then it spread them wide and took wing.

Elizabeth saw the snowy ground fall away from her, felt the beating of the bird's ragged wings. She flew higher and higher, the snow eddying with every beat of her wings. It tried to hide the world from the bird's one good eye, but Elizabeth still managed to piece together a pretty decent picture of the lay of the land. The bird could see no-one except her in the area around the old mill buildings, but Braddock was driving his trap along the road just the other side of reservoir number one, and a small knot of soldiers were advancing on him through the fields on his far side. The snow was too thick for the bird's one good eye to spot the Major amongst them, but Elizabeth guessed he wasn't there: she could see another cluster of red jackets behind the old works, and assumed that Webber would want to be leading the charge.

She pushed the dead bird up higher, until she could see past the old works and out across the valley. The sky was thick with snow now, and the clouds rumbled against each other ominously. She could just make out the light from the Sportsman's Arms up on the lip of the Goyt Valley, but that was the only sign there was of the village. Over on the opposite ridge, the darkness grew so thick that it seemed all light was being pulled into some bottomless pit. Just looking at it made her head ache worse. That was where the world would tear, and the Loa invade.

She didn't have long.

She pulled the bird down lower until she had the disconcerting visual echo of seeing herself through its eyes, then sent it swooping ahead. Bill pulled himself slowly to his feet and brushed down his knees in that way he always did. His cloth cap was a little crooked, and even now Elizabeth felt the urge to reach up and straighten it. Of course he knew what she was thinking, and gave her a little shrug of apology. He didn't move his hat, of course. He never had. He was, even now, a most infuriating man: it made her want to cry, and so she pushed on quickly between the reservoirs.

Her flying spy's one good eye kept track of the soldiers hiding behind the old mill, and she slipped round the other side. She kept in close to the rough stone of the building, feeling its ice chill even through her thick overcoat. The roar of the river, swollen with the snowfall, was in her ears: it fled from the mills as if it knew what was coming, and wanted to be far away when it arrived. The two water wheels clanked and turned with an alarming speed: Elizabeth half expected them to be torn from their housings and swept away, except that she could remember the women in the mill loading the wheels with the printed cloth, letting the river scrub the excess dye for them. The dye used to make anyone who bathed in the river water turn bright yellow, until they were banned from using that particular dye. No, those wheels would survive tonight and the next eighty years or so, all things being equal.

That thought made it impossible not to look across the river. It was empty ground now, nothing but stones and grazing for Whitecroft's cattle. But when the works outgrew its current home, it would spread across there. She could see the main floor rising up out of the snow, as if it had been hibernating there. The outbuildings loomed out of the snowstorm. And there was the gas room, where they made their own gas to power the machines and the lights hidden deep inside. She could smell burning hair, and it was all she could do to stop herself lurching forwards.

Bill was there in front of her. He tried to pull her away, but of course he couldn't touch her. He just held out his arms impotently, fingers just moments away. The ground shook and the sky trembled. This wasn't just an old woman's ghosts coming back to haunt her: reality was fraying. The Loa were breaking through, tearing the fabric of the world with their many teeth.

"I have to go," Elizabeth told Bill. She didn't know why.

He, of course, said nothing.

Lightning split the air and the wind howled.

She turned her attention back to the bird in the sky, but the growing wind was sending it spinning and twirling, perhaps in an echo of the moment it had first died. She could feel its attention being pulled away to the darkness up on the hillside as a greater power started to bleed through there. She would only keep hold of it for a few minutes more: best make the most of them. Flexing her will, she sent it up over the roof of the old works: the soldiers were there fretting and trembling, but she could see one blistering redcoat trying to bark them back into order.

Webber.

Even he could tell that something was starting to happen: he snarled his men into two groups that started to circle the building. It wouldn't take them long – it was little more than a shed with a handful of presses crammed inside. Bill stood out in the snow, looking left and right and then pointedly at her. She tutted at him – even now, she hated being hurried by anyone. Then she folded her arms across her chest and pushed back on her heels. The window behind her seemed to open wider, and then swallowed her whole. She disappeared inside its darkness.

Lightning crashed again.

It was too dark to see, but she could feel that the building was swelling around her. It was already twice the size it had any right to be, and some corners were starting to twist and tumble down into infinity. The dead bird followed her through the window, and could already rise up three times Elizabeth's height without troubling the rafters. It would only get worse as the night progressed: the floor trembled again, and she started to feel an otherworldly heat rising up through her feet.

She blinked her eyes, and spotted Bill across the room.

Of course he was here too.

There was another boom of thunder, and Elizabeth thought she heard the crackle of the lightning earthing itself in the ground. Then she heard the howl of the dogs, part panicked and part excited. The bird could see nothing of them, but the room was so wide now that its edges disappeared in the gloom. She could only assume that they must be guard dogs left here to watch the building overnight. Or else the edges of the world had already started to crack, and other creatures were starting to find their way in.

No, there they were. Their lips were specked with froth as they worked themselves up into a state: four bull mastiffs, their beady eyes already hunting out the intruders. She felt their gaze land on her, and her old heart gave a little skip. She took two steps into the room, two steps closer to the snarling dogs. They were already starting to circle her, their sharp claws echoing on the cold stone floor. They were scared, but she was something familiar, something they could comfort themselves with. Blood running through their teeth would calm them on this strange, disquieting night.

They were still uncertain: she didn't cower or bolt as their prey usually did. Instead, Elizabeth did her best to fix each animal in turn with a calm, cold stare. On any other night, that alone might have been enough to convince them to leave her to her business. But tonight was different: lightning burned to the ground again, and the walls of the building shivered against the cold. One of the dogs couldn't stand it any more, and it threw itself jaws agape at the intruder.

Elizabeth turned calmly to face it.

Its teeth seemed like they could easily cut through flesh and bone and sever whatever limb was unlucky enough to be between them. The steam from its breath brushed gently against her face as it launched itself up for her throat. For a moment it flew through the air, the moonlight glinting on slaver-wet teeth. Then from nowhere a dark shape swept down from above and buried itself deep in the dogs throat, pushing down and deeper with such force that the animal found itself thrown backwards even as it choked to death on the stone floor.

Elizabeth had been losing her hold on the bird anyway.

Bill averted his good eye.

Elizabeth remembered him, on cold nights, stretched out in front of a coal fire with their dog Lady resting on his chest. Lady was a poodle of vicious disposition, and looking at these slavering mastiffs must have put him in mind of her. She wanted to apologise to him, but they were past any of that now. His good eye never rested on her with approval any more, and his every movement made it clear that the life she lived now was not the one he would have wished for her. It was not the one she would have wished for herself, come to that. Despite the forty years she spent travelling from bokor to mambo to make herself ready for this night. If she had any other choice, she would have made it by now.

Lightning flashed outside again, and the snow hit the warping building with the force of hammers. The guard dogs circled and snarled, but not one of them would take a step closer. For all their posturing, they had learned their lesson. Elizabeth found a relatively clear patch of the factory floor, and knelt on the cold stone. The floor of the old works was all ashlar stone, reclaimed from mills and water wheels up and down the valley. As she brushed her fingers against this slab, she could feel that it had been round a culvert where a water wheel had turned. The taint of industry ran through it: it would be the perfect altar. She drew a small bone-bladed knife from her hip and started scratching a pattern into the stone. She had a vague awareness of the presses surrounding her, ghosts of copper and steel uneasy in their idleness. Her knees twinged as they tried to remind her she was sixty-three, not twenty-three any more. Everything else was the pattern on the floor, and darkness beyond.

On the train from Manchester, she had worried at herself incessantly with the notion that she would forget the vevé. The complex web of interlocking cogs and pistons had been her every second thought for the last twenty years. It was every dream she ever had. But still the thought was there that she would forget it. That everything she had planned would fade like the name of the first boy she kissed. But now, as she scratched the last cog into place, she knew that it would never leave her: the vevé was exact, the very same as she had first seen glowing with white heat on the floor of the new works in ...

Well, that was where the strangeness started in, wasn't it?

The recoil of a pistol echoed through the air. The bullet sped in her direction, intended to throw up the dust at her feet and add an extra punctuation to the vevé. But Elizabeth just happened to have her eyes in the right place. She saw the bullet head straight and true, only to glance away as if hitting something solid as it came over the vevé. She didn't think the gunman had seen it, but she had. So it was accurate. It was beginning to work.

She glanced over at Bill.

"Not long, my love," she whispered.

"Mrs Howkins," a singsong voice languished. "Put down the knife. Time's come to surrender."

Major Webber of the British Army.

Elizabeth afforded him as much attention as she did the dogs. She drew a small packet from the soldiers' knapsack at her feet. She allowed herself a moment to look at the dull cardboard box and remember. A box of tin spoons she had bought from the Woolworths in Manchester for threepence. She could remember putting them into her bag and forgetting about them, carrying them into work the next morning. After the fire, they were one of the few things she still had with her that had been part of her old life. But they were the product of a factory, and therefore the heart of the ritual. She scattered the spoons across the vevé, discordant music filling the air as they fell.

But the box she quickly folded and slipped back in her pocket. If this didn't work, there would be time again to look with sadness at the production date stamped on the bottom.

January, 1931.

"I'll shoot you," Webber called again, his pistol unwavering. "You know I will."

Elizabeth pulled a small glass vial from her jacket pocket. The liquid inside was inky black, and had been mistaken for blood on more than one occasion. She threw the glass against the floor and watched it shatter, the viscous machine oil seeping into the vevé and the spoons. She could feel electricity in the air, and the heat of a fire that hadn't burned for forty years, and wouldn't for another eighty if you looked at things chronologically.

"Madam Jenny," Elizabeth cried. "I demand an audience."

Webber tensed again for a shot, but never took it. The dogs howled as one as the roof above their heads bowed, bubbling and blistering like Bakelite melting. The blizzard invaded the room as if the walls and roof were no longer strong enough to keep them out, white flakes flurrying against a black sky. The air and the snow were suddenly pulled upwards, and a sound like nightmares crying echoed through the night. Above them, the roof melted clean away to reveal a sky in a constant turmoil of purple and grey.

There were things up there in the sky. Shapes that you couldn't quite see with your eyes. Gigantic, monstrous things that tumbled and fought without an inkling of the destruction even a single drop of their blood might cause to the tiny worlds below them. Webber had to avert his eyes, but Elizabeth stared up into the heart of them. She could see them. She could see.

"This isn't ..." Webber cried behind her. "What are they?"

"Don't be afraid," Elizabeth answered with a cold smile. "I'm here to kill them."

# 3. January 1854, Strines

The print works was barely more than a shed packed with a handful of gleaming engines that pulled the calico in and out of the plates and then span it onto vast spools, ready to be transported elsewhere. Sergeant Brierly had led the party that reconnoitred the building while they made their preparations for Mrs Howkins' arrival. Now she paced cautiously across the stone flags, eyes wide and pistol drawn. It was ten minutes since they had crossed the threshold, and they still had seen no sign of a printing press. Her team stayed pressed together in an anxious knot: they had already lost two soldiers in the darkness, and each man worried that they might be next.

They lost their footing as the ground trembled beneath them.

Brierly heard stone grind against stone as the building warped again.

"Please," Braddock whimpered, not even getting back on his feet. "Just let me go home. I won't talk to anyone."

Brierly looked back the way they had come in. The corridor snaked and twisted, branching here and there seemingly at random. There was no way to tell which passage they had come from, even if she could be sure it would still lead back to the same places. They were in the bloodstream of some vast and angry animal now: their only hope was to let the pulse push them on to the heart. Her men were back on their feet: she motioned for two of them to get Braddock on his feet, and then pressed on.

There were a thousand thoughts in her head. Part of her was convinced that the shot they had all heard had come from Major Webber's pistol. It could have been fired accidentally, it could have been fired on purpose. It could have been fired by Webber himself, or by Howkins or any number of potential accomplices or innocents there only by happenstance. It could be a warning or a summons: there were so many things that the shot could have been, and no time left for debate.

Her orders had been clear: arrest Braddock, then regroup.

With orders, she didn't have to worry about debate.

The ground bucked again, and this time Brierly saw the walls roll in on her. The air was filled with the smell of cordite, and she knew that lightning had struck nearby. She tried to shout to her men, but found she had been deafened by the noise. Somebody grabbed onto her arm, and then suddenly they were falling away from her. Brierly held tight as gravity shifted and they both tumbled up towards the ceiling. The roof spiralled away from them, pulling up into a never-ending sinkhole. Then the world trembled again and they both landed hard against a cold stone wall still dancing with electricity.

Brierly had only a second to gather herself. As she stood again, she saw her companion hadn't been so lucky. He lay dead at her feet, his neck twisted at a sickening angle.

West. His name had been West.

"She's never been able to do anything like this before," one of her men breathed.

"We don't know that it's her," Brierly heard herself say.

Braddock was there, looking anxiously from one soldier to the next.

"Who?" he demanded. "Who?"

Nobody answered.

"Mrs Howkins?" he whispered.

The world trembled again.

"We have our orders," Brierly said coldly. "After me."

The corridor twisted and bucked like an angry snake. But she led them down it regardless. It was easier if she didn't have to decide any of this for herself. If she took the time to think, she might not survive.

James felt his skin tingle with electricity. The air pressed hard on him, as if he was grasped within its clenching fist. The soldiers all around looked ready to shoot at every shadow, and they had been trained for this kind of life. The worst danger he faced was making sure every stranger in the Sportsman paid for their drinks. His heart felt like it was tearing itself to pieces in his chest, and he had the overwhelming urge to run – though he could see nowhere to run to: the corridors had closed in around them, and now they were bent almost double as the Sergeant pushed them ever deeper into this strange and impossible hell.

With every step he felt his fear blossom. A dark bloom, it grew and grew.

"We need to go back," he heard himself whimper.

The Sergeant didn't even look at him.

"We need to find the Major."

They pressed on.

"We need a gris-gris," James heard one of the soldiers mutter. "You remember King Zena? None of her tricks worked on him."

"I remember she shot him," his companion replied. "That worked."

"Please," James said, placing a hand on the soldier. "You know what's going on here?"

The man barely caught his eye.

"Hoodoo," he said. "Keep moving."

The air rumbled ominously again. Dust trickled down as the stones of the walls shifted uneasily. James could just see the vague shape of the Sergeant pushing on ahead. Probably she would never know if he just turned and fled. He glanced behind him: the corridor spun round and round over itself, and then disappeared into the thickest darkness James had ever seen. If he ran, he would be on his own. But if he stayed, he would only move deeper. His muscles twitched, but he knew there was nothing he could do. He was going to die here. They all were.

"She's a witch," one of the soldiers said, possibly to James. His eyes darted here and there in the gloom. "She won't stop even if we catch her. She'll spit out the bullets one after the other. This is it."

"You think this is it?" another asked.

"This is it," the soldier repeated, as if pronouncing all their dooms.

"This is what?" James' voice was ragged with tension.

The soldier looked at him sadly.

"I'm sorry you got pulled into this," he said, and pulled a pistol from a holster at his hip. He held it out, grip first. James just looked at it. "It's the end of the world, so there's nowhere you'd be better off. But I'm sorry all the same."

"I – I can't take that," James stammered.

The soldier frowned at him.

"She's a witch," he growled, his eyes dark. "She sacrificed her own husband to the Loa for power, and we've chased her from one end of the world to the other trying to stop her learning how to drag them here for the rest of us. Now she knows. Here, now: this is it. You can't use it on her, you might want to use it on yourself."

James looked down at the gun.

"Can you feel that?" the Sergeant called from ahead. "I think there's something there."

The soldier snatched the pistol away, James forgotten, and hurried ahead.

James felt the cold and the dark draw close.

It was impossible not to see that they were getting close to the centre of it. Every voice in Brierly's head was screaming at her to not step any closer, but gravity was pulling her in. The walls and the ceiling pulled that way too, with no more new paths branching off. Everything led onwards into the darkness. As the walls crumbled and fell, the stones fell sideways as they too were sucked in. The air was filled with the bass rumble of thunder, coming so often now it sounded like the rhythmic beat of some gigantic heart.

Brierly could see the presses now: swollen and throbbing, they prowled the cavern like restless animals. Each had been cut, bleeding machine oil onto the broken ground. There was snow on the ground too, the roof having been torn clean away. Looking up felt like she was staring down into the pits of hell. The air swirled with snow and falling stars, and was stained a deep, deep purple. There were shapes moving up there, pulling the sky out of shape as they tumbled and turned. Brierly felt the overwhelming urge to vomit, and scream and scream her throat raw.

She had seen many strange things as they had dogged the footsteps of Mrs Howkins across the globe, and not all of them she could explain. And she had learned what Mrs Howkins had: that in the space behind the real world, the old African gods still lived. The Loa, ancient and capricious deities that would just as soon grant you a lifetime of madness and infirmity as they would the power to raise the dead or curse your enemies. They would ride the souls of the living, jumping from host to host in an instant and ... well, not all of it was incredible, she admitted. But the Major had always dismissed it as heathen superstition waiting for a rational explanation, and Brierly had always been happy to follow his lead.

Until now. Now it was easy to look up and believe that the Loa were real, that they had their fingers deep in the fabric of this universe and would fold it at their own whim. Because there they were, the old gods. The sky was thin, and they were tearing through it. And the world was tearing with it.

She heard dogs howl, and saw them close by in a circle. They too had their eyes fixed on the sky, but in the centre of their circle stood two figures. The uniformed man and the white-haired witch.

"She's here!" Brierly screamed above the tolling thunder. "Positions!"

What was left of her men didn't move.

"Now!" Brierly barked.

Even the dogs jumped.

"This is it," one of her men muttered. But he moved with the others.

It took only a moment for every weapon to be trained on Howkins. She didn't spare them a glance, just reached into her pockets as she focussed her attention on the monsters in the heavens. It occurred to Brierly that her orders had been vague on this one point: she was to stop Howkins, kill her if necessary. But how could she tell if it was necessary? Perhaps her death would end this strange magic, or was she the only one who could act to stop it? Already she could feel her resolve slipping as alternatives started to bounce around her head. This was no good: she needed definitives. She needed orders.

"Sir," she shouted to the Major. He didn't move. "What do I do?"

His mouth hung open, but he said nothing.

Howkins spun. There was something in her hands, and she threw it to the floor around her. The motion was enough for one of her men, and there was the crack of a rifle shot. The bullet barely even made it an inch out of the barrelled before it was pulled upwards and disappeared into the sky. Brierly tried to see what had been thrown into the snow and dirt, but all she could see was a stain of red. But they caught the dogs' attention, who snarled and pounced at them, lifting them into their jaws and tearing at them. As one, her men screamed. Brierly felt phantom teeth tear into the flesh at her side, and she was shaken from her feet by invisible jaws. She could feel the heat of its breath envelop her, and then she was tossed across the room like a doll.

As she landed hard against the bricks, she saw one of the dogs pawing at the thing in its mouth. It was a doll, roughly knotted out of cloth and hair, and wrapped in a red-rag jacket.

The dog bit through the doll's arm, and another man screamed.

Brierly looked up. Howkins was the only one still standing. She was shouting something inaudible up at the sky, brandishing a knife that gleamed white in the moonlight. The old woman darted towards one of the bloated presses, digging her fingers deep into the pliable copper skin and hauling herself up onto its back to scream again at the stars. Her man had been right: this was it. There was nothing left for them to do, and no-one left who could do it.

Pain tore through Brierly's stomach, and she rolled as a chunk of flesh tore itself from her. Braddock. She could see him, cowering by one of the crumbled walls and looking like he wanted to run but had no idea where. His eyes darted from the dogs, to Howkins, to the sky in terror. But the phantom dogs left him be. Howkins would not have guessed they would bring him with them: there was no doll for him.

There was no doll!

"Braddock!" Brierly yelled. "Please!"

Her voice broke the spell. He looked at her, his eyes wide.

Then he turned and fled.

He tried to run, but the best he could do was stumble and grab the ground to stop himself flying. Nothing was steady. The earth shook and the sky looked ready to fall, and the constant boom of thunder had deafened him as the flash of bolt after bolt of lightning threatened to blind him. James had never really been a religious man. He had kept it to himself for fear of driving the devout away from the Sportsman, but he had found it difficult to reconcile himself with the Bible's views on wealth. But even he knew the Apocalypse when it was upon him.

It wasn't just the factory, he could see that for himself. The ground around them had changed, and he seemed to have emerged from the factory on the wrong side of the river. He could see none of the landmarks he should be able to, and the water of the river raged and foamed like it was boiling. In the strange purple light, it looked thick like blood. In the field where he found himself, trees had been uprooted and tossed hither and thither like discarded matchsticks. On the ground nearby, a strange sigil burned. Hell itself was rising up to claim them.

He glanced back behind him and saw the bloated factory start to crumble and warp. Grey stones bigger than men lifted themselves into the sky and were ground to dust in the maelstrom. He tried not to think about the people he had left behind in there. There was no helping any of them. It was every man for himself now. He decided to make for the copse that spread up the side of the valley towards Mellor. It meant running away from the pub, but might offer him some shelter from this impossible night. He moved as fast as he could, every step painful over broken ground, dodging the torn scraps of the factory that rained down around him.

Something unearthly roared above him, but he didn't dare move.

He made it to the trees, long silver birches that shivered begrudgingly aside as he pushed through them. There was no light here, and James was suddenly aware of how little he could sense of his surroundings. Looking up he could only see the rustling canopy of leaves. Around him the ghosts of trunks and blackness. The air still crackled with electricity, and he wondered if the wood would combust spontaneously around him. His heart pounded heavy in his chest.

The women barged past him, and knocked him to the ground.

He ended up on all fours, looking up at her back as she raced down the valley. She was heading for the factory – he tried to shout to her, but he couldn't even hear his own voice. She was dressed in black, silhouetted against the falling snow and the trees. For just a moment, she glanced back at him, and he could see she was bald-headed with some kind of smoked goggles hiding her eyes. James tried to shout again, but she turned away and kept running.

There was a sickening crunch, and a chunk of falling roof slammed into the woman. It slammed her into the ground, and James saw a viscous glob of blood spat from her mouth. The young woman shook her head, but couldn't right herself. Debris rained down around her. Some stones were bigger than she was.

There was nothing he could do. It was every man for himself.

He found he was running, his feet stumbling over themselves as he stretched his arms out towards her. There was an unearthly howl and a flash of lightning so bright James thought he must have been hit. A great wind whipped up, speeding down the hill to the ruins of the factory and dragging him with it. He looked up at the sky and saw something spin and circle, then dive down at the factory and swallow it in a mouth glistening with row after row of razor teeth. Chunks of stone fell from its mouth as it span back up, cresting on the stars like it was riding a wave. They fell fast and landed deep in the frozen ground.

His fingers brushed the woman's back.

He glanced up and saw a section of the roof spinning down towards them. She was curled tight into a ball and wasn't moving. James might have screamed something as he flung his arms up to protect himself. The factory roof struck the hard ground and tolled like a bell.

Then there was silence.

# 4. January 1854, Strines

It was impossible to tell exactly how much time had passed. It was dark. Even with all the snow on the ground, it was dark. The sky above was black with cloud, and the snow was still falling in thick, heavy flakes. It fell on the ruins of the works, the factory buildings reduced to a hump of snow and twisted metal. The boilerhouse chimney still stood, but the rest of the building had been ripped apart and scattered across the fields with the snow. Here and there, the earth still smoked. There was no sound, only the gentle pat-pat of the snowflakes falling.

It was cold, too. Webber's muscles cracked and ached as he stepped from one pile of rubble to the next, and the bullet still lodged in his shoulder from an old campaign burned like it had just struck him again. He'd come to a few minutes ago, slumped under the arch of a door that wasn't there anymore. Aside from a few knocks, he had escaped major injury. The only thing damaged was his pride. His men had not been so lucky: he found traces of some scattered amongst the rubble. Others had vanished completely.

That would have to be dealt with in time, but first he still had to find Elizabeth Howkins. On that, his orders had been clear. Nobody expected him to kill her, but if she did die nobody was going to be too worried about it.

Providing he could prove it.

He reached what he thought was the centre of the factory, the last place he had seen Mrs Howkins. He had to judge the spot by his position in the valley and the blueprints he had studied before coming here. There was barely any trace left of the presses or even the shape of the building. There didn't seem to be enough debris left behind – already the site was developing the air of an ancient ruin.

Something moved behind him.

He didn't turn. He knew better than that. But he did try to focus on the very edge of his vision, looking for movement or the hint of a shape. There was nothing. Possibly it had been an animal: some fox or badger disturbed when one of the corpses got up and started moving. All the same, his hand hovered over his service revolver. Just in case.

There were a few mounds of rubble that looked as they they could be big enough to cover Mrs Howkins' body. Webber quickly set to work shifting the stones from one of the nearest.

His senses strained for any hint of movement, both below him, and behind.

James woke groggily, his waking mind only surfacing cautiously as if afraid of what state it would find him in. He felt uncomfortably warm, sweat trickling down his neck and dripping from his nose. He couldn't move one side of his body, but he quickly discovered that was because it was pinned by rubble. There was a strange smell too – a mixture of sweat and flowers that made his nose twitch. When he realised it was coming from the unconscious woman wrapped tightly in his arms, his heart gave a little jump. He remembered reaching her as the roof struck, pulling her out of the way and into the shelter of his arms. Then a flash of white, and then nothing.

His eyes were growing accustomed to the darkness. He could just make out that a section of the roof had fallen directly on top of them, shielding them from any further damage from falling debris. He had no idea how much of the building was lying directly on top of them, but at least they had escaped death for a few more moments. He was of course an idiot. He had known that he should leave the unfortunate woman to take her chances, and now they were both going to end up dead. That was what happened when you tried to save everybody. Heroes never helped anyone in the end: much better if everyone just looked after themselves.

He could hear the shallow rasp of her breath. It was too dark for him to make anything but the rough shape of her out, and she was tucked into him tight with her back turned. He couldn't see her face, and nor did he have any idea of whether she was injured. He tried to feel for breaks or blood, but all he found was his own sweat. He listened to each ragged breath, his heart dying in the silence between each one. If they were going to die buried here, he at least wanted it to be him who died first.

Above him came a new sound. Stone grinding against stone as the rubble shifted and moved. James felt a few smaller stones fall across his face. He tried to pull her closer, but his arm was starting to go numb. Instead he closed his eyes.

"Braddock?" came a voice from above.

James opened his eyes. He could see a small gap in the rubble, and through it peered a bruised face. He couldn't make out the features, but he could see the dark crimson of the uniform jacket.

"Have you got Mrs Howkins there?"

James tried to speak, and coughed up a glob of blood.

"No," he managed to hiss.

There was a pause.

"Damn," he heard the voice say.

And the face went away.

It took the best part of an hour for Webber to dig through the most likely piles, but Mrs Howkins was not under any of them. What he found were several dead bodies – men and dogs – and three survivors. Braddock and the stranger were in relatively good condition, all things considered. He had dug them out to help with his search, although Braddock had insisted on making a fire instead and sitting with the girl he had found. The fire made Webber nervous: it gave away their positions, and meant he couldn't see out into the wider dark.

The last to be found was Sergeant Brierly. She was in worse condition.

"I saw her, sir," she said, dried blood cracking as her lips moved. "When the roof collapsed. She was right there. Then she was gone. I tried to get close, but then ..."

Brierly turned her head to look up at her arm. It disappeared at the elbow into a malformed lump of twisted metal that had once been one of the printing presses, pinning her fast to the ground. The metal was blackened and scorched, and the snow around it tainted red.

"Tell me what to do, sir," she said.

Webber felt the weight of his sword at his hip.

"I think we've lost her again, Sergeant," Webber said as he turned away from the fire, "There'll be a doctor in the village who can fix you up. Braddock will fetch him."

"I'm not leaving," Braddock piped up.

Webber ignored him, for the moment.

"A doctor won't be able to save the arm," Brierly said matter-of-factly. "Will they, sir?"

Something made Webber turn before he even knew why. In that moment – before Braddock screamed, before anyone moved – some instinct set the hairs on his arms quivering, and he spun. He barely even registered the shape coming out of the darkness, leaping down from above with claws bared. Webber's sword left its scabbard almost on its own volition, and he felt the weapon tremble and sing as he managed to bring it between claw and Braddock's face. Sparks flew as the claws struck the blade, metal screeching on metal. For a moment, the attacker was held there, an inch from Braddock's wide blinking eyes. Then the publican screamed, and the creature disappeared back into the darkness.

"Sir?"

From where Brierly was pinned, she wouldn't be able to see anything. Nor would she be able to defend herself.

"Braddock," Webber barked. "Braddock!"

The young man was spinning wildly, still screaming like a stuck pig. It was probably only because he had the girl pulled tight to his chest that he hadn't already started running blindly across the fields. Webber barked his name again, and it struck him like a hand across the face.

"What the hell was that?" Braddock yelled.

Webber didn't answer, instead kicking snow onto the fire and pulling Braddock up to his feet. The girl slipped from his grasp and almost fell onto the smothered fire. Braddock bent to steady her, but Webber snapped him back up to his feet.

"Keep your eyes open!" Webber ordered. "It's still –"

Something heavy barged into Webber from behind, sending him sprawling across the ground even as he felt the fabric of his jacket sliced open. A second later he felt the pain, as the cold air bit into the fresh claw-marks between his shoulder blades. His head hit something hard as he went down, and the sword slipped from his grasp. He heard Brierly shout something, and Braddock scream again. Everything tried to go dark. But he fought it, rolled with a hiss as the rubble scraped over his new wounds.

He rolled up onto his knees, his pistol aimed.

There was a flash, and the kick of the shot.

For a moment, he was blind. Then his eyes recovered enough for him to make out a dark shape spinning to the floor, clipped by his shot. For a moment, the figure was there, back to him and both hands down to the ground. He thought that his eyes still hadn't recovered from the flash. Then he realised that his eyes were telling him the truth: the creature was a black shape, insubstantial enough for Webber to see the ghost of Braddock's terrified face through it. As it stood, he realised it was a shadow: a living shadow, with steel-edged claws.

Then it disappeared into the darkness again.

"Sir?" Brierly shouted again, panic in her voice.

"Get to the village," Webber shouted, at who he didn't know.

Then, pistol in hand, he gave chase.

James' heart thundered in his ears, and his clothes hung soaked with sweat despite the cold night air. He couldn't see a thing without the fire, and he still expected the darkness to suddenly bare its teeth and snarl. For more than a moment, he was frozen to the spot. But even in the darkness, he could see the unconscious woman lying on the cold ground in front of him. Her chest barely seemed to flutter with each breath. He realised he could hear a voice as the blood came back to his skin.

"Mr Braddock," it was the sergeant, pinned to the ground and her voice edged with panic. "What's happening, Mr Braddock?"

"I'm sorry," he managed to stammer.

He scrabbled over to where the woman was lying and managed to pull her up into his arms. She felt insubstantial, as if she was already fading. As he strained to lift himself back to his feet, her head lolled gently into the nape of his neck. He could smell perfume, and feel the light touch of soft stubble as her head brushed against his skin.

"Mr Braddock?"

James spared the sergeant a quick glance. She was pulling furiously at her damaged arm, her teeth gritting against every wave of pain. But she was pinned tight: nothing was going to lift the machine from her arm. Nothing.

"I'll send help," he stammered.

"Wait. Wait!"

James took two steps, and felt the ground give under him. He went down on one knee just as he saw something move out of the corner of his eye. He let out a cry, and spun to see what it was. But there was nothing there, just more snow and darkness. He took a deep breath, and lifted the woman up in his arms again.

"The sword," the sergeant barked at him like he was one of her men. "Mr Braddock, the sword!"

It was lying on the ground almost by his feet, hilt towards him invitingly. James had no weapon, and for just a second the idea of defending the unconscious girl with his swordsmanship came to him. But he was just the man who kept the villagers happy from behind the bar – he'd never so much as used his fists in anger, let alone wielded a sword. And besides, he would need both hands to carry the woman back to his horse. The sword would be no use to him.

He made his decision in a moment, freeing one hand and taking the sword by the blade with it. He held the hilt out to the sergeant where she lay helpless on the floor. Maybe it would be some use to her. Maybe she could save herself from the monster, and live long enough for James to really send help from the village.

The sergeant looked up at him with her strange almond eyes.

"No, Mr Braddock," she said softly. "You must use it."

James didn't … oh.

"No," he stammered. "I never –"

"There is no time," she hissed at him. "We are under attack."

From somewhere in the darkness behind them came a shot.

Brierly knew that she was pinned, but still jerked round to try and see where the shot had come from. She couldn't see anything but Mr Braddock, and pain kicked her in the side of the head once again. The sword glinted as it stole a glimmer of light from somewhere, and a large part of Brierly voted to give up and move on. But the rest of her dug in. There was still hope.

"Now, Mr Braddock," she said firmly.

Her voice held a calmness that she didn't feel.

"Now."

He looked at her, and she had no idea how to read the emotions that were so clearly there on his face. All these years living with humans, and she was still no closer to understanding them.

"You'll die," Mr Braddock stammered. The sword looked like it might drop from his hands, and rust in the snow. "I can't ... it's your arm!"

"No," Brierly said, firmly. "It isn't."

There was a moment of internal debate. The Major had always told her that above all else – even above her duty to protect the life and reign of the monarch – Brierly was never to tell anyone the truth about herself. That knowledge was Major Webber's alone to impart, and when he did it was always with the agonised reluctance of one confessing a secret weakness that still afflicted them. He had told perhaps three people in all the years Brierly had served with him, and two of those he had ordered killed shortly afterwards. But there was no small voice of dissent within her: if she didn't do this now, she would die here and that would be the end of it.

"This is the arm of Helen Copley," Brierly told Mr Braddock, calmly and coolly. Like a doctor telling their patient the cancer had spread. "This is the body of Helen Copley and while she remains attached to every part of it, she is quite happy to leave it if it means our continued survival. We have debated: we have consensus. This is the only way for Brierly to survive. Please do as we ask, Mr Braddock."

Mr Braddock looked like he might just expire there and then.

"I am not a person like you, Mr Braddock," Brierly said, fixing him with her eyes. Keeping him on his feet these few seconds longer, and that sword in his hand. "I am a parliament. Within me are the minds and voices of a thousand people, and each has in turn given their body to us for us to use until we need another. And we are all agreed: if we must lose Helen's arm for us to survive, so be it. There will be other arms, and other bodies."

Now there was a look she could decipher: horror. Sheer, bloody horror at the monster before him.

"That's not ..." he stammered. "You're ..."

"I'm six-thousand years old, Mr Braddock," Brierly said, keeping her voice as calm and steady as she could manage in the circumstances. "I am a thousand souls, each one joining me openly and voluntarily. And if you don't do as I ask now, we will all of us die on our backs in this field. Please, Mr Braddock. Please."

Mr Braddock looked at her again. The sword lifted up as if under its own power. Brierly wanted to tell him to put it down again, to leave her and pray for her. That she had lied, and the world was of course the narrow place he had always known it to be. But instead she said:

"Higher. You need to get through the bone."

The sword whistled to itself as it came down, slicing the night air in two. Brierly let out a cry, but it was more of surprise than pain. For a moment, she thought that Mr Braddock had missed. But when her eyes opened, she could see the publican still standing over her, still holding the sword that was now almost blade-deep in the cold hard ground. Brierly tried to move, and the pain came. She bit her own tongue with the sheer force of it. But she still couldn't move.

"It's stuck," Mr Braddock was whimpering. "It won't -"

Another pistol crack in the air. This time, closer.

"AGAIN!" Brierly screamed.

Mr Braddock gave a cry of terror and snatched convulsively at the sword hilt. He nearly dropped it in his panic, but he managed to pull it free of Brierly's arm. She heard a crepitus scrape as the blade twisted out of her bone, and another wave of pain so strong she had to turn her head to vomit. The sword came down again before she could turn back, and then again. Sparks flew as it struck a chunk of rubble and spun out of Mr Braddock's grasp. He screamed again, and Brierly sat up.

She could see her elbow still lying in the snow. One end was crushed beneath the mangled press, the other severed razor-cut neat, except for a jagged splinter through the bone about halfway through. Thick black blood oozed from the wound, and dripped down from her arm.

She was free.

James felt his knees give way, and a sharp jolt of pain as he landed awkwardly in the rubble. He sat there, dazed for a moment as he watched the sergeant grab a handful of snow and rub it into the stump of her missing arm. The arm that he had severed. The snow melted instantly, dripping a thick black red into the shadows. Sergeant Brierly grabbed another handful, and rubbed it in again.

"Tie your belt around it," she ordered, her voice ragged. "Just above the wound."

"I just want to go!" James heard himself whine.

"I don't have long."

She was already scrabbling at her waist for something, leaving James to fumble his belt free and loop it around the arm. He knew he would have to pull it tight, but part of him flinched from causing any more pain. His hands were wet with blood as he pulled, securing it as best he could. The sergeant didn't even look, instead smiling as she pulled a handful of percussion caps from a pouch on her belt. She lay them quickly down on a reasonably dry stone and struck them with the butt of her pistol.

As the flame jumped into the air, she thrust her bloody stump into it.

The smell of cooking meat filled the air.

The sergeant cried out, then fell to the floor.

James looked at her for a moment, but she didn't move. In the burning afterglow of the flame, he couldn't even tell if she was breathing. He thought of the creature with the claws and looked quickly around himself. The sergeant's scream was still echoing around the valley: the creature must have heard it. It would only be a matter of time before … James jumped again, but there was nothing behind him.

For now.

The woman in the goggles was prone on the snow. Her dark clothes were growing wet as she slowly melted the ice. He could see the thick crust of dried blood over one ear, and he could imagine if she stayed there much longer, she would die. Probably they all would, when the creature returned.

James closed his eyes and stepped forward.

"Sergeant," he whispered, giving her shoulders a gentle shake. "Sergeant?"

Sergeant Brierly's eyes burst open, and her arms came up. She grasped at him with what she must still think were two hands, but her face showed no surprise when only one took hold. With unbelievable strength, she pulled James down until their noses were touching and stared deep into his eyes. Everything disappeared – the fields, the fear, the cold: in an instant, there were only two eyes growing bigger and bigger. He could hear voices, all talking at once, as if he was suddenly in the heart of a crowd of thousands. James felt himself slipping away.

"No," he heard the sergeant say softly.

She released him, pushing him back and away so hard that he stumbled. The voices stopped the moment that her skin broke contact with his, the silence so sudden that his mind couldn't quite believe they weren't still there. He looked across at the sergeant in disbelief, not quite sure what had nearly happened. She ignored him, pulling herself to unsteady feet with only one hand to steady her balance.

"You bring the woman," the sergeant panted, cradling her missing arm.

Then she staggered past, heading for the road.

Webber ran into the darkness. He had faced tougher and stranger challenges than this, particularly since Mrs Howkins had entered his life. In the five years that he had been charged with bringing her in, he had seen such things that made living shadows seem positively prosaic. Seen such things, and seen them off with his men, his pistol and his grit. And when he had seen this latest diversion off, he would get back on the old woman's trail and finally earn the crown for his collar. Sixteen years an officer: Mrs Howkins was delaying his timetable.

He stopped for a moment. Now he was out of the ruins, he should have a clear view up both sides of the valley and along the trickle of a stream that had carved it. But the snow was still falling heavily, and there was a thick mist hanging in the air that could easily be low cloud. He couldn't see more than a few feet in front of himself, and had already lost track of the others. There was a good chance that the shadow creature had simply doubled back as soon as it was out of sight, except that Webber imagined he would still hear the screams from this distance.

Something moved to his right, and Webber swung, his pistol pointing like an accusing finger. He did not fire: there was no target to see. He was an officer in the Queen's Army: he did not fire on ghosts and shadows. Except, of course, when circumstances required that he did.

A noise to his left, but again there was nothing. His ears ached as he strained for every sound, every hint that the creature was nearby. He could hear nothing, see nothing. It was as insubstantial as the air itself – what hope did he have of detecting it even as its claws were in his gut? A lesser soldier might have doubted he could prevail, but Webber knew that victory was just a matter of will. He had never lost, because no adversary could ever want to win more than him.

Something cracked loud in the darkness.

Webber held his pistol steady in front of him and advanced step by step. But as he pushed through the snow and the mist, he saw in front of him something large and white. Each step revealed more of it, until – as he was almost on top of it – he saw a gigantic wall of bluish-white curving up and around him. For a moment, he forgot the shadow and let his pistol waver. There came another crack, and Webber saw a section of the wall topple down and shatter on the hard ground. It was ice, he realised: a wall of ice so thick and cold that even as the outer edge creaked and melted, the inner core remained frozen solid.

He looked up at it curving gentling away into the sky. He couldn't see the top of it, but from the shape of it he could guess that he was looking at the inside of a dome. It must be some size – perhaps miles in diameter. Certainly large enough to enclose the village. Was this Mrs Howkins' handwork? For all the years he had hunted her, Webber was no closer to knowing what her ultimate objective was. But over those years, she had proved herself capable of many strange and impossible things …

There was something clinging to the ice.

He had just a second to identify it as the shadow, clinging like a spider. Then it kicked its legs, its claws drawing from the ice as smooth as a sword from its scabbard. The creature dropped casually down on Webber, one hand swinging to stab at his head. He managed to fire a single shot before the claws sliced through his shoulder and the shadow was on him.

It was almost too dark to see, and every time Brierly tried to get her bearings, the snow threw itself into her face and all she could see was ice. Her arm – her lack of arm – was throbbing alarmingly with each double-beat of her heart, and she could feel either blood or pus starting to trickle through her makeshift bandage. She didn't think there was much hope of this body recovering. She didn't want to think about that: there were so few candidates available, and she doubted Mr Braddock would stand as happy volunteer.

Somewhere out here was the horse and trap. It had seemed only a few paces away when the factory was still standing, but everything had warped and shifted so badly when Mrs Howkins had escaped that Brierly couldn't even be sure they were in the same valley. She was lost. All she could do was hope that Mr Braddock could find his way home: he stumbled on a few steps ahead of her, the strange woman carried in his arms like a sleeping child. That was something else that would need thinking about later, but for now his every step threatened to make him disappear into the storm. Brierly knew she had no chance of surviving without him.

Overhead, thunder grumbled loudly. Major Webber was still somewhere out there, alone. Brierly tried to put it out of her mind: she had her orders, and they would be obeyed. Get them all safely back to the village. Until she had done that, all debate must wait. She set her mind and her heart, and took another few painful steps.

He felt the shadow's claws slip easily into the flesh of his shoulder only because of the strange frozen sensation that spread with them. There was no pain, just the weight of the creature as it pinned him hard to the ground and brought its other hand up for the kill. Its eyes were already looking out into the night. It already knew it would win this fight: what mattered was finding its next target. Sergeant Brierly, most likely. Not that she would prove any harder to kill than Webber.

But he was not dead yet.

Webber pushed himself deeper into the shadow's arms, its claws pushing through his body until he felt its fingertips pressed against his flesh. The pain came then, particularly as he felt the tips of the metal blades make five clean cuts out of his back. But he knew that if he was going to win the battle he would have to stay out of the way of those claws. His only hope was to stay in close.

He tried to grasp the creature's arm in his, twist and break it. He didn't even know if the creature had enough substance for its bones to break, and he would never find out. It rolled with Webber's grip, sliding its claws easily out of his flesh to give itself the momentum to throw him over its shoulder. It didn't let its grip go, twisting him in the air so that he landed awkwardly against a half-buried rock. There was a loud crack, but it was only melting ice: somehow, Webber's bones remained intact.

The shadow again jabbed with its claws, but Webber managed to roll and stumble to his feet. It swaggered a little as it moved for him again, but Webber had the upper hand this time: he had snatched up the pistol from where it had fallen, and before the shadow had moved two paces had it loaded and aimed. A flash of fire, and a bullet tore through the creature's shoulder, leaving a wound the jagged twin of Webber's own. Webber could taste his promotion in the air.

The creature moved to attack again, but suddenly froze. Another loud crack of melting ice from high above them … no, this was different. Suddenly, there was a blast of intense heat and a bolt of lightning struck the ground between the two of them. Both were flung backwards, the shadow slamming into the ice wall as Webber felt his eyebrows singe. It was up again in a moment, ignoring the coming storm and calmly pacing towards Webber.

"Listen. Why don't you just surrender now?" Webber called as calmly as he could. "I'll ask them to go easy on you."

Another bolt of lightning struck the ground, and the air tore itself apart with a deep booming. The shadow took another step forward, and Webber quickly tried to formulate a plan of attack. None was forthcoming. The creature drew back its claws, and lightning again struck. As the flash blinded Webber for an instance, he heard the razor blades swipe through the air. He stumbled back, but as his vision cleared, he saw the shadow had not struck him. Instead, it seemed to have sliced a wound in the air itself, and with barely a glance back it jumped into it, leaving Webber alone.

Webber blinked, then started to laugh.

Iron will. The only way to win a battle.

The air was filled with the terrible growl of the thunder again, but it held no fear for Webber. He was thinking of his next steps – the Sergeant would regroup at the Sportsman's Arms, so it was there that Webber should head. She would bring the village doctor, and he would patch up Webber's shoulder. But for some reason, he couldn't move his feet. All the hairs all over his body had stood to attention, and were now pulsing with a strange energy. His heart started pounding an arresting beat, and his muscles ached for activity. His mouth was dry, and he was sure he could feel his eyes bulging.

For a moment, every single flake of snow in the sky froze. They stayed there, unmoving, like fat frozen stars in an overcrowded sky. Webber's breath froze in the air, and hung in front of him like a cloud.

"What the ..?" he breathed.

And then the lightning struck him.

# 5. Twilight, The Grey Town

For more than a moment, Elizabeth thought the only thing that had changed was that the wildlife had fallen silent. The night was just as dark, and she could still feel the snow as it flurried into her face. But as she reached up to brush it away, Elizabeth felt the snow smear between her fingers and looked again. It was ash. Fat flakes of grey ash falling from the sky as if heaven was burning.

She looked again. A cobbled street wound away from her, the shadows of factories being cast at either side. None of them looked substantial, and those that she could see were ruined and crumbling to dust. Where there weren't factories, there were machines. Cold grey monoliths of iron, rusting to white flakes. None of them looked as they they would work again, and many looked as if they had never worked in the first place. Everywhere was dead and grey. She looked for the red glow of the fire that rained ash on her, but there was no colour to be seen in any direction.

There was some relief in that. She didn't want to see a factory burn.

She looked again around her. None of Webber's men were there with her, nor anyone else for that matter. Except for Bill, of course. He had followed her there as he had followed her everywhere. He had promised to never leave her, and neither of them had imagined how true to his word he would be. He stood there now, as grey and insubstantial as the landscape. His bad eye stared at the ground, but he took his cap from his head as he leant back to look up at the sky. But it was empty too, pulled low with thunderous clouds, raining ash on everything, but empty nonetheless. He looked at her with questioning eyes.

Elizabeth had to admit that this was not what she had expected either. The years of training and practising had led her home to Strines and the old works, but somehow they had led her here and left her without a landmark. She had told Webber she was here to kill, but now she seemed totally alone. The bone knife was still in her hand, but of her prey there was no sign.

Elizabeth knew she had no real choice.

She slid the knife back into its sheath and started walking.

She hadn't been walking for long when they reached the crest of a hill, the broken cobbled road falling away beneath them into a deep valley. It looked as if it had been cut into the earth by dragon's claws, rock and stone torn through like paper and cast aside to crumble to sand. Along the valley floor ran a thin, grey stream. It had barely the speed to foam, but someone had seen fit to build a waterwheel across it anyway. The wheel turned lazily, fitting and started with its gears complaining loudly. Thin smoke rose from a chimney attached to the mill.

"What do you think?" she asked Bill.

He didn't answer, but Elizabeth started making her way down the valley anyway.

Inside the mill, there was no light, except for what little reflected back off the piles of white ash that lay everywhere. The gears and the rotors still turned, filling the air with the angry grind of iron and stone. It was impossible to make out any other sound, even though Elizabeth hovered on the threshold straining her senses before finally entering. As she crossed over, she forced herself to close her eyes. Her heart pounded as imagination brought wave upon wave of attacker into the room, but she retained control. That was all she had now: the ability to stay in control. What else could she lose, except her chance for revenge?

When she opened her eyes again, they had grown sharper. She could make out detail in the grey twilight. There was a machine, either half-built or half-disassembled, in one corner. A loop of chain ran from it to one of the gears of the waterwheel, rattling emptily as it turned on nothing.

Elizabeth stepped cautiously into the room.

"You're new," a hoarse voice croaked from one side.

Her mind began to race with the possibilities, rituals and incantations that would give her the upper hand in whatever situation this turned out to be. But she turned to the source of the voice calmly. For a moment, they were still hidden in the gloom. Then they moved a little, and the motion brought them into sharp relief. It was a man, extravagantly dressed in black and white save for a single splash of purple at his throat, a cravat badly tied and only just hiding an old grey scar there. He had hair so fine that it looked like it might drift from his head at any moment. In his hands were pieces of the machine, old and rusted. Like the man himself.

"Are you even really here?" he asked in a whisper.

Elizabeth considered.

"I imagine it's a genuine possibility," she replied.

The man gave a little snort.

"Well, we'll be the judge of that," he said, and turned back to his machine.

Elizabeth didn't move, waiting for the man to reveal his intentions. But he seemed content to ignore her, his myopic attention focussed solely on the ruined and useless cogs he was trying to fit together. Elizabeth tried to discern some meaning from the pattern, but machines had always been a mystery to her. Even when she had worked in the factory, she had performed her duties with the air of a ritual. Action followed action with no greater meaning than that they kept the unseen placated.

Bill settled himself in a corner of the room. He didn't spare a glance for the stranger, and instead reached into his pocket for his pipe. There was no smoke: Elizabeth liked to remember him sitting for hours, chewing absent-mindedly on the stem of the pipe because she had once remarked that she didn't like the smell. Had he always been such a saint? She had trouble remembering anything he had ever done to annoy her, but that couldn't really be the case. Memory was untrustworthy, but that was all she had. All of this was done in the name of a memory that was unreliable, but still clear enough to tell her that Bill wouldn't approve. She knew that it wouldn't make the memories of quiet nights side-by-side in the Sportsman any easier to bear. There was just nothing else to do.

"Sir," Elizabeth said. She had fallen into the habit of addressing strangers as young men, but this man seemed older than even her and so she was forced to adapt. "I don't suppose I could trouble you to tell me where I am?"

The man froze for a moment, and squinted up at her.

"If you were really here," he said gnostically, "you'd know where here was."

Elizabeth didn't answer.

"You wouldn't have a choice," he added, as if it explained something.

Elizabeth was not an impatient lady. The twenty years she had spent travelling the world to learn the secrets of the vodouists was testament to that. And then, finally, last year she had her audience with the Queen Mother of the Ewe People, and she asked the question. The woman had been much younger than Elizabeth, and had just cocked an eyebrow at her.

"Yes, I can tell you how," she had said. "But why on Earth would you want to?"

All so that she could be here for this one moment. Not for the first time, Elizabeth wondered exactly what she was doing with however little remained of her life.

She glanced across at Bill, but he looked away, disinterested.

Instead, she turned to the stranger.

"I seek an audience with Spinning Jenny," she said, as humbly as she could manage. "I think I'm correct to assume you wouldn't be her?"

The man looked at her for a moment, then laughed hard.

There were voices in his head. They didn't tell him to do anything – there were far too many of them for that. Instead, they just formed a constant babble, a background noise that often made it impossible for him to hear his own thoughts. Perhaps that was how control was exerted. Any voice that made it through with anything like clarity would have to be acted upon, whether it was his or not. And with such control in place, it obviously amused his master to let a thought such as that through.

With a start, he realised he was laughing. Why was that?

"Well," the old woman in the black uniform tutted. "I assume you won't be offended if I conclude you will be of no assistance."

Oh yes.

It was clear that whatever else she might be, the newcomer had no idea about where she really was or what was waiting for her. Which meant that she would just drag him into long and boring conversation about the nature of free will and reality, eating up time that would otherwise be spent productively on his escape attempt. He turned his attention back to the cogs in his hand, trying to see in them the platonic ideal they were strugglinging to fall back to. No matter how he tried, they only seemed to be interested in turning to rust, and that wasn't going to help him at all. He'd seen enough of that in his time here.

So important was his work that he had already put the newcomer completely from his mind. Which was why he was surprised to find a name pushing to the front of his thoughts, and the urge to speak it impossible to ignore.

"Betty," he retched, trying to choke the word off as it escaped.

Both hands clamped to his mouth. But it was too late: she had heard. A few seconds later and it wouldn't have mattered – she was almost at the door and gone. But now she turned, pacing catlike back into the room.

"I don't believe we've been introduced," she said in an undertone.

He told himself to ignore it. He had once been a soldier. He had been trained to discipline his mind and reject all outside influence, as a member of a people whose infants could instinctively identify and resist a foreign thought. But that was several lifetimes ago, and the problem was this thought wasn't foreign to him, not really. It was the whim and will of his very deepest being, as if the nuclei of his atoms had started telling him their secret desires.

Tell her everything.

It didn't even try to pretend the impulse was his.

"I'm sorry," he said. He spoke through gritted teeth, trying to trap the words in his throat. "I wasn't always like this. You can't understand. You don't want to: leave now if you've got any way to."

Tell her everything. The urge spread even as he tried to control it, suppress it. Everywhere it touched, it burned away a little of the fog that had grown over the centuries. Piece by piece, cell by cell, he felt his mind slowly returning to him. The mind he had fought so hard to lose. The threat was obvious. If he resisted the urge, within moments he would be clear-headed and sane again. He would know exactly what he had lost, and exactly how little hope was left in its place.

"Alright!" he spat. The old woman took a cautious step back, but otherwise her composure didn't waver. "Alright."

He took a breath, and the fog descended again.

The urge took him to tell the newcomer everything.

He laughed again.

"You want to talk with the Loa?" he asked. She just glared at him with the patience of a stream cutting a valley into cold, hard stone. "Then talk. Don't you realise where you are yet?"

His eyes fell back down to the dust and the dirt.

"This is her," he said flatly. "This is the Loa."

White ash on grey stone.

"We have been devoured."

It was a possibility she should have considered. She had planned her campaign meticulously, circling the globe more than once to learn the skills she would need to speak with the Loa. The auguries had given her the time and the place, but she had known in her bones where it would be. And at the factory at Strines, she had thrown herself into the Loa's path and demanded its attention. How did she imagine she would communicate with it? In the Sportsman's snug over a hot cup of Vimto?

Now the moment was here, she realised she had never imagined it. When she had lost her Bill, the seed of this moment had been sown. But in all those years she had never once thought of anything bar that he would be avenged. Elizabeth turned to Bill for guidance, but he just looked around her at the shadows of the mill, the hard grey stone and the white ash that penetrated even this darkness. How did you avenge yourself on a landscape? How did you destroy a world from within it?

She felt the weight of her knife at her hip.

Any way you can, she told herself.

"You've never seen one before," the madman said compassionately.

"Too often," she replied automatically.

But he shook his head.

"You've seen them when they are riding another soul," he corrected. He didn't need confirmation: somehow he knew. "Would I know you if I'd seen your shadow? You've never seen them in the ocean, have you?"

Elizabeth hesitated.

"Once," she answered, then corrected herself: "Twice. I saw them today, fighting behind the sky."

"Then you know something of what they are," the madman said sadly, as if acknowledging a heavy burden she carried. "They are a form of leviathan, swimming the ocean between the universes. Just by existing, they disturb the waters of reality. You're lucky you can't understand the tsunami that result from an attack."

"I cannot?" Elizabeth echoed archly.

"I'm sorry," the madman demurred. "I'd thought you were human."

Elizabeth said nothing: she'd thought the same of him.

"They do things to time, you see," he said sadly, contemplating the dust. "If you fall into their wake … I was born in another time, another world. The Loa killed my other half, and cut me loose. I'm adrift in causality. My future is my past and is my future all over again. It's no wonder I went mad."

Elizabeth glanced over at Bill.

"You're not mad," she said softly.

He looked at her with a strange light in his eyes.

"You would say that," he told her. "They've driven you mad too."

It was, she knew, a possibility she should have considered.

The madman seemed to have spent himself. With barely another glance up at her, he went back to his rusted cogs and dented machinery, fitting it all together with all the care and intuition of a bird building itself a nest for the spring. She wondered if he even knew what he was trying to do. Certainly she could not tell … although … No, she was mistaken: just for a second, she had thought she had spotted some ulterior design in the broken machine. But it was just a mirage. She had spent too long talking with the insane, on one plane or another.

No.

Her instinct had been correct. There was … something.

"What is it for?" she asked him.

He looked up at her blankly.

"The machine," Elizabeth explained slowly. "What are you building it for?"

He just grinned and went back to it.

But there was the echo of something there. One cog slid against another, and Elizabeth thought she knew where the next should go. The space between a mess of bolts and pistons seemed somehow suggestive, and she realised that the places the madman wasn't putting things were just as important as where he was. She had been fooled by the form into thinking he was building a machine. Perhaps even he thought he was, but he wasn't. This was something else – there, at the heart of the broken machine, was the thing she had recognised. It was the vevé she had seen burned into the factory floor when her Bill had died. The symbol of Spinning Jenny.

"Is it ..." Elizabeth hesitated. "A gateway?"

The madman stopped and looked at her with something like respect.

"Yes!" he said, excitedly. "You can see it?"

"I've seen it before," she answered flatly.

She was seeing something else.

"You fell into their wake," the madman announced.

The factory floor. The calico works in Strines, the new works across the gas bridge from the old, feeding material to the machines every second of the day so that they never went hungry. It wasn't the kind of life she had ever really expected for herself, but it hadn't been a bad one for all of that. The machines hissed and spat so loud during her shifts that she thought she would lose her hearing before she was twenty-four. But her Bill had taught her a sign-language so that whenever they caught each others eye they could share a few words, no matter what was going on around them.

She closed her eyes. She couldn't think of him without the anger coming in.

"I fell into their wake," Elizabeth echoed.

The fire had come from nowhere. She couldn't even tell you how or where it started. One moment, she was feeding cloth into the machines and the next the air was filled with grey choking smoke. The screams were just as thick, just as deadly. Before any of them had even seen a lick of flame, panic had taken hold and the entire workforce seemed to be determined to escape by climbing over the bodies of their friends and neighbours. They were all thinking about the gas room just behind the factory, where all the gas used to power the station was made. Once the flames reached it ...

The flames rolled in, licking their way across the roof and down to the bodies below. The air choked with smoke and the sound of bones breaking. And there had been Bill, appearing suddenly as a cloud of grey smoke rolled aside. He caught sight of her for just a second, the words on his lips trailing off into nothing: for all his good intentions, nobody would have heard them anyway. She screamed for him to get out, but he had the presence of mind to sign. He told her he loved her, told her to get out through the back window. Told her he was going to make sure the storerooms were empty, and then he disappeared into the grey and the dust.

"She killed my Bill," Elizabeth told the madman.

Because Elizabeth hadn't escaped. The people she spent every daylight hour with pushed past her screaming to crush each other to death in the doorway, but Elizabeth couldn't leave. She followed her Bill as he went deeper into the fire to make sure everybody else was moving in the sensible direction. She wouldn't let him go in there on his own. She would find him, and tell him he was being a selfish idiot and then drag him back out again by the scruff of his neck.

But she didn't see Bill. Instead, she saw a fat old woman dressed in a deep purple ball gown, striding through the smoke and the crowd. In her hand was a champagne flute filled with what looked like stout, and every corner she turned she seemed to find something else that tickled her well-padded ribs. The fire lapped at her like a kitten with its mother, but never got so close as to singe the tip of a single hair on her head. Elizabeth was transfixed, and she followed her deeper and deeper into the inferno.

Amongst the fire and the screaming, Elizabeth could hear the woman humming to herself. An oddly jaunty little tune, like a funeral march in waltz time. Then she took a last turn into the heart of the factory – the biggest workshop, filled end to end with oiled monsters of iron and steel. The woman laughed a hearty laugh and took a last sip from her drink. Then she slammed onto the floor, sending stout and glass dancing through the fire. For an instant, grey smoke jumped into the air. When it burned to nothing, the woman had vanished. On the ground where she stood, the vevé burned in liquid fire. Even as she closed her eyes and turned away, Elizabeth saw the after-image burned onto her retinas.

Then the gas room had gone up.

Looking up, looking past the smoke, past the fire, past the roof and past the world. Elizabeth had seen something she had never seen before: the view from behind a thick curtain blown aside in a torrential storm. She saw the Loa, twisting and turning in the seas. Its features were indistinct, but she could see the shape of a mouth opening wide – a scream, a cry, a laugh. Tears had rolled down Elizabeth's face, and she reached up to her eyes with the genuine intention of plucking them from their sockets.

She heard Bill scream somewhere in the heart of the fire.

The Loa dived at her, and the world fell away.

She was gone.

For a long time, they didn't speak. The mill grew a little darker, and Elizabeth assumed that night must have fallen. She wondered if she would see stars if she could see the sky. Would the moon be there, shining down on the grey world beneath. Or would she see the Loa dancing in the sky again, and pluck her eyes from her skull. No: she wasn't afraid any more. She wasn't anything. Just a grey husk of an old woman, filled with an anger that would not burn, and haunted by the ghost of a love long gone.

The madman lit a fire, though he showed no sign of being cold or cooking a meal. The flames stayed low, struggling to bring any light into the room, only making the shadows dance around them. After a while, Elizabeth sat down beside him and started moving the pieces of his broken machine where she thought they should go. The first time she did it, he raised an eyebrow at her. By the time she had half the vevé laid out in ironwork across the floor, he just glanced and nodded his approval.

"It took five years for me to find out what it was," she said, possibly to the madman. "Of course at first I was just trying to make sense of where I was, what had happened. When I was, I should say."

The madman gave no sign at all that he was listening. Elizabeth glanced up at him whilst he concentrated on threading a chain around a rusted hunk of metal that might once have been a flywheel. Did he have any idea what she was doing? Did he even know what he was doing, more to the point? His tangled hair fell down over his face, but Elizabeth could see the grey puckered scar barely hidden by his purple cravat. What had happened to him? At least that much she knew: he had fallen into their wake.

Elizabeth carefully slid a piston from where the madman had placed it. Slowly, dangerously, the pattern shifted.

"A hundred years doesn't seem like that long a time," she said, watching him still from the corner of one eye. "You wouldn't think the world could change so much in a hundred years. But it had, of course. I tried to think of the good I could do. End the war before it happened. Or women's suffrage years in advance. But it was all I could do to stay alive for those first years. And my every thought was of her."

"You christened her," the madman said. "Did you know that? No, I don't suppose you did. But you were the first to name her Spinning Jenny. You'd think that might evoke some sense of responsibility."

"Not me," Elizabeth tutted. "The girls in the factory. Every shift, we'd offer up a half-meant prayer to Spinning Jenny. To the hungry machines. Don't be eating my hair, Jenny. Don't chew on my arm with those big metal teeth of yours. Did we make her real, do you think, with those silly little prayers?"

The madman just shrugged. Elizabeth slid two great cogs together, and the room grew a little lighter. Not much, maybe a flickering candle flame's worth. But it was definitely there. And there was something else: that growing headache in the air, the nagging pressure of a thunderstorm about to break. Something was changing, they could both feel it. He looked at her with a grin that Elizabeth couldn't return.

"Where will it be a gateway to?" Elizabeth asked.

"Does it matter?" he answered. "Away!"

Elizabeth supposed that he was right.

She could barely think what she had done in those first five years. When she tried to remember, there was nothing but a vertiginous lurch in her stomach and the burning vevé scarred onto her history. It wasn't so much the loss of everything that she had ever known. Just the loss of that one thing. She would have coped admirably if her Bill had been with her. Really with her. Together they would have beat this little corner of the past into something resembling a comfortable shape, and just got by. But he wasn't, and so everything went to shadow.

But now she had focus. She had purpose.

She would get revenge.

The mill seemed to swell as he tightened the last screw into his machine. The space inside the darkened room grew by sizes bigger, and the crumbling stone walls bulged uneasily to accommodate it. The room grew lighter, as if the growing pressure was making the air spark and glow. It wasn't a pretty machine by any stretch of the imagination, looking like an explosion in a cog factory for a moment frozen in time. But it would work. He knew it would. There was a single inviting lever piercing the stained metal of the casing, and when he pulled it he knew he would be free.

He waited for the voices to coalesce into an instruction.

But they remained silent.

"Well," the newcomer reach out for the handle, "I suppose now –"

He grabbed at her wrist and held it so tight he could feel the thin blood pumping through her veins. She was an old woman: he could probably snap the hand clean off if he wanted to. But instead he tried to pull it away from the lever. The machine was his. He would be the one to start it, that was all. It was reasonable. But as he tried to move the newcomer's arm, he found her set as solid and unmoving as stone. She looked up at him, her face a passionless mask.

"Let go. Now."

He felt the muscles in her arm tense, just a little.

"I won't ask again," she said.

"The machine is –" he started to say.

The old woman twisted only slightly, and suddenly he was pressed upside down in a corner of the room. Pain started to run up and down his back, and he felt a trickle of blood matt his white hair. She stood exactly where she was, her uniform not even ruffled. But her eyes burned bright with fire.

"Twenty years," she hissed. "Finding someone who could tell me what the vevé was, which of the Loa it described. Learning everything I could be taught and then going and finding what I couldn't. I don't ask you to understand. But I will be the one to complete the ritual. Please don't touch me again."

He felt a flash of pride, and he thought for a moment of jumping to his feet, of showing this upstart little monkey something of how a true soldier responded to such a slight. And he looked at her again, and he thought better of it.

She reached for the lever, and pulled.

She whispered Bill's name as she grasped the blade stuck into the heart of the iron vevé. It bit into the flesh of her palm roughly, and a thin trickle of blood ran down the steel. It fell into the very centre of the mess of cogs and pistons, turning black as it dripped and ran. The black blood turned to white steam as the pistons started to pump, screaming loudly as their rusted skin started to blister and break. She felt her heart beat once, twice, three times. Bill wouldn't look at her. Not even in her imagination would he condone what she had done in his name. She closed her eyes, and tried to imagine what it was she felt.

"It worked," the madman breathed from the darkness.

When she opened her eyes, she could see a line of light making its way up the stone wall in from of her. When it reached eight feet from the ground, it turned at an angle and moved to the right before turning again and falling quickly back to the ground. Within seconds, a doorway had been etched in glowing quicksilver in the cold grey stone. The room swelled and contracted as if they were trapped in the lungs of some enormous creature, and the gateway rattled on invisible hinges.

"It worked!" the madman cried again, bounding for the door.

He stopped as his hand was almost on the handle, and looked quickly back at Elizabeth. He didn't say a word, just swallowed hard. Elizabeth tried hard to feel something, but the anger had gone. She had done her piece, struck her blow. Nothing else mattered now.

"Go on," she sighed. "Open it."

The madman smiled in excitement, and pulled on the handle. With a loud pop! the door pulled open, to reveal … nothing. On the other side, there was nothing but a thick impenetrable darkness, flecked here and there with white as if snow was falling. Otherwise there was nothing. The madman stared out into it as if he was looking over a sun-kissed valley dappled here and there with bluebells coming into bloom. But he hesitated still on the doorway.

"Aren't you coming?" he asked her.

"It doesn't matter now," she answered.

Elizabeth unbuttoned her collar and folded her legs to kneel next to the steaming vevé. She let her hands fall into her lap as if they couldn't think of anything else they could be doing. The madman couldn't wipe the wide grin from his face, but he still managed to look at her with something like concern.

"The machine won't last," he told her. "Once I close the door behind me, that's it."

Elizabeth let her gaze fall to the floor.

"You won't be able to escape," he urged.

"The door won't close," she told him.

He stopped for a moment. Blinked at her. She felt the air start to move around her, and wondered if he'd noticed it yet – it was pulling at that purple cravat of his, so she couldn't imagine that he hadn't. His hand stayed on the handle of the door, and he hovered on the threshold.

"Of course it will," he said.

Elizabeth didn't contradict him.

"The machine –" he hesitated, then shook his head. "Of course it will."

He pulled on the door to try and close it, just a little. But it didn't move. He tried again, then reached for the handle with his other hand and pulled hard. The door didn't move, but the air did. It was picking up speed now, its momentum rising at it fell inexorably down through the gaping doorway. The door pulled in the madman's grasp, opening wider as more of the air fell through it. He had to shout now over the wind:

"What have you done?"

"What I said I would," Elizabeth answered quietly.

The wind was starting to pull at loose bricks and roofing tiles, and first one then another flew perilously close to the madman as they were sucked through the doorway. Still he hesitated. Elizabeth couldn't decide if it was the thought of what she had done or the thought of finally being free that scared him the most. It barely mattered: in a few moments the pull of the gateway would be so great that everything inside the Loa would be sucked through. But perhaps he would feel better if he made a definite decision – hadn't that been how it was with her?

"You should jump," she urged. "If you go now, you might survive."

Bill walked up and stood behind her, wrapping his insubstantial arms around her as if trying to protect her against the storm. Part of the wall behind her gave way, sending up a cloud of brick and dust. It swirled in the air for just a moment before it suddenly fell under the gateway's influence and was pulled into a spinning typhoon out into the nothing beyond. For a moment, it looked as if the madman would be sucked away with it, but at the last moment he managed to push himself aside. He hit the floor hard, but bounced up again with a foolish grin across his face. The mill gave a single shudder and then fell, the entire weight of it falling down hard on Elizabeth and the madman. He threw his arms over his head as if intending to catch the roof and throw it to one side. Elizabeth didn't move, Bill still wrapped around her.

But again the gateway saved them. Even before they could fall, the bricks trembled and sped away to oblivion. The building disassembled itself around them, and neatly packed itself away. Within seconds, they were both sitting on a patch of grey wasteland under an ominous sky. The door was in front of them, no wall or frame remaining and yet somehow still somehow obviously a gateway. Elizabeth felt herself pulled up to her feet by it. This was it.

Her heart fluttered.

"I'm coming, Bill," she whispered to him.

He didn't answer, but opened his mouth as if he might.

And then the door slammed shut.

For a moment, there was complete and utter silence. Elizabeth found herself blinking in the greasy twilight, and half-wondering whether she had actually passed through the gateway. Perhaps this was the other side, the afterlife nothing but the reliving of the moment of her death over and over. She turned, and saw Bill step away from her with a look of ... he looked terrified. Of her? He seemed greyer, more insubstantial than ever. He held out a hand to her and then suddenly rippled apart.

Stepping through the last vestiges of the ghost came a man: squat, dressed in a three-piece suit that had obviously been tailored to fit someone else. His cloth cap was tilted back to reveal his face, his good eye on her as the bad surveyed the heavens.

"How 'bouts I come to you instead?" he asked.
The silence pounded in her ears. "Bill?" she said.

# 6. January 1854, Strines

They had just managed to drop onto the back of the trap when the village shuddered around them and the snow froze in the sky. A million fat white crystals hung motionless in the sky as if gravity had been given the night off. The horse gave an unsettled whinny, and Mr Braddock looked to Brierly with his mouth agape. Then another bolt of lightning broke the silence, and the horse bolted. Brierly tried instinctively to grab the reigns with her phantom limb, but it was Mr Braddock who reached them first. He gritted his teeth and pulled hard, trying to assert at least the pretence of control over the beast. Brierly clung on with her one good hand, wrapping her legs around the unconscious woman to keep her from sliding off.

The horse galloped up and out of the valley at such a pace that it felt like they were driving through a raging blizzard. But as she squinted up through the darkness above her, Brierly could see that the flakes still weren't moving. This was not something she had seen before: not even a single voice spoke up to suggest an explanation. She doubted that the aggregated wisdom of the British Army would be able to provide much more. She felt her arm ache dully, and she closed her eyes.

As the trap reached the crest of the valley, it turned right onto the main road through the village. The pub was only a few yards further along; Mr Braddock had only just enough time to bring the vehicle under some kind of control before it appeared in front of them. The lights were on and the front door wide open, but there were no shadows moving within. Brierly could see into the snug and the small kitchen behind it, but both were completely empty.

Mr Braddock said nothing and brought the trap to a lurching halt.

He leapt down without a glance at his two passengers. Just a hand moving to wipe the snow from his lips as he walked through it. Brierly considered trying to drag the woman into the warmth of the pub, but she knew that it would only mean both of them lying in a heap on the threshold. Instead, she swung her legs unsteadily to the ground and wobbled inside. She would have to wait until the publican could be reminded of his charge.

Inside, the Sportsman's Arms was silent. A fire burned cheerfully in the main tap room, and several half-finished pints rested on tables as if their owners had only just set them down. A few meals were gently cooling, forks set down mid-mouthful. But the only living soul in the entire building seemed to be Mr Braddock, standing mute in the middle of the room trying to comprehend. He spun as he heard Brierly stagger in, as if expecting the entire village to be there, just returning from a quick trip to the toilets and ready to fill the pub with life again.

"Where are they all?" he whispered.

Again, Brierly had no answers.

"I need a proper bandage for my arm," she said. She waved the bloodied stump at Mr Braddock. "And the young woman outside needs to be in here where it's warm. That should be enough to occupy us for the time being, Mr Braddock."

Her legs gave way and she had to fall into an empty seat beside her. There was a whiskey and a half-pint of beer on the table, but she doubted either would be much good to her now. She could feel the stump of her arm burning hot.

Mr Braddock did as he was asked.

Bandages weren't something that James kept a supply of. If someone came into the pub needing them, they would usually have to push past the doctor to get to the bar anyway. James looked across at his usual seat: his pipe was resting unlit on the table, the chair not even pushed back. The doctor had been sitting there when James had taken the trap to collect Mrs Howkins, and now he was gone so neatly that he hadn't even disturbed the furniture. James turned away: there was a clean sheet in the bedroom that could be sacrificed if it would save the sergeant.

If.

When he came back down with it, for a moment he thought she had died. She was sat unmoving in the same chair she had fallen into, a few drops of blood pooling on the wooden floor beneath her. Her eyes were fixed glassily on the window. The pub was built on the valley wall, and the back door was a whole storey below the front. It meant that the windows at the back of the building gave a spectacular view out across the Goyt

Valley, when the air was clear. Now all he could see was grey night and snowflakes floating impossibly in the air, refusing to fall.

"I thought I saw –" the sergeant said hollowly.

There was a flash that brightened the whole sky, and both of them flinched. The air crackled, and outside every flake of snow instantly melted. The air was filled with a million droplets of instant rain, hanging expectantly for a moment. Then they boiled away to steam, to nothing, and the night sky was suddenly clear. Another fork of lightning struck the ground, and the entire valley was illuminated in a cold grey-blue light. They saw the solid white curve of the barrier encasing them, and suddenly everything was dark again.

James felt his stomach turn.

The sergeant reached out her hand for him, and for a moment he felt the cool touch of her skin. It felt something like a comfort, but then he realised she was just reaching for the sheet. He let her take it, and then watched as she used her teeth to tear it into thick strips ready to wrap around her arm. Some small part of him added the cost of the sheet to the tab he had mentally opened the moment the army entered his pub.

He watched as she made a few unsuccessful attempts to bind her arm, and then took pity on her. He flinched as he touched the sticky, puffy flesh of her stump, but within a few minutes he had it wrapped. The bandage looked far from professional, but it looked like it would last the night, which was more than he was willing to say about the sergeant herself.

"There," he said. He paused awkwardly, before adding: "It'll be all right now."

The sergeant looked at him with a raised eyebrow.

"I don't think there's any chance it isn't infected," she said, oddly calmly. "There was no time to sterilise anything. I wouldn't imagine there's more than a few hours of consciousness left."

James didn't know what to say, but she just gave him a smile.

"But it is a good bandage," she said.

Lightning cracked again outside the window. It showed the extent of their bounded world. At the furthest edge, James could see the crumbled remains of the works. Nearly all of the people who should have been waiting for him in this pub had worked in one of those factory buildings.

The rest, like him, were only here to make sure those men, women and children didn't die, starve or go cold during the few hours they weren't feeding the machines. Perhaps it was for the best that the villagers had vanished: certainly there would be little left for them in Strines now that the factories were gone.

The thought gave him a chill.

"You're not going to die," he told the sergeant quite firmly.

She cocked her head at him.

"I'm surprised to hear you say that," she said.

"I don't want to be here alone."

For a moment, neither of them said anything. They both looked out of the window, but everything had gone dark again. All they could see were their own hollow faces reflected back at them. James could see there was something the sergeant wanted to say to him, but didn't quite dare.

"The major is still out there," she hesitated. "He would protect you, of course."

"I wouldn't put too much faith in that."

Neither of them turned. Neither of them had spoken. But looking into the dark mirror of the picture-window, they saw a figure in the doorway. A short figure, their body nothing but a shadow. They held onto the door frame with both hands as if afraid the world might suddenly tilt out from under them, but they made no move to come into the warmth of the room.

"Your companion is dead," they continued lightly. "Or else if he isn't, he will be in moments. There isn't anyone else."

James couldn't move. He recognised her instantly, of course. Not from the shaved head or the round dark goggles hiding her eyes: it was her posture as she hovered on the threshold, the shape of her body and the turn of her head. It was the woman, the one who had been injured when the factory had collapsed. She was awake. She was talking to him.

She smiled and stepped into the room.

"We're the last living people in the universe," she said. "So what do I have to do to get a drink?"

"My name is Isabella," she said. She spoke softly, certain that everybody was listening. "I know more about what is happening here than any of you do. I will fix this, I promise you. I just need you to give me someone to talk to while I do. Does that sound reasonable?"

In the time she was talking, Isabella had gently lifted herself up and over the wooden bar in the corner and pulled a bottle of single malt from the shelf. She glanced across at Brierly and Mr Braddock for just a moment, before pulling the cork and pouring herself a double measure. Brierly couldn't quite decipher the look in her eyes: the young woman might as well have been wearing her goggles.

"I'm taking silence as agreement," Isabella said, and downed her whisky.

In a sudden fluid movement, she swept all the bottles from the shelf behind her to the floor, save for one of whisky that she deigned superior enough to save. There was the sound of glass crying out as it met its doom, and Isabella peered deep into the mirror revealed behind them. Not seeing whatever it was she was looking for, she leapt back over the bar and started pulling chairs and tables away from the walls. Wood splintered and cracked, and more drink and glass crashed onto the wooden floor.

"What the hell are you doing!" Mr Braddock screamed.

He reached out to grab her, but she danced and spun and suddenly he was nose deep in the nearest wall. The sound of his impact was only just drowned out by the crunch of breaking bone, and blood joined the alcohol on the floor. Isabella skipped lightly through into the snug next door and started tearing the photographs from the wall. More glass crunched underfoot. Brierly's hand went for her weapons, but none were there: a small part of her mind told her she had no chance of stopping the young woman with only one arm. Was it worth risking further injury merely to prevent a little property damage?

"Are you alright, Mr Braddock?" Brierly asked.

He was holding his nose, gingerly trying to stem the flow of blood.

"She broke my nose!" he spat.

Brierly stepped forward.

"Perhaps you should answer his question?" she said darkly.

Isabella didn't even look at them: something about the spot of wall revealed when she removed the dartboard had caught her eye, but after inspection it was apparently not what she was looking for. The board crunched to the floor and she rushed back into the tap room, eyeing the large picture windows suspiciously.

"Remember: me know what's going on. You, not so much," she said, almost as an afterthought. "I'm looking for something. I'm sorry about your nose, James, but you brought it on yourself."

Her voice trailed off as she focused on the fireplace between the two windows: there was a fire burning merrily in the hearth, intended to warm the outsides of the missing customers as thoroughly as the alcohol did their insides. The flames flickered orange, and she approached them cautiously.

"Get me some water," Isabella ordered.

"No!" Mr Braddock spat.

"It's still snowing outside. We'll need the fire tonight," Brierly said, trying to sound reasonable. The realisation that she was going to have to act on incomplete information was dawning on her. She didn't like it, and tried to push it away. "Perhaps if you told us why, we could reach some consensus?"

Isabella laughed, coldly.

"Trust you to want that," she said.

Brierly felt a chill. How much did the woman know?

"It's not snowing," Isabella said with a resigned sigh. "We're completely sealed in: there isn't any weather any more. But the barrier is somewhere around absolute zero: what you're seeing is the water vapour in the air freezing and falling to the ground. Next it will be the oxygen: that fire won't be any good to you. The only hope you have is to let me find the way out."

Brierly couldn't help but look out of the window at that. The snow was falling in fat heavy flakes again. The sky was still dark, although there was the distant growl of thunder to suggest that wouldn't be the case for long. Thunder, lightning and snow all without clouds in the sky: perhaps it was something she shouldn't believe, but she had seen far stranger. Even Mr Braddock seemed convinced by the certainty in Isabella's voice: he stepped forwards to better see the night outside, his hands dropping from his broken nose.

"Everything you thought you knew is gone," Isabella said, still stalking the fireplace. "The barrier is the outside of a space-time bubble. This is the inside. You saw the things fighting in the sky? They swim here. They bend reality just by existing. When they fight, they can tear whole chunks of it away. In the normal run of things, we'd already be dead."

"Then why aren't we?" Mr Braddock asked.

"Something has been manipulating this bubble. It's beginning and its end have been sewn together in a loop," Isabella explained casually as she reached out for the flames. She pulled one out of the fire and watched it die in her fingers for a moment. "Once the timequakes subside and the temperature normalises, this bubble will go on happily existing until the heat-death of the multiverse. You will live the rest of your lives getting colder and older in this little village."

She looked at Mr Braddock and gave him a flash of a grin.

"But maybe that's what you intended to do anyway," she said.

"And you," Mr Braddock said quietly. "You walked into it. I saw you."

Isabella just smiled.

"Now I want to get out of it," she said. "You should, too."

"And why does that necessitate putting the fire out?" Brierly asked.

Isabella took a step closer.

"Because there's someone hiding in it," she whispered.

Brierly felt her stomach drop.

"Who?" she asked.

The flames twisted and danced, and Brierly suddenly realised she couldn't hear the crackle of the logs burning. Then there was an arm reaching out of the fire. It grasped Isabella's neck tightly, the nails pressing so tight that little beads of blood appeared at her throat. Within a second, there was a man there: he was dressed in an orange robe, with what looked like a circlet of bronzed barbed wire wrapped around his head. He was a good head taller than Isabella, and as he unfolded from the fire he lifted her effortlessly into the air.

Behind him, a second man appeared, his exact double.

"Us," he said.

For a moment, nothing moved.

Isabella felt the thick fingers pressing into her neck, felt her lungs start to pull deeper of their own accord, just to keep the air coming. Being held in the air by your neck was painful. That probably wouldn't surprise anyone, but there you are. She was damned if she was going to let either of these two see it, though. She would have them thinking she osmosed air through her skin even as the brain cells started dying.

"You know an awful lot about the situation here," the man who wasn't holding her neck said casually. "For a native, I mean."

"I know a lot more than you think," Isabella said as best she could.

Was that a bone in her trachea breaking? No, surely not.

"Put her down," came an authoritative shout from across the room.

Isabella had to admit that she was a little impressed. The sergeant – Brierly – had lost an arm, God knew how much blood, and every member of her little taskforce. But there she was, standing firm and barking orders at the two guardsmen as if she had a hope in hell of even comprehending what they wanted, let alone defeating them. It showed spirit and determination, even if it exposed a general lack of any self-preservation instinct.

The man holding Isabella up snorted.

"Associative lifeform," he tutted to himself.

"Dependent on their internal communication protocol," the other finished the thought seamlessly. "Let's see what happens when we reboot it."

The soldier waved a single finger in Brierly's general direction, and Isabella tensed. Brierly stood firm, still trying to look as if she and her army were in control of this situation. Isabella could see the sergeant had no idea what was about to happen to her, but she doubted that the knowledge would provide any comfort. Certainly it didn't make Isabella any happier.

"I ..." Brierly began to say.

Then she let out an ear-piercing scream as the parliament of internal voices that controlled her every action was suddenly and forcibly dissolved. She crumbled to the floor in an uncomfortable knot, trying to work up the resolve to keep her own heart beating. Poor James tried to help her back to her feet, his broken nose dripping blood onto the sergeant's red jacket. The two soldiers didn't even smile in self-congratulation.

"Bright," Isabella choked.

The two soldiers turned their attention back to her. The grip on her neck tightened reflexively.

"And your friend," Isabella tried to indicate the second soldier without moving her head. "Cobden. Isn't that right?"

The two soldiers looked at each, but not a word passed between them.

"What else do I know?" Isabella smiled grimly. "And do you need to find out before you kill me? That's what you're thinking."

The grip tightened.

"That's the wrong question," Isabella said. "You should wonder if I'm alone."

Beside them, a single claw cleanly sliced down through the still air. A wind briefly picked up from nowhere, and a glowing hole into nothing hung in front of them. Out of it stepped the clawed shadow.

It attacked.

James had no idea what to do. He wanted to help – of course he wanted to help – but this wasn't the same as stepping between two lads knocking seven shades out of each other on a Saturday night. He earned his money, he paid a reasonable amount of tax: the whole of society was there to protect him. That was how it worked. But this … society was just him and four other people. The idea that he was the only one of them who thought the way he did, knew the things he knew … that was more frightening than anything else he had seen that night.

And so he hesitated. And in those few short moments, the shadow lunged at Isabella and her attacker, its arm raised ready to strike. James heard himself cry out, but he didn't move. He saw it slash at Isabella's throat, felt his heart spasm as she fell to the floor and bled away to nothing, all while he stood there and did nothing. But that wasn't what happened: instead the shadow swung its arm lightning fast towards her attacker, the tall man in the strange purple dress. James didn't even see it move, but the blades on its fingers went right for the man's throat.

And he casually reach up with his free arm and caught the shadow's wrist.

For another second nothing moved.

"Sombras Que Corta," the man said, not a hint of strain in his voice. He looked for all the world like someone at market sizing up a pig he had no intention of buying. "I suppose that settles that question."

"I had no idea there were any remnants of the Faction still in existence," his twin said idly from the other side of the room. "I wonder if it is merely coincidence."

The man holding Isabella and the shadow considered for a moment. James could see the shadow twisting and writhing in his grasp. Somehow, even though its face had no features, he could sense its surprise. This was not the way that Isabella had intended this to play out.

"I don't suppose it matters," the man said.

And from his face, his eyes, came a suddenly blinding white light. Even the sergeant, who was barely in her right mind and crawling around at James' feet, covered her eyes. James squinted through his fingers to make out what was happening. All he could hear was Isabella screaming as the touch of the light burned like lava. The light had a much worse effect on the shadow: its insubstantial flesh blistered and burned, and soon it turned to ash and blew away on the air.

His hand suddenly empty, the man in purple wiped it carefully on Isabella's jacket.

She didn't stop screaming.

There had been something here once. What was it? A thing. Many things. Something with clarity and purpose. A voice. Many voices, together as one, eventually. But now there was just discord and loud angry noise. And pain. Even just curling into a ball and lying here waiting for it to end was an agony.

What had once been Brierly barely even heard the screaming.

Cobden-Bright allowed himself a breath to recover his composure. Truth be told, it wasn't all that much of an exertion, but he found that taking everything at a steady pace led the lower orders to see a certain inevitability to every action. Which of course there was: it was inevitable that he would

66

carry out his orders and finally get to leave this empty distraction and get back to the rest of the guard. It was inevitable that his punishment would be forgotten and he could rise again, this brief hiatus forgotten and buried. The sooner he popped this stubborn little bubble and left, the better.

"I assume we can consider whatever petty intrigue you intended over now?" he asked the Faction agent in a sarcastic drawl. She rather ruined the effect by screaming in agony over his words. "Fine. If you have no pithy last words –"

Something struck him on the side of the head.

Cobden-Bright staggered a little, his free hand touching his temple to find a little blood there. He looked at the tips of his fingers, not quite understanding how they had grown red. Another bottle flew through the air, this one sailing harmlessly over his shoulder but attracting his attention none-the-less. He let the screaming Faction agent fall. The apeman was behind the bar now, pulling broken bottles from the floor and hurling at him with a surprising lack of accuracy.

Cobden-Bright had to admit he was unsure of what to do.

James threw bottle after bottle, scooping them up from the floor one after the other. The business man in him made him pick the broken ones first, but soon they were gone and even the bottle of Spayside malt Isabella had left on the bar became a weapon. It rolled in a lazy half-revolution before hitting the man in purple cleanly on the nose, knocking him back and down to the floor. And so this was the moment when James had to consider just what in the name of Hell he was doing.

Isabella curled into a tight ball, her screams subsiding into gasping sobs.

James cleared the bar in a single leap, and then stumbled as he fell and landed in a bruised knot next to her. The man in purple was already getting back to his feet, and his twin at the fireside was only two strides away from breaking James' neck. James put his hand on Isabella's shoulder and tried to think of something useful to say. Instead, he pulled her to him, and suddenly they were both on their feet and lurching away from the angry twins.

"Sergeant!" James hissed. "Help me!"

But the sergeant was going to be no help to anyone, least of all herself. She was still curled into a tight ball and spasming without the slightest hint of self-control. James knew that he should help her, but he doubted he could. The twin nearest him was blocking the exit. The other was approaching calmly, as if he was just as aware as James how little hope there was.

"Leave her," Isabella managed to gasp. "Leave me."

The door behind blocked, the other twin reached James and paused for just a moment. He had a look of reluctance – as if he realised that James was such a low-level annoyance that dealing with him would only demean all involved. His hand came for them both, and James gave a scream of panic and punched the man in the face. It felt uncomfortably like he'd just punched the prime minister, or more likely a prince given the crowns they both wore.

There was no crunch of bone. Evidently the twins' noses were made of sterner stuff than James'. He didn't even rock back, but he did turn away slightly as if in respect to the effort involved. James didn't wait, and pulled Isabella with him, running for the picture window in the corner of the bar. He could see the snow and the lightning outside, and for just a moment his greatest fear was getting cold and wet. Then together he and Isabella struck the glass, and he wondered if it would break or if he would bounce off it and land at the twins' feet, dazed and embarrassed.

Then the air was filled with broken glass and snow, and he felt his stomach lurch upwards. For just a moment, he felt like he could fly, that he'd be able to stretch out and leave all this madness behind him. Then something hard pushed his feet into his neck, and the wind from his lungs. He rolled a little way down the hill, fairly certain that he was screaming as he went. When he came to a stop, he realised that Isabella was gripping tightly to his hand.

The idea of moving never seemed further away.

The snow flurried in through the broken window. It started gathering on the table nearest to the window, slowly melting as it hit the warmth of the fire. By the time Cobden-Bright reached the window, there was nothing to see outside but a few vague trails in the snow and the encroaching darkness. Even the lightning seemed to have a moment's rest as Cobden-

Bright tried to find the apeman and the Faction agent somewhere huddled against the cold. Or perhaps the bubble was starting to settle into its new unnatural existence. Hopefully not – that would mean there was not much time.

He reached out, his hand sliding into a pocket of spacetime that was folded into the surface of the bubble. A bubble on a bubble. It had been prepared before they had entered, and they had drawn it through once they were here: standard procedure in such circumstances. His hand pulled out again, and dangling down from it was a small black bat, clinging upside down to his fingers with sharp little claws. It started to twitch even as the atmosphere inside the bubble touched its wiry fur, its beady eyes blinking in the half-light. It chittered maniacally to itself, and rolled a thin, dry tongue across its pointed teeth. It flapped its wings experimentally: vast leather folds that could have easily enclosed the whole of Cobden-Bright's head if it so desired.

Cobden-Bright stepped to the broken window.

"Let's be done with this," he told the bat. "Quickly."

He held out his hand, and it flew out into the darkness.

# 7. Twilight, The Grey Town

He didn't take her face in his hands and rain kisses on it, one for every moment they had been apart. He didn't even rain as much as a single kiss on her: her lips, her cheeks, remained unmolested. Her Bill didn't even take her hand in his, and of course Elizabeth found that she couldn't quite bring herself to do those things either. There was too much time between them, she was surprised to find. Too many years that she had lived without him: she suddenly realised it would be like kissing a stranger. For him, she meant: it was clear that he was exactly the same old Bill, not even a single day showing on his face. But then, of course, he was dead.

It was she who had remained, she who had changed.

She felt the urge to apologise.

"I suppose there is a chance that this is some kind of a trick," Elizabeth managed to say, her lips dry.

Bill just smiled wryly.

It was such a familiar thing, and she realised then how long it had been since she had seen it. She had thought she had taken him with her, but the grey ghost who had haunted her wasn't her Bill. His features had grown exaggerated with every passing day, his bad eye growing worse until it never pointed in her direction. And she hadn't noticed. Every day the real Bill had slipped further away from her, and she hadn't noticed. It was only now he was here that she could see how badly her memory had tainted.

"You closed my doorway," the madman complained limply.

Bill didn't look at him. Instead, he took the hat from his head and let the rim run through his fingers, like he did when he was nervous. But there was no sign of it in his face: it was just the dead echo of the emotion. He looked around him, and seemed unsurprised that the wheelhouse was no longer there. His eyes were on the horizon, and the dusty scrub surrounding them.

"We could go for a walk?" he said hesitantly.

"Twenty years," was all Elizabeth could say. "If you knew half the things I'd done, you wouldn't even speak to me. This ... I wasn't prepared for this, Bill."

Bill just tutted.

"Don't be daft, love," he scalded gently. "Let's just walk, eh?"

And he crooked his elbow, offering it to her. But not like old times, nothing like that. She remembered the way he used to just bend his arm without even looking, knowing that she would take it. Not even considering that she might not be there. But this time, he didn't have that confidence. He thought she could still turn away. But of course she couldn't – the years hadn't changed her so much, after all.

"Let's walk," she agreed.

They didn't go far, of course. There was a heap of rubble across the road, and he walked her over to it and took a few cautious steps up before thinking better of it. He lowered himself carefully onto a large stone, and Elizabeth went to stand dutifully next to him. She could still see the madman and his door. Now it was just a frame standing in an empty wasteground, firmly shut. But the madman circled it like he was afraid it might suddenly come to life again, and then pulled frantically on the handle before giving out an agonised scream of frustration. Bill just watched him, his face as blank and grey as slate.

"Why are you here, Bill?" Elizabeth asked.

He didn't answer, just shrugged slightly.

"I missed you," she said, not able to meet his eye.

"I know," was all he would say.

Elizabeth looked him up and down again. Not a day had passed for him since the fire. His skin, his eyes, his hair, all had the sheen of youth. People had always said they were such a well-matched pair – on their wedding day, Gordon Yarrow had joked they looked like more like brother and sister. But now his skin was fresh and smooth, whilst hers was cracked and dry, her fingers soaked in old blood.

"Well," she said with a sigh. "Isn't this a fine little pickle, William Howkins? So what is going on here? I suppose I can't assume that you're here to come home with me again? I don't suppose there's any way we can set off where we left it."

Bill smiled again at that.

"When did you get to be such a daft old bird, Betty?" he teased with easy affection. "I'm dead, love."

Elizabeth couldn't trust herself to answer that. Already she could feel a tear pricking the corner of her eye. It had been ten years since she had last cried for Bill. The day she had learned about Spinning Jenny and set her mind to revenge was the last. She told herself that she would cry again once the Loa was dead, but she honestly doubted she would be able to even then.

"Aren't we all, Bill?" she whispered sadly.

"I've been here since the fire," he said. "Me dying – everyone dying – that was something someone did on purpose. To feed her. So we died and we all came here. It's not much of an afterlife, I suppose. But it's the only one I have."

Elizabeth looked over at the madman, beating on the closed door with his fists.

"And if I kill her?" Elizabeth asked.

"Well then that's the end of all this," he said, looking around. There was still that twinkle in his eye: she could tell there was some part of him that was still gauging the best place to plant the cabbages in all this dust. "Me too. But don't worry about that: you aren't going to kill her."

"Is that so?" Elizabeth bristled.

Bill just rested a hand on her knee. It felt rough and cool, but not uncomfortably so. His skin had always been rough to the touch – too many years of scars on scars, love-bites from the presses.

"It is so," he said softly.

The ground trembled ominously underneath them.

"You're going to save her," Bill said.

She was a leviathan, there was no doubting that. There were only very few who ever got to see the Loa swim, but that was how all of those that did described it. The space between the universes was a wild ocean, stars cresting the tips of the waves, and through it all the Loa glided. Their scale was so impossible that it seemed like they moved the same way mountains did, cresting and falling across geological ages. But they moved so fast that time and space simply buckled around them.

Spinning Jenny twisted, flicked her tail with a power that sent universes trembling. Her jaws yawned open, revealing claw-tipped teeth falling in rows down her throat. Her chest trembled as she gave a magnificent roar, but there was no sound in that ocean. Only this balletic mime of pain and anger.

The other Loa dived with the same grace and slow-seeming speed. He was larger than her by far, his hide a rough thick purpley grey that was pock-marked and scarred. Each scar was the token of a battle such as this: there is no natural predator for the Loa save themselves. His jaws gaped white, revealing the same barb-ended teeth, and with a flick of his tail it spun into her underbelly and took away a great bloody chunk. Her mouth opened again, no sound shaking the ocean waves.

Loa blood washed away on the ocean.


"Baron Samedi?"

"He's come because someone from your plane has drawn him," Bill said. Elizabeth felt a little shiver of loss: the conversations that they used to have in their little house in Strines never involved anything more metaphysical than whether Bill would get away with last Sunday's tie for church. So much that neither of them would ever be able to unlearn. "Her too. They got them here to fight."

"Then she will die," Elizabeth said. "Samedi is the head of the Guédé. What's Jenny to him?"

"Just a kiddie," Bill agreed. "He's nearly won already."

The ground trembled again, just to make his point.

Bill looked around him briefly as if to check that they were all still here. Then he slapped his hands on his thighs and pulled himself up to his feet. His arm crooked again for Elizabeth to take, but this time she hesitated.

"No point hanging around here," Bill said, as if to himself. "Best get to it."

"Are you leaving?" Elizabeth asked.

Bill started to smile again at that, but then he saw the look in her eyes and he had the heart to stop himself. Instead, he gave her a look of apology and took her face in his hands. She moved almost imperceptibly towards him, and his dry lips brushed momentarily against her forehead. For just a moment, they stayed like that, and the whole imagined world around them faded into nothing.

"Sorry, Betty," he whispered. "No way out of here for me now."

And then they were walking again, heading back over to the madman and his doorway. It was still firmly closed, and he seemed to have given up on it completely now. He sat in the dirt with his back to it, a sulky look on his face that said he had never intended it to open anyway.

"So what exactly would you have me do, William?" Elizabeth asked.

"You'll do whatever you want to do," Bill said with a sad chuckle. "I'm not so daft that I don't know that. Somebody has to save her. But if I were idiot enough to ask you, that would as sure as damn it mean you went out of your way not to. You were always a wilful woman, Elizabeth Howkins. I doubt you've got any less so without me around to keep you in check."

"But if I don't save her, I can't save you?"

Bill didn't say anything to that. Elizabeth didn't think she really wanted him to: the only reason she wanted revenge was because – even with everything she had learned – there was never any hope of saving Bill. Even this, this grey wasteland of ghosts and industry, wasn't his salvation. Perhaps it would be best for all of them if they were laid to rest once and for all.

"Come on," he said. "Time to get going."

Bill reached out and pulled the door open in one easy movement.

"That's my door," the madman grumbled, not moving from the ground where he sat. "You can't stop me going through."

Bill didn't even look at him.

"You can't go out there any more," he said.

The madman didn't say anything, just nodded sullenly as if he had remembered something that he was pretending to himself that he had forgotten. Bill motioned for Elizabeth to move. She stood at the threshold and looked through. There was no wind, no howling void. Just a doorway in the wasteland, and darkness beyond it. She thought of the ocean that boiled outside the leviathan's thick skin, and wondered whether she was about to find herself drowning in it. But what choice did she have?

"I could stay," she ventured.

Bill gave her an odd look.

"Why on Earth would you do that?" he asked.

She frowned.

"To be with you, idiot."

His eyes flickered a little, and for a moment Elizabeth thought she saw something of a real emotion burning there. Then the grey sheen came back down, and he just shook his head sadly. But it had been there, just for an instant. Some raw, real part of her Bill, still living after all this time: his terror.

"No, Betty," he said grimly. "Whatever happens to me, I don't want you here."

No heaven here, then.

"I can't make any promises," Elizabeth said sternly.

"Oh go on with you," Bill said.

She hesitated, then gave him the barest peck on the cheek. Then she was gone.

She felt the cold before she felt anything else. Not the absolute lack of anything warm that she could sense whenever she tried to commune with the Loa, but the heartless chill of a winter night far from the city. There was no sensation of movement, but as soon as she stepped into the doorway she was back again: standing on frozen ground, snow swirling all around her and looking down the valley into Strines. Back on almost the very ground she had left who knew how long ago.

But something was wrong.

The air was thick with cloud and there wasn't much light, but it wasn't as dark as it should be if time had passed inside the Loa as fast as it had out. It should be a few hours before dawn, and the snow should have been much deeper on the ground if it had kept up at this rate since she left. Elizabeth looked around quickly, straining her eyes for some sign of what time it was. There were none, but she could tell that she had slipped through time anyway.

She was on the moor at Mellor, one of the villages on the crest of the valley that looked across at Strines. It was rough, hilly ground, but there were still farms up here. All the animals had long been taken into their barns, though: anything out in this snowstorm would be dead within hours. If this was still the same snow she had left behind, then she knew it would keep falling until all the lines in and out of Manchester were completely blocked. The city would have two days of nothing but its own company, perhaps the first two since the Romans first built their fort there.

Looking down the slope, she could see the train line running from Manchester to Sheffield. There was a steam engine racing along, determined to beat the snow and get safely home before the end of the night. It looked identical to the one that had brought Elizabeth home to the village, but then didn't all trains look the same anyway? She turned her head in the opposite direction, and could just make out the road running down into the valley and then up again to the station.

There was a small horse-driven trap rattling along it.

James Braddock, on his way to meet her.

"So that's your game, is it, Bill?"

Elizabeth reached into her jacket pocket and pulled out a small silver hip flask. She took a sip of brandy, and then closed her eyes. This was something she had done so often since that first Haitian houngan had taught her how that it had become second nature. She usually didn't even need to concentrate to pick up the scent of the Loa in the air – she doubted she even really needed the brandy any more, except your usual next step was to try to call to the Loa you had identified. The Loa were always much more ready to come to you if they thought there might be a drink in it for them.

But this time she was nearly knocked from her feet by the force of their presence. They were practically on top of her, getting closer every moment: two separate scents enveloping her. They were both hungry, both eager – moving with such urgency that she doubted they had noticed each other yet. She remembered what Bill had told her: this was Spinning Jenny and Baron Samedi, summoned here to fight and shake the walls of creation.

And Bill had sent her here to stop it.

She didn't know if she could.

She didn't know if she wanted to.

Suddenly the wind turned, and Elizabeth heard a distant shout. She couldn't make out the words – quite possibly there weren't any – but she could hear the fear and the pain behind them. She turned her head and tried to pick it up again, but just at that moment the train carrying her younger self to Strines raced by underneath and all she could hear was the rattle of its wheels and the scream of its engines. Pressure began to build uncomfortably in her ears: the Loa had seen each other, both intent on the same prize. She knew it would only be moments until they fought.

She had known Bill right from school. He had been a little older than her, and had always seen her as a young annoyance. But all the same, when she was older, he had taken her to Marple Cinema and sat on the back row sharing a bag of mint humbugs with her. There had never been anyone else for either of them from that moment. They hadn't made any plans together – they had just instinctively known what the future would hold. Love, happiness, a little hard work and then – one after the other – three lovely little children to raise and love. It wasn't just Bill that the Loa had taken from her, it was those three freshly-scrubbed little faces. It was the steady certainty of what tomorrow would bring. It was any sense of hope, of security.

It had been a surprise just how much that hurt her. How much it physically hurt; like a wound that had been salted and rubbed every day to stop it from healing. All she could do was think how there would be no end to it, because there was no way for her to get that life back again. That was why it had been such a relief to find out about the Loa, to formulate a plan for her revenge and take each measured step towards achieving it. The idea that she might be able to make the something responsible for that pain feel even a fraction of it ...

The shout came again.

She still didn't know her own mind, but whichever way she chose to go, she might as well see the true face of what she was dealing with.

Elizabeth didn't need to hear the cries to find him, but they grew louder the closer she went, just in case. She could feel the Loa circling each other, the pressure of their briefest touch on the wall of this universe making her head ache unbearably. When the first of them took a bite at the other, Elizabeth felt a shooting pain run from the tip of her finger right down into her heart, and she felt like she might collapse and die just there on the hillside. But she took another swig from her hip flask and put one foot in front of the other all the same.

The snow was growing thicker, and it was hard to see more than a few inches in front of her. She doubted it was coincidence that the worst storm in a century had hit just as two Loa fought practically overhead, and it didn't bode well. She had escaped the consequences of the fight through her ritual, but now she was going to have to live through them or die trying. She could see the factory looming out of the blizzard below her, but had no way of knowing whether her younger self was already inside. She doubted she had long, though.

Another few steps and she found him. He was lying in agony, writhing and screaming on the ground. Each scream made him pull tightly at one of the ropes that had him pegged to the hillside. The robe he wore was tattered and drenched in blood, and his hair was thin and neatly trimmed. But even distorted in agony, Elizabeth could recognise the face of the madman she had just left behind with Bill. His neck was a still raw wound, slashed open with a sword or knife, but none of the blood there was fresh.

Most other people might have thought that he had a chance, but not Elizabeth. She could see the other wound: as well as his throat, someone had sliced open his soul. His biodata – the genetic record of his journey through time and space – was exposed to the air and bleeding everywhere. It was thick and black, flecked with oil and death. There was no doubt that this was what had attracted the Loa: Elizabeth could feel the taint of both of them on him, and each would fight to claim him as their own. From the few minutes she had spent inside Spinning Jenny, Elizabeth knew which was destined to win.

So at least she knew now what Bill wanted her to do.

"Please," the man saw her and croaked. The pain from the wound in his throat must be bad, but nothing like as much as from having his entire history bleeding out of him. "Please: kill me."

It was an idea: with nothing to fight for, there was still a chance that the Loa might simply fall into empty posturing. Spinning Jenny could save some face and retreat, and Bill would be saved. The echo of something that might once have been Bill. Or else it was just another of those bitter ironies that seemed to give the Loa sustenance. To convince her would-be-killer to save her life – that was the kind of irony that would earn the new Loa a little respect from the others of her kind.

But Elizabeth knew none of that really bothered her. The question she struggled with was simple: was she able to do something for someone else, not just herself? A man lay at her feet, bleeding both physically and metaphysically. And still she hesitated. Just what sort of a woman had Elizabeth Howkins become?

The madman reached a hand up for her, but it could barely lift more than an inch from the ground before the rope bit tight at his wrist. He fixed his eyes to hers, and she didn't flinch from them. If she was going to leave him to his fate, the very least she could do was acknowledge the fact to his face. His mouth opened, probably to plead for death again or merely to scream. But Elizabeth felt the sudden urge to turn, a vague vertiginous feeling in her stomach trying to pull her away.

She moved at the last moment, and the claws only snipped a lock of hair from her head. Elizabeth's heart jumped in surprise, and she found herself facing an insubstantial black shadow, claws bared and glinting in the moonlight. Just the sight of it gave her that odd feeling in her stomach again, and just as she was wondering how much she could trust its warning, the shadow leapt for her again. This time, she was just a little too slow and one of the razor fingers sliced a line of blood across her cheek. Elizabeth was turning even as she fell to the ground, and as the shadow rolled and rose again it was surprised to see its intended victim fleeing at speed towards the old works.

It gave chase, and the madman was left screaming to nobody once again.

But only for a moment: then he wasn't alone.

Elizabeth ran through the snow, but it wasn't a blind panic. There was no point in staying with the man – the shadow had chosen that battleground, and besides there was nothing to offer any kind of shelter there. Elizabeth had learned well enough that she didn't need to carry weapons to protect herself, but this was an entirely new situation and the possibility of somewhere to hide wasn't to be ignored. Perhaps the shadow wouldn't even follow her – probably it was merely guarding the madman, and would leave her be once she proved herself uninterested.

She glanced back over her shoulder.

The shadow was giving chase.

Elizabeth tried a few simple wards and discouragements as she ran, but there was nothing for them to get purchase on. She tried reaching out to the Loa, but Baron Samedi and Spinning Jenny had given up on cautious circling, and it was impossible to be heard over the shock waves from the blows they dealt each other. The shadow was fast, and Elizabeth was – despite everything – old: there wasn't any chance she could outrun it, and even if she reached the factory it would only be a matter of moments before the Loa lashed out and destroyed it all.

The shadow leapt at her. She tried feinting to the side but it had already second-guessed her. Its claws sliced through the thick cloth of her jacket, and its weight pushed her down into the snow. The shock of the cold was enough to make her hesitate, but she knew if she did she would be dead: resisting the urge to look, she tumbled twice down the hill and spun up into a crouch. The shadow had its claws deep in the snow where her heart had been, but quickly drew back: it looked at her and somehow managed to convey its deep annoyance.

At first Elizabeth thought that the hill had shook, but her other senses quickly told her that in fact it was their whole plane of existence. The Loa were so close now she could practically see them fighting in the sky above, spinning around each other, biting chunks out of anything that came close. The hillside's grip on the rest of the universe was shaken loose, but it managed to claw itself back by the tip of its metaphorical fingers. Another blow like that and all of reality might fracture: even the shadow sensed it, and paused in its attack for a moment to look back up the hill. She should have run, but instead Elizabeth followed its gaze: she could see silhouetted on the crest of the valley a small figure holding its arms aloft. The goggles resting on her head glinted in the moonlight, as did the knife that paused there.

The knife, Elizabeth could tell, was carved from an impossible bone.

She had carved it herself.

The knife fell, and the air screamed.

Elizabeth turned and raced down the hill, so quickly that the air moved too fast for her to pull it into her lungs and her legs threatened to get left behind with every stride. The knife had reminded her of another way to escape the shadow: the same way she had escaped whatever happened here before. If she could reach her younger self as she managed to breach Spinning Jenny's hide, they could both wake up inside the Loa and give her Bill the surprise of his life. Perhaps they'd both get sent back here to try again – perhaps there was already another slightly older version of herself taking full advantage of this poor foolish Mrs Howkins leading the shadow away from the sacrifice.

She felt a push like a gentle tap on the shoulder, and suddenly her arm was wet with blood. She knew it was the shadow, but she didn't allow herself to stop: instead she launched herself forward with a scream that was half pain, half desperation. She let go of any semblance of control and let herself spin and tumble the rest of the way to the edge of the factory. She hit the base of one of the old work's walls with enough force to crack a tooth, but she at least remained unperforated for those few moments she had been falling.

But that was it. She had no more strength left to fight.

Elizabeth stayed where she had come to rest, her neck pushed awkwardly against the rough brick of the wall. She opened her eyes and looked up, and could see the shadow standing there. It didn't hurry – it could feel the air throbbing with the force of the Loa's battle, and knew there was no hope of Elizabeth ignoring it long enough to escape. Her eardrums pounded with it, and as she looked past the shadow she could see a small black figure running from the site of the sacrifice. In the air all around them, Elizabeth could see teeth: Spinning Jenny dived and swallowed the madman whole, and the universe shook with her victory. Then Baron Samedi petulantly took a great bite from her flanks as she twisted by, and everything shattered.

There was a moment where everything was the piercing ring of crystal resonance, and Elizabeth couldn't stop herself from crying as her ears burst and her teeth popped. She could see nothing, because for that one terrible moment everything shuddered and everything rippled to black. She felt herself lift and violently fall, and thought for a moment that she had been thrown. But then she felt that the snow, the hill, the wall at her back had come with her too and she realised that it was reality that had been thrown. A vast chunk of it had ripped away as the Loa still fought and snapped, and now it was only a matter of time before it collided with something and was gone.

Elizabeth felt the wall shudder behind her, but everything was already black when the first bricks started to rain on her. She heard someone – she thought it might have been Mr Braddock – yell "Stop!" and then everything was silence.

# 8. Now, Inside the Bubble

There were voices everywhere. They shouted, they whispered, they cried out in fear and anger and frustration. Some tried to cajole, others comfort, but in the end all they were was noise. A thousand voices shouting impotently into the dark. The idea of anything as coherent as "a thought" or "an idea" in that maelstrom was ridiculous – an impossibility that frightened the voices almost as much as the reality of being unheard. And yet ... somehow amongst all that chaos, a single thought did fight to emerge. A single idea, flitting from voice to voice and trying desperately to find some fertile ground to grow.

This was the thought: this isn't how it should be.

At first, the idea bounced off a few of those voices without making the slightest impact. But then just one of the other voices seemed to hear it, and for a moment started to shout the same thought. Maybe as few as ten in all those voices found themselves changed by the thought, united by it into something like a conscious will. Slowly, painfully, the consensus that had been Brierly started to re-emerge.

For a single moment, she was there enough to understand that most of the voices were within, but a tiny minority were without. She trained all her will on picking out those two foreign voices, built enough of an idea of herself around the desire to understand what they were saying that suddenly she tipped back into being. She could feel the outside world again – the rough grain of the pub floor underneath her fingers, the fingers she had borrowed from a native woman when her last host had withered and died.

"Alright," said one of the external voices, "that wasn't the smartest thing we've ever done. Perhaps we should have secured the gateway before we released the bran-puca."

The words almost felt like they meant something.

"But the quicker we're away from this hole the better," echoed the second voice.

And then there was enough of Brierly there to open her eyes – to actually see the two men standing over her prone body. Two identical men in dusty purple robes, a twist of bronzed barbed wire wrapped around their temples. They didn't even look down at Brierly's body as they stepped over it to make for the door. They didn't say another word to each other as they stepped out into the village, and away from Brierly's one line of sight. The door swung shut, and they were gone.

Brierly's new-found consciousness trembled and tore. The voices that had been united in their desire to hear the two outsiders suddenly split on how best to cope with their absence, and Brierly hadn't recovered enough of herself to fight for consensus. She felt the world slip away from her again, and Brierly went under once, twice, and then for the third and final time.

But then there were her orders.

The thought came from nowhere, but it quickly bounced through her synapses and quieted nearly every voice. None of them were convinced that she had orders, but the idea that she might be able to get some gave her something to cling on to. The life-raft thought floated there appealingly, and she grabbed for it with both hands. She was sure that even if she had no clear orders, she still had a duty. A duty to ensure the safety of the men under her. Who were all dead. A duty to report to her commanding officer and obtain new orders, and be ready to carry them out.

For a moment, there was silence in her head.

The parliament was gone now, and would take time to rebuild. There were techniques, tricks she'd learnt as a child, to bring all her disparate personalities together into groups and alliances but there were no short cuts: building the trust that allowed them to act and interact was a long process, but without it no one voice would ever let the result of any vote stand. It wasn't an easy process or a quick one, but it meant that her actions had the power of a conviction and a consideration that no one mind could ever hope to achieve. But there wasn't a single one of them who couldn't be tempted to let some dominant outside influence take the decisions and relieve them of the frustration of reaching compromise.

She had joined the army out of necessity, but it was becoming an addiction.

Brierly pulled herself back together as best she could around the thought that somewhere out there, Major Webber might still be alive. And if he was, he would have no doubts, no nagging contradictory voices, about exactly what their next step should be. Brierly couldn't quite make it to her feet, but inch by inch she crawled to the door.

The snow was still falling, but only in light drifts. The sky was growing lighter, and it was that as much as the long hours he had been awake that made James think it was morning. Except of course it couldn't really be: there were still no clouds, but James couldn't see any trace of sky. There was a grey mist that seemed to rise from the frozen earth and thicken the closer it got to the heavens, but beyond it James could still make out the frozen blue sheen of the barrier. It was hard not to believe that outside it was nothing but empty space, and that the light leaking through came from some other sun in some other sky. But that was madness. Wasn't it more sensible to think that the world was still there, outside the barrier? That somebody outside was already trying to cut their way in and save them all?

Neither idea seemed particularly sane, that cold winter morning.

He pulled the curtain over the window as gently as he could. He had seen no movement across the road in his pub, but he didn't want to take the chance of attracting the men's attention. Doubling back up the valley wall with Isabella in his arms had been nerve-wracking enough, but as soon as he had felt the first touch of the frozen winter air he had known they wouldn't last long out in the open. Now they were inside, however, he couldn't shake the worry that Mary Devlin was going to burst into the room demanding to know just what he thought he had done to her kitchen window. Mary had a good stock of bacon and eggs in her pantry, but it wasn't just the thought of a smoking chimney that kept him from them. Instead he hid in her bedroom, gnawing on a crust of bread that must have been stale yesterday, and kept watch on the the unconscious girl on the bed.

She seemed to be sleeping peacefully now, but every now and then her face would crease as if she remembered momentarily that she was in pain. He knew he should have built her a fire, but there would be the tell-tale chimney and so instead he had piled as many blankets as he could find in the house on top of her. He couldn't imagine they were keeping her all that warm. Something else he had failed to do properly, now that he couldn't pay someone to do it for him.

Isabella suddenly sat bolt upright, pulling a huge breath into her lungs. James jumped so high he fell over onto his backside, and then panicked that she might be about to scream and give their position away. But the girl had her eyes closed, and instead of screaming she held onto the breath as if it was the only one she would ever need. James felt his heart beat ten times before the breath finally escaped her, easing out from between her lips in a thin stream of frozen air.

Her eyes opened, and she looked at him for a moment.

James didn't say anything, just blinked loudly.

"You got me out of there?" she asked lightly.

James found that if he concentrated very hard, he could nod at her. She looked at him for another moment without expression. The light in the air glinted off the googles that were pushed up onto her bald head. Her eyes sparkled a little, like the ice still hanging in the air. Then she gave him a grin that seemed to appear from nowhere, and go back there just as quickly. He couldn't help but return it, and tried desperately to think of something to say that might bring it back again.

"Thank you, James," she said.

The idea that he had saved her life came to him. He was surprised by how brave and capable it didn't make him feel.

"I feel a little sick," he said, and let himself fold to the floor.

Isabella looked concerned, but she couldn't move fast. Even as she tried to lean towards him, the pain came back to distort her face and she let out a breath that was more than half gasp. She didn't try to move again.

"Are you okay?" she asked instead.

James fought the urge to put his head between his knees.

"I'm fine," he said. "I've just realised how much those bottles I threw cost."

Another little smile. God help him, it almost made it worthwhile.

"It's okay," she said gently. "You're bound to have a touch of shock. You were two steps from being dead. They would have killed us all. But they didn't, because of you. Just hold on to that until the panic goes away."

James did his best to obey. "Who were they?" he asked her.

She looked at him with an odd look in her eye for a moment, and when she started to speak he realised that she was deciding whether to tell him the truth. And of course when she did speak, what she said sounded so insane that he had no idea which way the decision had gone.

"They were agents of the Great Houses. Minor agents," she corrected herself with a click of annoyance. "You would call them aliens. Or maybe policemen: they like there to be order in the universes, so they have strong opinions on something like this bubble. They're here to collapse it. Whether or not we're inside, apparently."

"And you can stop them?" James asked hopefully.

She shook her head.

"Not a hope in hell."

Isabella had every grain of salt in the house poured under every window and door before she would even consider letting James raid the pantry for anything as inessential as food or water. She didn't think there was much chance that they would send tracker-beasts after her, but now she was shadowless she couldn't afford many risks. The thought gave her an odd chill, and she reflexively reached out that part of her mind that was joined to her shadow. All she felt was a yawning vertigo as everything fell away to a recursive nothing. It was gone. Dead, well and truly. Even if she hadn't been completely alone, she wouldn't have known how to bring it back again.

Perhaps that was why she had let James follow her downstairs. He followed in her footprints like a surrogate shadow, but she doubted he would be as much use if they met Cobden and Bright again.

She felt a little pang of something when she noticed his nose was bleeding.

"James," she said.

It seemed that in her years alone, she had lost the knack of starting a difficult conversation. Perhaps the part that was easily able to apologise had lived in her shadow, and was forever lost to her too.

"Yes, Isabella," James answered.

He spoke a little bit too quickly, scanned her face for an unexpressed intention a little too deeply. It made her uncomfortable to think how comfortable she was with that.

"I am sorry about your nose."

He looked surprised.

"That's fine, really. It doesn't –" he brushed a finger against it to wipe away the blood, and then winced as if punched again. "Actually, it does hurt. But I can ignore it. It's fine."

"It is? Oh good."

Isabella turned her back on him and peered again out of the narrow kitchen window. It was hard to see anything out there, and not only because the window was frosted and cracked. The ice had started shaking loose from the bubble wall again, filling the air with a combination of mist and snow that at least made it unlikely Cobden and Bright would see them hiding out here. But it also meant she could only see a for a few yards. Outside that shallow radius, anything could be readying to strike. Or nothing – possibly Cobden and Bright would simply retreat and collapse the bubble remotely, not caring about capturing her. Either way, she would need to act fast if she had any hope of salvaging this.

"Actually," James said a little sharply from behind her. "No, it's fine. Although you didn't have to hit me."

"You were the one who grabbed me," Isabella countered calmly. "I can't always control my reflexes."

"And that thing, that creature –"

"The shadow whose loss I am still grieving?" Isabella replied coldly.

"It attacked us down in the valley," James retorted.

"It attacked the Major," Isabella corrected. She decided not to point out that if it had attacked James, he wouldn't have been around to complain about it.

"I think it might have killed him."

Isabella paused for a moment.

"It isn't impossible," she admitted.

"Because you told it to?" James asked. Isabella didn't stop, didn't answer. "What am I doing? I should just go back to the pub. At least that would feel normal."

"You'd be dead before you got ten paces."

"I'll be dead whatever!"

For a moment, they both stood looking at each other across the kitchen table. He looked afraid that she might beat him into his grave. For good reason, she had to admit. He didn't deserve this: whatever else, he was a passable shadow surrogate.

Isabella held up her hands.

"I surrender," she said. "Major Webber is a dangerous man. Dangerous to me. And dangerous to everyone if he tried making the Great Houses submit to the will of the Empire. You don't know him like I do."

"I don't know you either," James answered quietly. But his guard was down.

"No," she said with a half-smile. "But tell me you don't trust me."

James turned his head away, but not before Isabella caught sight of the schoolboy blush he was trying to hide. She smiled again: perhaps James wasn't the only one who had let their guard down, just a little.

"What do you want to know?" she asked him.

Just for a moment, Isabella thought he might actually ask. The question that was written all over his face, in the roll of his shoulders and the tremble of his hands. In the half-light of that dirty, dusty kitchen, he looked pretty enough that she might even answer. But instead, he swallowed a breath and let the moment pass. She couldn't completely blame him, of course.

"I don't know anything about you," he said. It was a statement of fact, an expression of regret. "I don't know what to do."

Isabella took his hand gently.

"My name is Cousin Isabella," she told him. "If I had a name before that, I don't choose to recall it. I was initiated into the Faction when I was eight years old, and they have been the only thing that is worth knowing about me ever since. I am nothing outside of the Faction. There is nothing more to know."

"Faction?"

"Faction Paradox," Isabella answered. There was still a little thrill from saying the name aloud. She hoped it would never fade. "If the Great Houses are determined the universe should be neat and ordered, then the Faction are the shadow they cast. We deal in paradox and impossibility. We won't let the universe be reduced. We know it is bigger and madder than that, and we strive to make it more so."

"I don't understand," James admitted.

"If I killed you now, the universe wouldn't care," Isabella said. James backed away a step. "I'm not saying I will: it's an example."

"That's very comforting," James said.

Isabella couldn't help smiling. He smiled back, if nervously.

"If you killed yourself now," she tried again, "it wouldn't matter."

"Again," James said, "I find myself comforted."

"But imagine you could go back in time. Imagine you stepped into a time machine now and went back to yesterday. What if you killed yourself then?"

James started to say something, and then stopped.

"That's ridiculous," he said eventually.

"It's Paradox."

"But it isn't possible," James spluttered only a little. "You couldn't actually do that."

"That's what the Great Houses would say."

Isabella let her hand brush gently across James'. He watched it move away again with a look of endearing confusion.

"Well, alright," James said. "But they would be right. It isn't possible."

"There's a ritual in Faction Paradox. Something a Sibling can do to show their ultimate dedication to pure paradox. They go back in time and they kill their younger selves. Hundreds have done it and lived to tell the tale. Their very existence gives the lie to the Great Houses' stilted laws and regulations: you don't need a law forbidding crossing your own timeline if paradox is impossible."

"But ... hundreds?"

Isabella looked out into the village. She told herself that she was checking again for tracker-beasts, but her gaze was dreamy and unfocussed. Whatever she saw, it wasn't the snow and the mist of that village in the bubble. She was seeing something else, something far colder and older than that.

"That's how I joined the Faction," she told James. "Sometimes the younger self wins."

She turned back, and found he was looking at her with a look of undisguised sympathy on his face. It made her shudder just to look at it. She could see it, towering over her, the sheer horror of her existence, ready to crash down on her.

"You said you were eight," he said softly.

She would not let that wave fall.

"Come on," she said sharply, turning to the door. "We can't waste time. We've got to get moving while we can."

"Isabella –"

No.

"Come on!" she snapped.

She reached for the handle, looked once more to see what she could outside. Very little, as before: she might open the door and step right into Cobden and Bright's waiting arms. She didn't know if James would be following.

"Isabella – wait!" But of course she didn't. "Where are you even going to go? There's nothing we can do – you said as much."

"I said I couldn't stop them," Isabella corrected.

"But your Faction can?" he asked.

Isabella knew she would be able to move much faster and effectively if she just stepped into the mist and left him behind. There was no reason not to. She knew what she had to do, and none of it relied on him. If she did kill him here and now, why should Isabella care any more than the universe?

"Isabella?"

"The Faction are gone," she said. "Wiped out. There are several versions of how: the details aren't important. I survived. Somehow, I survived. Just me."

"I'm sorry," James said.

She felt his hand on her shoulder, and didn't shake it loose.

"They'll have a tunnel," she said eventually.

"The Faction?"

"The agents. They're only minor agents. They won't be trusted with a Ship, and you couldn't bring one into an unstable bubble anyway. They'll have a tunnel between the bubble and the real world. If we can find it, if we can get past them, we can get back before they collapse the bubble."

"And that's where we're going? This tunnel?"

"Yes."

"Where is it?"

"I don't have a clue," Isabella admitted. "But it will need a strong connection to the real world. The place where the bubble wall is the thinnest would be the obvious place. And that is where the Loa has her place of power."

"I don't understand," James said. It wouldn't be the last time.

"The works," Isabella said. "We can escape if we get to the works."

His hand was still on her shoulder.

Webber awoke suddenly – one minute he was in total blackout, and the next he was blinking in the morning sun. It took him more than a few moments to piece together the last thing he remembered, but then he recalled the lightning strike and understood why the darkness had been so total and complete. Obviously he had been injured, possibly he even had only minutes left to live. He blinked again to focus, and his hand went up to the wound on his chest.

There was no pain. There was no wound.

He looked down and saw his uniform, charred and singed where the bolt had earthed itself through him. The fabric was burned clean away, as was the shirt underneath, but beneath that the skin was as pink and fresh as a newborn baby's. Somehow, he had survived. And survived unscathed – the only problem as far as he could tell was a cold pressure against his shoulders ... something that he was relieved to see was caused by him leaning against the icy wall of the barrier.

He was still in the village, then. And the village was still under attack.

"Major Webber?" an unsteady voice said.

He blinked again. He realised that he was not alone. Kneeling in the snow at his feet was Brierly, looking exactly the way that Webber had expected himself to look: her uniform was in ragged disarray and her eyes were red-rimmed and wild. Her skin had the look of dried parchment, and there was a bleeding stump where her arm used to be. He could guess how she had escaped being trapped. But worse was the look on her face, a mix of concentration and hope that made it clear the only thing keeping her together was the expectation of his command.

"I can't do it without your permission, sir," she said.

He looked at her blankly, looked around himself. He wasn't where he had fallen. Somebody – he assumed Brierly – had dragged him from the field and almost all the way up to the railway station. The only thing stopping them from reaching it was the thick barrier that had appeared since the previous night. Or was it perhaps still night – looking up, he could see darkness on the horizon where the village should be, and the ornamental lake that should be beside them was similarly invisible in the dark. But he and Brierly were sitting in the cold light of a winter morning: that was almost as impossible as his survival.

"At least we'd die truly together," Brierly was saying.

Webber felt his face drain as he realised what he was seeing. The village wasn't in darkness. It was gone. The darkness was moving, a sea of black flapping wings and everywhere they weren't there was nothing. They moved at a pace that was incredible, devouring and destroying until everything inside the barrier was just black and empty space. Webber tried to stand, to reach for his weapon and start the counter-attack. But his legs were traitors, and all he could do was watch.

A flock of the bat creatures whirled overhead. Brierly let out a cry as they dived, but they weren't going for her. Instead they struck the barrier at furious speed, their tiny teeth breaching it with ease. They swung up again into the sky even as more of the creatures dived down at them. Webber could hear the roar of the oxygen escaping the barrier, and the cold empty vacuum outside rushing in.

"Too late!" Brierly cried. "This is it!"

The world ended.

# 9. Now, Inside the Bubble

And then life went on.

For a moment, Webber lay on the ground with his eyes closed and waited for the darkness to take him again. But nothing came, and soon he opened his eyes again. Instead of blackness, there was a cold haze floating above his eyes, and it took him a moment or two to realise he was lying on his back looking up through a winter mist. Snow was packed around him, and drifted over him, but the ragged hole in his jacket and shirt smoked where the lightning had ignited it. The flesh underneath was still pink and unmarred.

The mist washed over him like smoke across the battlefield.

His thoughts did their best to follow.

"Sir," slurred a voice beside him.

He turned his head, and was surprised to find what an effort it was. The muscles had locked tight, and he suspected he had been lying on the ground for most of the night. Beside him was Brierly, in less disarray than she had been just moments ago, but her eyes were mismatched and hazy. His first week in the army he had seen a quartermaster drink nearly a pint of rum from his own stores. That quartermaster had stared through him with that same unsteady intensity as Brierly attempted now.

"Are ..." his voice cracked, and he fell into a cough.

"You alive?" Brierly said, reaching out a comforting hand that missed and landed knuckle-deep in the snow. "Sir?"

Webber tried again, his throat a paper-dry rasp.

"Are you drunk?" he hissed.

Brierly just stared through him glassily.

"Pull yourself together, soldier," he barked, and tried to follow his own orders.

Brierly flinched a little, and her eyes closed for longer than they really had a right to. When she opened them again, they were both the same colour. That was a start. As for himself, Webber struggled up onto his elbows and tried to take a deep breath. He had, he realised, a broken rib. It would need strapping if he was to go anywhere. He realised his breath was coming in sharp pants, and willed his lungs to slow down. Looking around, he found that he was lying exactly where the shadow and the lightning had left him. Was it only the night before? And if so …

"Where are the bats, Sergeant?" Webber asked, wincing again with each breath.

"Bats?" Brierly echoed, but she seemed in that one word to find something of herself again. "I don't understand."

"Give me some water," Webber ordered.

Brierly smiled a little, and reached for a flask at her hip.

"Yes, sir," she breathed.

Her eyes rolled back into sharp focus, and Webber suddenly found all of her attention on him. In all the years he had known her – man and boy – he had learned that she could be most disconcerting. The only real way to cope was to let anything short of open insubordination pass without comment. He had seen too many officers drive themselves mad to try anything else. In some cases literally.

The water eased the rasp in his throat a little. He took another gulp and passed the flask back. His head had almost stopped swimming long enough for him to try and piece back together what he knew.

"There were bats in the air," he told Brierly, looking for some sign of recognition on her face. "Too many to count. Thousands. You were there: you saw them. They were tearing the village apart bite by bite."

"I've been in the Sportsman's Arms most of the night, sir," Brierly told him. That at least went some way to explaining that, then. "It didn't go well. I came to report."

Webber carefully removed his jacket and shirt.

"Then report," he wheezed.

As Brierly began her report, Webber quickly checked himself for injuries: he had fresh cuts and bruises from his fight with the disappeared shadow, and of course the broken rib … which, if he was lucky, might only be badly bruised. He had a bandage in his pack that he wrapped cautiously around himself, being careful to keep his face impassive in diffidence to the dignity of his command. But with each wind of the bandage, a new thought came to him. They fell one onto the other, building a structure that was impossible to ignore.

"The girl," Brierly reported. "Her name is Isabella."

He had been lying some way from here, nearly back at the station.

"She knows what's happening here, sir."

His rib had not been as painful. In fact, he had barely noticed it.

"She found two men hiding ... in the pub, sir."

But it had been broken. Now he thought about it, now he tried to remember, he knew it had been. Broken, and bound. Just as he was binding it now. So he could manage the pain as he tried to master this impossible situation.

"They are the men behind this, Major Webber," Brierly said firmly, her eyes briefly flashing indigo. "They did this."

Webber looked at her.

Whatever had happened five minutes ago to him, she had no knowledge of it. Because it hadn't happened five minutes ago to her. Most likely, it hadn't happened to her at all. Yet. Most likely, it was going to happen to them both again, some time soon. He closed his eyes and for just a moment allowed himself the feeling of giddiness that swam over him. It was always the same whenever he came up against Mrs Howkins: nothing would stay the same.

"Alright," he said to Brierly. "Tell me about them."

If she was honest, Brierly would have to admit that she couldn't clearly remember the moment that she started looking for Webber. She couldn't remember when she had left the pub, or how she had pieced herself together voice by voice. Her memory ended as the man in the barbed-wire circlet reached his finger out to her, and started again in this field as she found herself crawling towards Webber's prone body through the frozen dew. It wasn't the gap that troubled her, though. It was the vivid memory of how dispassionately the man had taken her thoughts from her. He hadn't even smiled.

Brierly was nothing to these men. Nobody was. They had a job to do, and would do it as quickly and efficiently as they could. Any resistance they met would simply be removed.

Brierly didn't think that even Webber had a chance against them.

"Sir," she said, as tactfully as she could.

Webber wound the last loop of bandage around his chest and tied it tight. He pulled his ripped and burned jacket on with a reverence she had never been able to replicate. Bodies were just clothing to her, and the things that they wore much less than that. But Brierly had learned long ago that Webber saw his uniform as the very fabric of his contract with his monarch. Every button was a solemn vow, and could not be fastened easily.

"We are under attack, Brierly," he said, pulling himself wheezily to his feet. "Possibly just this village, but likely the country and perhaps even the whole Empire. This is the first stage of an invasion."

"Isabella-"

"Isabella is a child. She might have some grasp on the situation, but I would be remiss if I were to rely on it. Especially receiving it second hand."

"Of course, sir," Brierly answered. She continued before Webber could start up again: "But she was right about the men. She may be right about the rest. If she is, then this may not even be part of the Empire any more. And even if she is wrong, our force is not at full strength. We should make use of what local resources make themselves available to us."

Webber paused for a moment. Brierly could almost hear the debate in his own internal parliament. Except of course he had none: he was one man alone, trying to decide the best thing from one narrow point of view. She wondered how he ever managed to decide anything. He brushed his uniform down, straightening it and himself. The buttons flashed like stars in the strange half-light.

"You don't have access to the full gravity of the situation," Webber said. He looked away across the snow and into the heart of the mist. "Whatever is happening here, our first duty is to warn our superiors. What happens to us after that is irrelevant."

"Sir," Brierly said again.

"We are going to breach the barrier and get word to General McAllister. You have your orders, Sergeant."

He was wrong. Brierly knew that he was wrong, as did the majority of the members of her jury-rigged replacement self. Even with everything he had seen and done, this was beyond him. The right thing to do was to find Isabella and do whatever she told them should be done. But Brierly hadn't come to Webber because she knew he would be right. She had come to him because he would tell her what to do, what to think. She was just too fragile to argue this through for herself: she wanted orders. Cold, unambiguous orders.

And now she had them.

"Yes, sir."

"The first thing we ..." Webber's voiced trailed off as he stared up at something in the sky. "We don't have much time."

Brierly looked up, but all she could see were black dots circling in the sky. Birds, or something very like them. But Webber looked as if he had heard the first shots fired in a very uneven battle.

Brierly could guess which side they were on.

Isabella was weakening. She tried her best not to let James see it, but her left arm had gone completely numb and she could feel the sensation slowly draining away from her legs. They kept as close to the line of terraced houses as they could, edging down the road cautiously until they dared make the dash across the open fields and down into the bed of the valley. Isabella told James that they had to move carefully in case Cobden and Bright were on the streets, but at that moment her only real goal was to not end up face down in the freezing snow. They had burned her shadow away from her - boiled its very essence until there was nothing left. James had seen how much it had hurt her, but he didn't know anything of the web of ritual and history that bound them together: he had seen it move on its own, make its own decisions, and die while she lived. Why wouldn't he think it a separate thing to her?

They had burned her shadow, and the truth was it had left a gaping wound in her bio-data. With every step, she was leaking history. She would have had more hope of surviving if they had torn out her heart.

"What ..." James stopped, afraid to break her train of thought.

She looked at him and tried to smile.

He was peering up through the mist.

"What are they?" he asked.

Isabella barely needed to look. She glanced up anyway, and saw the dark shapes circling above. They were well below the barrier, only a few feet above their heads. They were getting the lay of the land now, finding out exactly how much space they had to play with. But any moment now they would start to attack. Isabella looked through the mist and tried to judge how far they were from the works: still some way, and there was a long sprint downhill across open ground. She might still make it, if she could convince the bran-puca to concentrate on James ...

Isabella had always known that coming here would be dangerous. That a single untrained Faction initiate would struggle going up against the Great Houses' elite. She had never thought that she might lose her shadow, though: some part of her had imagined it surviving even if everything went badly, making good its escape and finding another host to train. The next generation of Faction agents, raised from the impossible dregs of the last. But losing it hadn't been the only surprise: she also hadn't counted on her desire to save James. If it came to it and only one of them could escape ...

You're going native, Isabella. Focus.

"I think ..." James said. "Are they getting closer?"

Isabella dived.

"Get down!" she spat.

She pulled him down to the snowy ground of somebody's well-kept garden, his head striking an ornamental gnome with more than a little force. It was just in time: the bran-puca that was diving swooped inches above his head and instead sank its claws into the rough brick of the terrace. Its head burrowed deep into the brickwork, sand flying out in its wake, and then it was off again into the air. James stared at the large hole in the side of the house, his mouth agape.

"But that's –" he started to say.

"That's nothing," Isabella interrupted sharply, pulling him to his feet. "We have to move. Before you find out how much worse it can get."

Another bran-puca swooped down at them, but Isabella had already dragged James into the road. They were going to have to take their chances: if Cobden and Bright found them, there was nothing Isabella could do. But if they stayed put, then the bran-puca would devour them without a moment's pause. It wasn't that far to the hedges, and then down to the factory. Of course, if she was wrong and the tunnel wasn't down there, then it would all be pointless anyway.

"Look out!" James screamed.

A cloud of black mouths fell from above, narrowly missing their heads and instead flying through the hedges just in front of them. When they flew up again, the hedges were completely gone, not even a ragged edge to remember them by. But there was no time – the creatures spun round and dived at the two of them again. There seemed to be more of them every second, and every one of them wanted to be the first to taste flesh. Within seconds, the field in front of them was nothing but a vast dark cloud: Isabella stumbled and found herself leaning more heavily into James than she had intended.

"We have to find some shelter," he said.

"They can eat the fabric of the universe," Isabella coughed, tasting copper in her mouth. "What were you thinking of hiding behind?"

More bran-puca had landed on the road, and were starting to tear great chunks out of it. Each cobble disappeared in seconds, revealing the frozen earth beneath it. Then they devoured the earth, and beneath that … was that the glistening underside of the barrier Isabella could see? Damn it. They couldn't go forwards. She could barely go backwards: she clung tight to James arm.

"The houses," she hissed. "We need time."

They both looked up.

It was a long way back to the terrace.

In the darkness, she could hear nothing, see nothing. She lay for a few moments, just savouring that feeling. The world had been taken away … no, she had been taken from the world. Pulled outside and left there where it couldn't touch her any more. She didn't have to worry about any of it, ever again. The very idea sent a shiver of bliss down to her toes, quickly washed away by the guilt. She had thought that too might have been left back in the world, but no. It had sniffed her out, hunted her down and sank its teeth deep into her soul. It worried her from side to side, and made even this comforting nothingness a prison of sorts.

He had been there. Her Bill, or an echo of him so perfect that it didn't matter so much if it wasn't. She had been given the chance to save him, and instead she had hesitated. Had it ever really been about Bill? Had she told herself the truth about any of it? She had spent so long trying to live with the fact that he was gone, was she so afraid that he might possibly be back?

Elizabeth lay in the dark for a long time. She could feel how thick the air was in her dark space, and instinct told her there was no point even trying to stand. The chimney had collapsed on her, and she was buried. She tried to lie quiet in her grave, and accept the peace that death must finally bring to her.

And outside, Spinning Jenny would swim on.

She had only ever wanted to live with Bill. Marriage, work, children: she hadn't wanted any of that for herself. That wasn't to say she was against any of it, or that she hadn't loved what little she had got. But that had been what Bill wanted, what he needed. He had told her he couldn't live if she wouldn't be his wife. She had just needed him to be there. And then of course there came that one day when he wasn't, and she had found the second need in her life: the need to ensure that the hungry god who had devoured her life would know no more of it itself.

Now that was all gone. No chance for any of it.

Down there in the dark, who could tell if she cried.

---

The door burst open and they both fell through it. With a kick of his foot, James slammed it behind them, but how long that would keep those creatures out he had no idea. Not long, it was safe to guess. Probably they were already swooping down at the blistering wood, even as he and Isabella lay panting on the hearth. His arms were still locked around her body: she had no substance any more, and he had barely even felt a strain as he hefted her across the road. She would make no good meal for those ravenous creatures out there. They would both be gone in seconds.

He tried to resist the urge to sob.

Isabella drew herself up into a ball, and James jumped up to sneak a peek out of the window. He could make nothing out, just a swirl of mist, snow and darkness. The creatures had been devouring everything in their path: was there actually anything left out there to see?

"Isabella –" he said.

"Quiet!" she snapped. "I need to concentrate."

He could seen the strain trembling through her body. Her eyes were closed, but he could see the left eye twitching alarmingly under the lid. She was holding her breath, but it shook her hard as it tried to punch its way out again. He could feel the room grow colder around him, but he had no idea what she was trying to do. He had no idea if there was anything he could do to help.

She screamed, so loud that James jumped back and nearly fell through the window and back out into the street. She screamed until her throat was ragged with it, and then screamed just that little bit more. It didn't sound like pain, it sounded like frustration.

"Nothing!" she spat, a drop of blood falling with it to the floor.

He felt such a wave of concern. He wondered if it was for her, or for himself.

"There isn't a tunnel?" he asked.

"There must be," she growled. There was more blood staining her mouth. "But I could be standing right on top of it and … I'm not at my best, James. I'm sorry. I don't think there's any hope."

James swallowed.

"There's nothing we can do?" he asked.

The floor above them creaked ominously.

## 10. Now, Inside the Bubble

Isabella dug her fingers into the table and hauled herself back to her feet. Her mind was racing with every ritual she had ever performed, every one she had ever seen, even those that she had only heard about and doubted had ever really happened. Somewhere in all that history, there must be an answer. Something that would stop the bran-puca without draining the last bit of life from her. There would be something. There must be something.

But instead of answers, she found herself staring out of the window. The world out there had been softly buried under a snow that wasn't snow. The water had frozen and fallen a long time ago: now the snow was the air itself, freezing as it touched the bubble membrane and fell back to the ground. If the answer didn't come soon, they would need a fire just to melt enough oxygen to keep them alive. But in truth, they would be dead long before that became a problem.

It was as black as night out there now, what little light the barrier gave off blocked by the sheer mass of chittering, furry bodies. The house trembled and rocked with the impact of the little creatures taking bite after bite out of it. For a moment, the sound of their voices was drowned out by a rumble as one of the other houses in the terrace collapsed. If she could think of anywhere else to go, she would.

"There's someone up there," James hissed, pointing up at the ceiling.

He had such a strange, soft face. Particularly when it was trembling with fear. He swallowed hard, but made no move to stand. The atmosphere around them continued to freeze, and it was starting to get so cold even in the house that he was shivering through his clothes. She wondered if James had ever considered dying before, if he had any concept of all the things the universe might still hold for its dead children. Even the impossible was only a matter of time. She wondered if that would comfort him. Somehow, she knew it wouldn't.

"It's them," she sighed. "They'll have eaten through the top floor."

He looked at her in disbelief.

"What are they?" he asked. "What are they doing?"

"Destroying the bubble," she answered. She let herself slip down to the floor again. "Devouring it, piece by piece. Tidying up for the Great Houses."

Something thumped loudly against the door to the kitchen. It echoed dully but didn't open. In a second, it would be devoured. In a second, so would they. She had miscalculated. This was it.

"James ..." she said.

He looked at her.

The door burst open, and then was slammed shut again. A figure dressed entirely in black rested its head against the wood for a moment, and then turned to fix them with a questioning glare.

"What are you two doing in my house?" asked Mrs Howkins.

James had no idea how Mrs Howkins was here again. He had seen her in the works when it had been destroyed. When it had been devoured. He hadn't even considered the possibility that she might have escaped, but the exact method seemed irrelevant now they were all doomed. The house shook again, and a section of the ceiling tumbled in. James reached out and pulled the old lady out of the way of the falling rubble, but even so she looked at him with that same impassive composure he'd seen as she stepped off the train. It seemed she was unconcerned about the building having the sheer bad manners to fall on her, and that James was merely the first of many candidates who would have helped her eventually.

He wondered if the knowledge that she was going to die here would stir that calm demeanour. Somehow, he doubted it.

"Are you all right?" he asked.

Mrs Howkins didn't answer. James glanced towards Isabella, but the young woman looked uncomfortable and didn't offer any help. He didn't know how long they had left – looking through the crumbled ceiling he could see that the top floor had already gone. But he supposed it would be best to try and share those last moments with as many people as he could. To savour his last taste of human comfort, before ... He had never considered the possibility of an afterlife before. It had always seemed somehow unlikely. But was it any less unlikely than the world Isabella had opened his eyes to? Perhaps this was all just the pause before judgement and revelation.

He thought about the money under the boards of his pub, hidden there and gathering dust for some future date. He thought about camels, and saw the snow falling gracefully down.

"Mrs Howkins," he said. He found he wasn't sure what words would come next. "Please. Can we just hold each other?"

Mrs Howkins looked at him, and he noticed for the first time that the sharpness in her eyes was gone. Like the village around them, the darkness had descended and now it was too hard to make out anything there at all.

"How much do you know?" Isabella said.

"Enough," Mrs Howkins answered. "They're gone. Yes?"

Isabella seemed to gather her strength.

"They might still be out there now, fighting," she answered, pulling Mrs Howkins down beside her and resting a hand on her dry skin. "Time does strange things in these places. Somewhere, none of this might have happened yet."

James saw Mrs Howkins close her eyes for a moment, as if half-remembering some passing fancy. Her brow creased as it passed again, and she shook her head almost without knowing it.

"They're gone," she echoed flatly. "I can't feel them."

"You haven't even tried a summoning," Isabella chastised.

Mrs Howkins bristled, and for a moment her eyes were clear.

"I've been doing this a good deal longer than you, young lady," she tutted. "I don't need the paraphernalia to know I can't reach them. There's no-one listening, if they're still alive. That's it."

The house shook again. Everything that wasn't attached to something rattled across the floor and the far wall disappeared into a cloud of dust and teeth. Suddenly they were out in the open, the bats swooping and circling overhead. James tried to look for the rest of the village, but there was nothing but broken earth and dust. Everything had been devoured. The bats screeched in delight.

"Let me lend you my strength," Isabella yelled.

"Why?"

Isabella paused.

"To say goodbye?"

There was no time. Elizabeth tossed the table to one side and quickly scratched a circle onto the dusty floor with a finger. Mr Braddock looked at them as if they might be seeking a human sacrifice to add to the trappings, but this was perfectly adequate. They weren't asking for anything, after all: just peering into the water to see if anything was moving.

He stayed outside the circle as Elizabeth and the girl fell inside. She wished that they had drawn it a little bigger as she found herself uncomfortably nose to nose with the other, but then there were only moments left. The bats circled and chittered above them: they had devoured the village piece by piece and now they were devouring the ruins. Perhaps the two of them might catch the last glimmer of the Loa as it went, but that was the most they could hope for: Elizabeth had no doubts that the ritual would most likely fail, and then they would die.

Which begged the question: why was she bothering?

Did she really think there could be some last message for her ... even perhaps something like satisfaction? She had taken her chance and squandered it, allowed herself to be distracted by the memory of the woman she no longer was. She wouldn't have to live with that knowledge for very long, but there must be some better way of spending those last minutes. But the girl had insisted. Somehow, that seemed important.

"Why are you doing this?" Elizabeth yelled above the noise.

She didn't receive an answer.

Instead, Isabella grasped at Elizabeth's elbows and held tight. She stared deep into the older woman's eyes, and Elizabeth had no choice but to stare back. She could feel youth bleeding out of this girl. Strength and power flowing into her, even as it drained away through some invisible wound.

"I know you," Elizabeth said.

She tried to pull away.

But Isabella simply smiled and closed her eyes. Elizabeth felt her stomach turn as their spirits spun together, rising up through the air and quickly melting away from this misty echo of the real world. By the time they reached the wall of the bubble, they were no longer really there. They swam out into the space beyond, bleeding together at the edges until Elizabeth could no longer tell which part was her and which part the young girl. Her heart strained to near breaking, and an edge of panic tainted their shared existence: Elizabeth had only ever performed rituals with another whilst she was training, and she had never enjoyed it. It made her feel raw and open, her every emotion scraped clean and brought out into the light.

"There," said a voice, and she didn't know if it was hers.

In the distance, she could just make out the aura of the Loa. They spun and danced around each, Jenny and the Baron. Elizabeth felt she was watching them through a thick sheet of glass, warped and clouded with age, and with every long slow moment their battle led them further away. She tried to reach for them, felt Isabella urge her onwards, but something pulled at her from behind, trying to drag her back down again. She couldn't even make the Loa out as separate shapes when she felt the something stretch and tear ... and suddenly rip away from her with a pain she could barely understand. For a moment, she was lost, spinning alone in space and certain that something vital had gone. Then she found herself back on the floor, wheezing raggedly.

Mr Braddock was looking nervously down at her.

"What happened?"

But Elizabeth wasn't even sure.

Isabella wasted no time.

As soon as the connection was broken, she was up on her feet. She swayed a little, but on the whole the ground stayed where it should. She closed her eyes and concentrated, but could manage no more than a few seconds before she doubled over retching loudly. It was no good – she was just in too bad a way. After everything, it looked like she would die here after all.

James was still fussing over Mrs Howkins when he heard Isabella, and the clash of conflicting emotions that played out on his face almost made her smile. Instead, she struggled back up and tried to steady herself, just to show him that she could. Mrs Howkins needed him more, and that was only to be expected. The old woman looked up at her with clouded eyes disappearing into grey paper skin. Isabella knew that she too should be trying to help the poor woman, that she could do more than James could ever hope to. But there was too little time, and her goal was just too important. When you are building a better future, the hardest thing to accept is that you can't bring everyone with you into it.

Something of her thoughts must have shown on her face: Mrs Howkins grasped James' arm with bony fingers, but didn't have the strength left to pull herself up.

It was too late, anyway.

The bran-puca were holding back, just for a moment. There could only be one reason why. There was a rush of cold air, and the snow and the mist suddenly swirled around them. The flakes of frozen atmosphere whipped around with such speed that Isabella was sure she felt one draw a thin cut across her face. James pulled Elizabeth to him, but Isabella stood firm and tried to peer into the heart of the disturbance: a thousand tiny black wings, packed tight together and flapping almost as one. A million razor teeth, biting through existence and swallowing it down.

The creatures swirled once more, and out of their heart stepped two figures.

"Well," said CobdenBright tetchily.

"Still alive then," BrightCobden tutted.

Elizabeth wanted to stand, to face the two strangers and demand to know what they thought they were doing. This had been – would be – her house, and it was that that had brought her back to it when she had awoken in the rubble of the factory and seen the world ending. She had wanted it to end on her own terms, where she chose. And she wasn't going to let anyone spoil that. But there wasn't anywhere near enough air: she wondered if they might finally have used the bubble's finite supply up, since every ragged breath she pulled into her body seemed to have barely enough to keep her heart pumping. But the others were young, and they didn't seem to notice. Mr Braddock was shielding her in his arms, something which would normally have earned him a sharp rebuke but which she would have to live with, under the circumstances. The girl, Isabella, simply stood firm and gave them the kind of impassive glance that Elizabeth herself would have wanted to be behind.

But then this girl had been expecting the men. She had been expecting everything that had happened to them so far, including most likely Elizabeth's own presence in the village. Elizabeth had no doubt about that, because she had finally recognised Isabella. Before all this had started, a small shape in black on the lip of the valley, reaching out into the void and drawing the Loa here to feed.

That had been Isabella.

What was she playing at?

"You've got one chance," Isabella said. Despite the chill, Elizabeth could see sweat running down her neck. "Don't get on my bad side and maybe we can talk about this."

She stood for a single breath, looking every bit as ominous and still as a becalmed ocean. One of the strange men stepped forwards, and she didn't flinch. Instead, an eyebrow raised and she opened her mouth to speak. No sound came, and then the man's hand was at her throat. He lifted her off the ground, leaving Isabella grasping at his fingers and bicycling furiously in the air.

"Please!" Mr Braddock pleaded, starting and then stopping as the second man glared at him. "We just want to go home."

The man holding Isabella didn't even look.

"Believe me," he said apologetically, "this is the part of the job I dislike the most."

He raised his other hand.

"One question," Isabella croaked.

She raised her hands in surrender. Isabella hung for a second, supported only by the man's fingers around her throat.

"You're quantum entangled, yes?"

He didn't answer.

"Isabella?" Mr Braddock couldn't hide his concern.

"Each cell in your body mirroring his," she coughed, and Elizabeth thought she saw a little blood at her lips. "Two brains but one mind. But the circlets – they're the clever bit. You can control each body separately, with those."

The two men didn't glance at each other. But then if what the girl was saying was true, they wouldn't need to. One stepped closer, ready to finish the job they had come here for. It didn't really matter which one of them it was.

"So you can act independently, after a fashion," Isabella said. She reached up and wiped flecks of blood from her lips. "Which of you was it that killed my shadow?"

There was a moment of silence.

"That would be me," said the closest man.

The fingers clenched so tight, the nails broke the skin and Elizabeth could see the muscles in the neck start to strain and tear. Mr Braddock gave a cry, and moved to intervene, but the second man simply pushed him to the floor. Isabella closed her eyes, and anyone else might have thought she was slipping away. Elizabeth knew better: she had seen adepts at work before. She could feel electricity in the air, and not the ominous crackle of the previous night's thunder storms.

The air grew thick, and what light there was left began to burn brighter. No, Elizabeth knew immediately that she was mistaken: it was no lighter. But the shadows underneath Isabella's dangling body grew darker. The second man seemed to notice it too, and both started to look. It was already too late: the shadow leapt up from the ground, its arms outstretched before it. Its hands were black claws inches long, and they quickly pierced the first man's belly. He dropped Isabella and fell to his knees, his hands scrabbling to hold in the blood that blossomed at his neck. Elizabeth looked to his companion, but he had fallen too, as the claws swept up puncturing his throat.

Isabella whispered something as she rolled to her feet, and Elizabeth watched the muscles and bones in her neck start to stretch and pop. With a final twist of her head, the girl's neck knitted itself into something like its normal shape. Isabella stood over the bleeding man with a bestial snarl on her face. She reached down and plucked the barbed wire crown from his head before tossing it casually away. The man watched it go in terror.

"It got better," she told the man.

And then the creature swung its arms, and the man was dead.

James didn't know what to do. The shadow was there, right in front of him. He could see its claws, somehow dark and intangible and yet dripping with the blood of its victim. That shadow was part of Isabella, but he couldn't bring himself to believe it meant him no harm. To one side, he could see Mrs Howkins still slumped on the floor and looking like she would never stand again. On the other, he could hear the dead man's twin coughing and hacking up the blood that was suddenly in his throat. Isabella stood in front of him, wiping a hand across her hairless head and trying to get her breath back. She didn't even look down at the dead man.

She looked at James for a moment, and smiled the sweetest smile he had ever seen.

"What have you done?" he asked her.

She didn't answer. The one man was dead, the other dying. But the danger wasn't over: above them, the bat creatures realised that something had happened. Whatever command had held them back was suddenly lifted, and they massed and swirled. And dived. They were going to die. He looked to Isabella again, but what comfort could he hope to find there? He expected to see cold shadow steel plunging into his chest.

No.

The two men had meant to kill them. Isabella had saved them all. Now they would escape together. James doubted she had any other choice than to do what she had done. He would have done the same, if he had the nerve and the opportunity.

Of course he would.

"We don't have long," Isabella said.

The shadow twitched at her side, as if anxious for more blood.

"I've got my shadow back," she said, with something like a reassuring tone. Her eyes were fixed only on him. "I know where the tunnel is."

James gave a sigh of relief.

"We can go home?" he asked.

Isabella didn't move.

"Yes," she said.

Her shadow did.

"And no."

James barely even saw the attack. The shadow was as dark as the night, and moved faster than anything James had ever seen. The first he knew of it was when he felt the cold suddenly in his belly. He felt it run from the bottom of his stomach all the way up to his throat, and it was only when it reached there that he noticed the shadow in front of him. It pulled its arm out of his flesh, and he saw the claws glisten with something wet and hot. He still hadn't realised what it was.

"I'm sorry," Isabella said, and sounding like she meant it. "No other way."

And he felt his belly explode.

Elizabeth knew that she had to stand, had to fight. Whatever her plan, this young girl's intention at that moment was that Elizabeth Howkins should die. There could be no doubt about it. But the air was still thick and heavy, and it refused to give Elizabeth any strength even as she struggled to pull it into her lungs. She watched the shadow disembowel Mr Braddock and was no more able to do anything about it than he himself was. All she could do was wonder if Spinning Jenny would claim her once she was dead, so that the cold dead echo of herself might gain some comfort from being near the cold dead echo of Bill. More likely, the Baron would take her, just for the twist of the knife.

The shadow paused for a moment before it drew its claws from Mr Braddock's neck. It didn't seem to have any eyes, but still it looked at her. The blades slid easily out, but there was no blood. For a second, Mr Braddock's mouth moved as if he was about to chide the creature. Then a mushroom cloud of thick purple light exploded from the gaping wound in his chest. The shadow slipped quietly back underneath Isabella's body, and Mr Braddock disappeared completely. In his place was a hole in the wall of the universe, sparking with energy and twisting away into infinity.

Isabella stood in front of it, the winds released from inside rippling her clothes.

"You're coming with me," she said firmly.

Elizabeth braced herself to be hauled up by the young girl, but instead she went past her and grabbed the dying man. He was still coughing and choking on his own blood, and had no strength to complain: Isabella pulled him in front of the gateway and with a firm kick pushed him through it.

He disappeared instantly, and the gateway gave a little belch of its deep purple light. Elizabeth found a little of her strength was starting to come back to her, but at that moment it only allowed her to look up at the young girl and frown.

"I imagine I am staying here," she said.

Isabella nodded grimly.

"Sorry," she said. "You just get in the way of things."

Isabella pulled her aviator's goggles down over her eyes and stepped into the gateway. It belched a little more light and smoke, and then in that instant closed again for good. It left in its wake a prone publican, lying unconscious on the floor with no sign of any injury. No-one would guess that there was anything unworldly beneath his skin – and Elizabeth had no idea at all how the young girl had revealed the gateway – but perhaps it was still possible to escape that way.

Except … Bill was gone, Spinning Jenny was gone, and she was just an old woman with no idea of what to do next. Escape was one thing, but how would she cope with more of this life afterwards?

With a single shriek, the sky swooped down on her.

The last thing she felt was relief.

## 11. Now, Inside the Bubble

There was a crackle of something electric, and the knot of trees exploded into flame. Private Farquharson was standing just too close, and the force of the blast toppled him over the edge of the cliff and onto the jagged rocks below. The other men had heard Major Webber's barked warning and managed to get to some kind of cover. Another shot came at them, this time striking a rock and sending lava flying up into the air, but fortunately they all stayed down.

Webber looked around him: the island was small, and from some vantage points it was possible to see from one end to the other. To his left there seemed to be nothing but olive groves and lemon trees, and behind him there was nothing but the crystal Aegean. The shots had to be coming from the hills sloping up to his right, but he still couldn't see any sign of what was firing on them.

"There!" shouted the Sergeant, pointing.

There was a flash of light, and the air burned.

"We need cover!"

The men were starting to panic. He needed to assert himself, before the whole situation crumbled. He would not be bested here. Webber glanced around and saw the two hidden trails that led back down to the beach: they could get the cliffs between them and the gunman – possibly even sneak their way around the edge of the island and back up to the enemy encampment before they knew what had hit them.

"Men!" he shouted.

Something niggled at the back of his mind. Going down to the beach was the best option, but something told him he shouldn't take it. Actually, something told him he shouldn't even need to make this decision again: hadn't he already done this? Hadn't he been somewhere else just a moment ago …

The men were looking at him, and he knew he had to seize control or lose it forever.

"Regroup on the beach," he commanded.

Most of the men didn't need telling twice. Webber let them speed ahead of him, keeping an eye on the hillside where Brierly had seen the flash. There was nothing – perhaps they needed to reload? Brierly panted up to him, steering the men back toward the trail.

"How's your arm, Sergeant?" Webber asked. She was a dead shot with a rifle – might even take out the riflemen from this distance, but there was little chance of her making the shot with her arm in the state it was.

Sergeant Brierly looked confused for a moment.

"Arm?"

There was another electric crackle, and the Sergeant quickly pulled Webber over the lip of the cliff and down onto the hidden path below. Most of the men had made it, and were now tramping down the narrow path as quickly as they dared. It wasn't really designed for rapid retreat, and one false step would see them all following Farquharson to a bloody death below. Webber looked out to sea in the vain hope that he might see some naval support arriving: they had managed to get a message out before the invaders' blockade bit, but who knew how long it would take to reach British ears? No, these few men would have to rise to the challenge: the invaders had sealed off the island and intended to make it their bridgehead into the rest of the world. They were the only ones who could stop them.

"Sir," Brierly said, her voice low.

The scrub around them started to shiver. Webber turned just in time to see a flash of red, and hear the angry bark of his attacker. Teeth sank into his arm as he threw it up to protect himself, and the fox bit savagely deep and then again, and again. It didn't even bother with its pistol – none of them did: all around him, Webber saw his men falling under the tooth and claw attack. It had been a trap.

Of course it had.

"Sir?" Brierly said again.

He blinked, and suddenly shivered. In the Mediterranean heat, he had almost been tempted to remove some of his uniform. Now, all of a sudden he felt the chill of a savage English winter. The fox had gone, but he still found himself jerking away from its attack and falling, ending up rolling in the snow. He felt the Sergeant's hands on his shoulders, trying to prop him back upright, but in his mind they were the sharp claws of the foxes trying to tear out his heart. He batted them away and kept rolling.

"Sir!" she snapped.

He looked up at her, saw the bloody stump of her arm.

"Sergeant?" his voice cracked.

"Yes, sir?"

Of course.

The sky was thick with the bat creatures now. They had appeared out of nowhere, and multiplied until they were the main reason Brierly couldn't make out anything more than six yards away. Isabella would know what they were, possibly even how to escape them. But there was no way back to Isabella now: Brierly had needed the certainty of Webber's orders to coalesce herself around, but those orders had led her to their certain deaths. Such was the multitude of voices within her that there were even some that could enjoy the irony in that.

"The strangest thing," the Major said, his tongue seeming a little too big for his mouth. "I was back in the Lakes. You remember – when the night foxes invaded Skiathos? Must be twenty years ago now. It felt so real."

Despite herself, Brierly remembered. It had been a terrible battle: the night foxes relied on sheer weight of numbers to prevail, and their band of twenty tired soldiers had been severely outnumbered. Not many had survived, and Brierly thought she remembered that she and Major Webber were the only two still serving.

"It looked bad," he said dreamily.

"It was bad," Brierly corrected.

"But we dug in. We struggled." he barked, some of the colour coming back into his cheeks. "That's something we could all do with remembering, I think. Victory goes to those who want it most."

Brierly thought that victory had gone to those who were the luckiest: if Corporal Devlin hadn't found that cache of night fox weapons when he got separated from the rest of the party … and of course it hadn't done him any good, in the end. Apparently he hadn't wanted to survive enough.

"I'm not ready to give up just yet, Sergeant," Webber said suddenly. "We'll get out of this. Trust me."

"I do, sir," Brierly said.

He looked at her for a moment, and then nodded.

"What are we doing here?" he asked.

"There isn't anywhere else," Brierly answered.

The bats were raining down around them, wings outstretched and claws digging deep into whatever they could sink themselves into. As they rose gracefully upwards again, more and more of their surroundings vanished. Webber looked confused, and then had to stumble out of the way as one of the black little creatures aimed for him. His knees buckled, but he just gritted his teeth and kept his balance. Brierly was in no doubt that determination and stubbornness could take you a long way. Now she feared she was about to witness the limits of that doctrine.

"Do you have a firearm?" Webber barked, trying to take cover.

"No, sir. I have my sword."

"Stones, then."

Webber pulled a rock from the ground and threw it up into a mass of the bats. There was no way he could miss at least one, but the one he struck did little more than wobble in the air. One of its companions swallowed the stone whole before it even struck the ground again. Webber looked around them.

"Tough little blighters ..." he muttered, and tried to take cover behind a wall that had been neatly bisected by the icy barrier. Brierly scuttled over to join him. "Remember the foxes, Sergeant. This is just the start. If they succeed here, they'll raise their barrier and carry on across the Empire. We must get through to warn them."

"Isabella –"

The world shook, and there was an ominous rumble from the sky above. Webber didn't even look, instead snatching the sword from her and starting to hack maniacally at the icy barrier that surrounded them.

"Sir?"

"Help me," he barked. "For God's sake, Sergeant. Help me!"

Webber knew that he should act with a certain regard to his rank and standing, but even so he couldn't help himself. He hadn't wanted to distress his Sergeant, so hadn't intended to mention the little detours his mind had been making since the lightning struck. He had spent two minutes at his brother's wedding whilst she reported back the events up at the Sportsman. She had stayed with him regardless, and duty told him that if he could save her, then he had to. But part of him whispered that if he could get her away, then it couldn't have been the future he had been to that first time he had detoured.

"Sergeant?" he said, looking back for her.

She was still there, her eyes on him. She looked concerned.

Of course he couldn't send her away. How would that look? Her place was with him, right to the very end if that was what was coming. He allowed himself a second, closing his eyes and holding his breath. It was only natural that he would feel a little doubt, with everything that he had been through and everything he knew was coming. But he had never given up in his life, and he had achieved incredible things. This was going to be the most incredible: there would be a way out of this. He just had to work hard enough to make it.

He felt something push him into the barrier, and his head struck the ice hard. Even as he slid down to the earth, he saw the bat flying up and away, devouring a chunk of his flesh. Brierly was at his side in a moment, but he batted her away.

"Assess the damage," Webber croaked. "Can we make it through?"

Sergeant Brierly hesitated for a moment, but then she knelt over him to inspect the wound he had made in the barrier. The snow was falling again. Webber could see the barrier rising up into the sky. He could see it sweeping down into the earth, apparently unbroken. The Sergeant looked back at him nervously.

"Nothing?" he asked.

She knelt on the floor and pressed both hands against the icy wall. From where he was standing, he could see some of the white had been chipped away from the barrier. Sergeant Brierly pressed her nose against the clear patch and looked hard for any sign of damage.

"Nothing," she echoed.

As she stepped through, Isabella felt a blast of heat so strong on her face that she feared a fire. The light was bright enough to be painful, and the air on the cusp of the tunnel howled like a detuned radio. Her heart fluttered for a second, and the urge to stay rose up in her. But she knew it for what it was, and ignored it as best she could. She pushed through, and heard the static whisper deep into her ear before everything suddenly went silent.

She had to blink a good few times before she could make anything out in the tunnel. It wasn't particularly bright in there, but given the chill and the gloom of the collapsing bubble it was positively radiant. Everything was a deep, dark purple and it felt uncomfortably like standing inside the veins of some giant creature, except that the walls danced and swirled like oil on water. Through the swirling walls, she could make out strange shapes and darker shadows.

But the one thing she couldn't see was her prisoner.

The tunnel snaked and turned, and bent a full ninety degrees only a few yards ahead of her. It could be that Cobden was simply lying unconscious safely out of sight around that corner. But this was his home ground: it was equally possibly that an entire guard were waiting for her, with a fully recovered and regenerated Cobden standing at their head, waiting for his revenge.

With a pop, the tunnel entrance closed behind her. Isabella might have spared a quiet word for Elizabeth, except she was distracted. Just as the entrance was at its smallest, mere milliseconds from closing for good, something small and black came darting through it. The little creature didn't make allowances for anyone who might be standing in its way: it flew straight into Isabella's chest with such force that it actually knocked her from her feet. She landed on her back on the tunnel floor, which set it undulating and groaning in a most alarming way.

Isabella gave a sharp cry. The creature fell onto her chest in a stunned heap. It was the bran-puca, snub-nosed and sharp-toothed. Those teeth were capable of eating their way through the very fabric of the universe: Isabella didn't want to imagine what would happen if it decided it wanted a piece of her. Even if it didn't, there was every chance it would decide to take a few chunks out of the tunnel, and that would not be good for any of them. As it shook its head and tried to focus on her, Isabella snatched at the creature with both hands.

It gave a loud shriek and lifted up into the air. As it sped upwards, it did a quick somersault and doubled back on itself. Isabella was still on her back, watching as the creature dive-bombed at her heart. She brought her feet up over her head and rolled back, not even waiting to see if the branpuca would react in time. She spun on a heel and ran as fast as she could for that bend in the tunnel: if Cobden was there, at least he could deal with his pet whilst Isabella thought of a decent excuse for killing his quantum twin.

She had only gone a few steps when she realised she wouldn't make it.

She could hear the bat creature behind her. It was chittering to itself in a most alarming fashion, possibly just trying to echo locate itself but maybe venting its frustration that Isabella wouldn't just sit still and be eaten. Either way, it meant she could hear how far away it was and how fast it was moving. She was still half a yard from the corner, and it would be on her in another couple of steps. Picturing it burrowing head-deep into her shoulder blades, Isabella dived forwards and rolled back to her feet. She looked up and saw the creature sailing over her head.

Its wings open wide, it gracefully turned in a sharp arc. Its dark eyes were fixed on her and with two flaps of those leathery wings it was back up to attack speed. Isabella took the momentum of her roll and let it carry her forwards. The creature began gnashing its sharp little teeth: the speed they were both moving at, Isabella could well imagine it would punch a hole clean through her. With everything that had happened, it would be a particularly undignified end, but possibly no more than she deserved.

It screeched again, inches from her chest.

Dark claws slashed down and knocked it to the floor.

It smashed down against the tunnel floor and bounced dramatically, rebounding up and off the wall before it came to rest a few steps ahead of her. Isabella didn't stop running. The creatures were designed to survive in the hostile null space between the universes: it could survive in the kind of environment that even naked singularities found too unforgiving. There was no way that anything a shadow could do to it would be anything worse than annoying for it, particularly a shadow that was newborn and weak. More likely the creature would tear her shadow to pieces, but that didn't stop Isabella leaving it behind to guard her retreat.

She was at the turn now. She felt just a momentary unease when she thought that her shadow would be unable to protect her from anything up ahead, but she pushed it to one side. If Cobden was waiting, then he was doing it with one hand keeping his severed neck closed. Isabella had purpose, will and determination on her side. She knew what was at stake and that she couldn't let anything stand between her and victory. If Cobden was there, then he would lose. Isabella just needed to win too much.

The bat creature screeched behind her again, and she felt the blow as her shadow was swept from its feet. Then Isabella was around the corner.

For just a moment, she stopped. The inside of the tunnel was a magnificent sight, even to somebody as well-travelled and jaded as Isabella. It stretched up so far and out so wide that it was impossible to see its boundaries, and the thick air rippled and rainbowed as the deadlights from outside pushed their way in. The guard had obviously only been using it as a way to get from the universe into the bubble, as the entire space was empty of any buildings or road ways. Even so, there was room enough to build a city that would dwarf London. The place was so big that it even had rudimentary weather: black snow powdered the ground here and there.

Lying face down on the ground a few steps away was Cobden. He clearly wasn't preparing his grand counter-attack.

As Isabella ran closer, she could see thick purple blood pooling around his face and neck, and his hand was up near his throat where he had been trying to hold the wound closed. Isabella gave a quick glance behind her, but there was no sign of the creature or her shadow. A hand went into her greatcoat pocket, and when it returned a silver blade flicked out of a pearl handle. She gave a quick swipe at Cobden, and then pulled a long strip of his robes away. Within seconds, she had wound it around his neck as best she could. Then she tried to drag him to his feet.

He murmured something, but his eyes stared wide and unfocussed.

"Don't fight," Isabella snapped. "You're coming with me."

There was a roar from behind them, and Isabella glanced over her shoulder. Her shadow came stumbling into the vast chamber, its right arm hanging loosely by its side. Its left arm swiped and swung at the bat creature as it darted and zipped around it, its teeth flashing in the thick purple light. Neither creature looked like they were about to finish the other off, but Isabella could clearly see that her shadow wasn't about to win the fight. Given time, the bat would disable the shadow limb by limb.

Isabella was determined that it wouldn't get that time.

"If you want to live, do as I say."

Cobden didn't answer. There was nothing in his face to say that he was still alive, let alone that he wanted to stay that way. But Isabella wrapped an arm around his chest and dragged him away from the fight anyway. For a panicked moment, she realised that she had no idea where the other end of the tunnel was. But then she centred herself and did her best to reach for a moment of calm: it wasn't the most zen moment she had ever found, but before the second breath had left her body she could feel the direction she needed to move in.

"Come on," she shouted back to her shadow, then set off.

Fortunately, the exit was relatively close to the entrance: if it had been across the other side of that chamber, then she could easily imagine needing two or three days to march across. Instead, it took only minutes until she was at another curved, membranous wall that puckered into a tight little sphincter. It didn't create comfortable associations in Isabella's mind, but at least she knew that the Great Houses would dislike it even more. They had denied their biological nature since before the first stars formed, and they were much more comfortable when their technology was made of steel and plastic. It was, therefore, a very Faction kind of gateway, and that was good enough for Isabella.

The ground gave a massive lurch, and Isabella found herself thrown to the floor again. Cobden fell in front of her like a sack of potatoes, and didn't move. Isabella quickly looked behind her for the bat's follow-up blow, but she saw that it and her shadow were still some way back, each surprised by the shifting geography. Behind them, the alcove leading back to the entrance vibrated wildly and then suddenly stretched so wide it tore itself open. The cold dead space between the universes took a bite at the tunnel wall, and hungrily devoured more and more.

Isabella knew immediately what had happened.

The bubble had collapsed.

The other end of the tunnel was now attached to nothing, and the whole structure was unravelling around them. It was like being inside a balloon as it popped. Isabella shouted back to her shadow, and it swiped one last time at the bat before running to catch them. Isabella didn't have time to reassure herself that it would make it: she closed her eyes and sliced into her arm with the knife. Blood arched through the air as she lost her footing, and a mess of her black bio-data sprayed across the closed exit. Even as she tried to get back onto her feet, Isabella was chanting under her breath, but the tunnel wasn't listening.

The walls unravelled at the speed of sound, and Isabella felt the ground underneath her heels dissolve into nothing. For just a moment, she teetered on the edge of the edge of space. A single breath would send her spiralling through the dark seas for ever, or at least until one of the creatures that swam there decided she might make a tasty meal. She screamed the name of her preferred Loa aloud, and her blood on the far wall suddenly bubbled and steamed. The collapse of the tunnel slowed, then stopped completely. Then it began to reverse, the vast chamber behind her reassembling itself just as fast as it had fallen to pieces. The closed sphincter of the exit gave a gentle shudder and started to open.

Isabella didn't hesitate. She grabbed Cobden up by the waist and swung him around like a hammer, sending him spinning towards the widening exit with his limbs limply flying. She launched herself after him, and spat out another command: the exit began to tighten and close again. First Cobden, then Isabella fell through the gateway. A short moment later, Isabella's shadow dived through with its arms outstretched. As the sphincter slammed shut, the bat creature swooped into the narrowing gap.

But the gap slammed closed too soon.

The bat struck, then hit the floor.

Isabella had escaped.

Brierly was down on her knees, her nose almost touching the barrier. She could feel the cold radiating from it, threatening to take the tip of her nose as a sacrifice. This close, the barrier was nearly all that she could see: it swept up and down, left and right, and filled her line of sight with nothing but its curved white impenetrability. Except for a small patch directly in front of her eyes. It was barely a foot in diameter, but it told her why the rest of the barrier was white.

When she had first seen it, she had thought it must be made of some solid white substance, hard and unforgiving like bone. But the cuts that had failed to even scratch it had still had one effect: it had chipped a little of the thick ice shell that had formed on the barrier. She could see the crystals starting to reform, spreading across the bare patch like some kind of living creature, painting the surface cold and solid white again. But it was clear. Smooth and transparent like glass, and barely an eighth of an inch thick.

Brierly could see through the barrier to the other side.

"Nothing?" Major Webber asked urgently behind her.

She knew he wasn't ready to see this.

"Nothing," she lied.

She watched as the window slowly closed, swallowed up by thicker and thicker crystals of ice. She could just see the ghost of her face, staring intently back at her from the darkness. Beyond that, she could see almost nothing. It looked like space, but like no space she had ever seen: it seemed to flow like treacle, and gave off a faint purple glow. There were no stars, no planets, nothing. Except that just at the edge of the limits of her vision, she could see vast monsters swimming. They tumbled over each other, impossible mouths open to reveal impossible teeth, each rolling and twisting to take a chunk from the other.

Brierly knew that these were Mrs Howkins' Loa. But more than that, she knew what they weren't: they were not the road leading up to Strines station and a track heading out to the rest of the world. Isabella had been right, and Major Webber had been wrong: they were not simply cut off from the rest of their world – they had left it completely. They were in a bubble torn from their own universe, with no hope of ever getting back. Every voice inside Brierly was silenced. None had any idea for what they should do now.

The ice closed in, and the barrier was sealed again.

"Brierly?" Major Webber breathed behind her.

He sounded strange. There was something in his voice that Brierly had never heard before, and when she turned her head to look back at him she realised what it was. In the moments she had turned from him, something had happened: he stared down at her with such open relief on his face – he drank her in greedily, as if he had never seen the like for a hundred years.

Sad as it was to think, Brierly knew that the strange sound in his voice, the one that she had never heard there before, was unguarded emotion.

"Brierly!" he cried. "You have no idea how good ..."

Brierly looked at him, unmoving.

"Sir?"

But he had taken his eyes from her for a moment, and was snapping his head one way then the next. Brierly realised that he had no recollection of where he was, and was trying to quickly piece his memory back together again from the surrounding scenery. And it was clear that he had succeeded: his face fell a little, and he turned back to her.

"I'm here again?" he asked sadly.

"Sir?" Brierly said again. She didn't quite know what to say. "Are you feeling all right?"

He smiled thinly.

"Sergeant Brierly," he said, with something of that old composure. "I am severely incapacitated, and should not be relied on. Case in point: in a few moments, I will have no recollection that this conversation has taken place. Not that it matters."

"You are injured?"

"I honestly don't recall," he answered with a dry laugh. "Physically. When the shadow attacked ... were you there? I don't recall. When it attacked I was struck by some kind of lightning. Since then I have been travelling through my own life. I haven't seen you for ... it must be ten years. I imagine that sounds strange."

"I have worked with you for over twenty years, Major," Brierly answered softly. "Everything has been strange."

The Major gave a loud chuckle at that.

"There isn't any time, Sergeant," he said, his face blistering with the words he was holding inside. "Even if there was ... I have travelled through every day of my life again, often more than once. Every second, from birth through to now. It has been ... Every second, Brierly. But only once have I been any further forward than this second, this moment now. There is no time. I think I am about to die."

Brierly looked around her, but there was nothing she could say.

"I don't know how long you have left, Sergeant," he said sharply, drawing her eyes back down to him. "But I do know this: it was a lie, all of it. Sentiment is for imbeciles and the French. It is every man for himself, and that is all it has ever been. If you have the chance to save yourself, you must take it. You cannot save me."

Within Brierly, there was uproar. Every voice suddenly clamoured to be heard, even those that had never spoken since they had been invited in. The din was overwhelming, and she found herself putting her hands to her ears as if their cries were out there in the bubble with her. She had no idea what they were saying, what action they were trying to convince her to take, but she could sense the general mood. They might not believe in Webber's prescience, but they didn't doubt the truth in his words: death was upon her.

"There is something I can do," she told Webber. He looked at her with sad eyes. "You know what I am. You know there are many personalities in me. They are there because I invited them, and they accepted. I don't make an invitation very often, Major. Each new voice takes time to assimilate."

Brierly looked across at him, fixing her eyes on his.

"Major Webber," she said firmly. "I'd like to invite you to join me."

Brierly thought that the clamour inside her might silence for a moment, shocked by the enormity of what she had offered even now. But no. Each voice was still too concerned with its own survival, its own plan for escape. She felt a sickening vertigo in her stomach at the idea of such tiny parts of herself taking advantage of the confusion to make whatever grand decisions they wanted. But in the end, there was nothing she could do. She had to listen to the consensus, no matter how small the margins.

The Major, however, didn't seem to be listening.

"Major Webber?" Brierly asked hesitantly.

He seemed to jump, and then looked down at her again. She saw his eyes go from her face, to her uniform to the bleeding stump where her arm had been. Perhaps he was thinking about the state of the accommodation he was being offered, no matter how temporarily. He swayed a little, and then blinked. Brierly suddenly wondered if his prediction had been correct after all: he looked like a man with not long left for this world. Perhaps he wasn't even strong enough to make the decision himself. Brierly wanted to reach out and pull his mind in regardless, but there was no protocol for this kind of situation. None of her kind had ever invited a sick mind in before – why would they? It had only ever been the strongest, the best, and always the procedure was the same.

Despite everything, Brierly found she was still a slave to tradition.

"I can't do it without your permission, sir," Brierly urged.

He looked at her blankly.

"At least we'd die truly together," she said.

Brierly tried to keep her eyes fixed on him, to will him into decisiveness with the sheer burning power of her need for it. But he just blinked and looked around him vaguely. The bats were the sole fabric of the bubble now. They were so numerous that the sky teemed with them. Their were only a few things left to devour, and they chose the most obvious: they struck the barrier at speed, their tiny teeth breaching it with ease. Brierly could hear the roar of the oxygen escaping, and the cold empty vacuum outside rushing in.

"Too late!" Brierly cried. "This is it!"

A hole the size of a cannonball opened up in the barrier, but it soon cracked and crumbled until it was large enough for a man to stand in. Brierly tried to press herself to the floor as the rushing air pulled at her, but there was almost nothing to hold. Everything around them that wasn't part of the ground disappeared through the hole, and Brierly could feel herself starting to slide that way too.

But Major Webber stood tall, staring into the void with a look of peace on his face.

"This time," he yelled above the noise. "This time I make it."

He took a step, two. Then he was running.

"Sir!" Brierly gasped.

But it was too late. He ran to the edge of the hole and didn't stop, launching himself into the void as if he was doing nothing so dangerous as the long jump. Brierly turned and saw him already disappearing into the darkness, arms outstretched as he grasped for nothing. No, not nothing: Brierly could see what he was trying to do. The creatures were still out there, distant but suddenly interested now that the bubble was pouring all its impossible energies out into the void. Like sharks sensing blood in the water, they circled closer and closer. As they did, Webber reached out to them. Brierly couldn't see his face, but she felt sure he was shouting to them.

One of the bat creatures dived again at Brierly, this time its teeth taking a chunk out of her shoulder. She let out a cry and swatted at it, and the creature was knocked from her. It tumbled towards the hole, its wings flapping to try and save itself but there was no hope. It tumbled away into the void. Brierly didn't try to stop the blood falling from her wound – if she lost her grip now, she knew that she would follow the Major and the bat and that would be the end of that. But she did manage a last glance after Major Webber, and saw him disappearing into the darkness. The creatures left him to fly past, more interested in the blood on the water.

There were tears at the corners of Brierly's eyes. She shouted something up at the bats, but the words were snatched away. They too fell out into the void to be devoured by the creatures that swam there. A bat fell on her again, then another. Soon she was covered in them, disappearing bite by bite by bite. She didn't move even as she was eaten alive. Brierly was gone.

The bubble burst, and all was darkness.

## 12. October 1853, Strines

It was still early, and the curtains were firmly shut on the world outside. The pub was quiet and empty, the customers long ago sent home for the night. There were the remains of a fire in the hearth, the embers glowing red from the night before, but otherwise everything was cold and silent. Except for one thing: in the middle of the main room, a large hole gaped. Purple smoke belched out of it in a single plume, rattling the bottles that lined the shelves behind the bar. The hole burned with a blue flame, flickering and screaming as it did so.

With a pop, a figure fell through it and landed hard on the floor. Blood started to seep sluggishly into the wooden boards from the slowly healing wound in his neck, and if you watched very carefully you could see each shallow breath as it trembled through his frame. Then the hole screamed again, and a tight ball of limbs and obscenities came rolling through. As the ball struck the ground and rolled into a corner, the hole quivered and shook, before folding up on itself. As it puckered to a close, it pulled around it the shape of a man.

The gateway closed, and James Braddock fell to the floor.

In the corner, the ball gave a little groan.

Isabella stood up, rolling her head around to loosen up her neck muscles. She lifted her flight goggles and set them back up on her shaved head, and then quickly moved over to James. He was still breathing, and his heart was beating a healthy little samba in his chest. She found that she was smiling a little, and couldn't really explain why, so she left him where he was and instead moved to the window.

Pulling back the curtain, she could see that the sun was just starting to come up. The sky was a mess of purples and oranges, and the air had the brittle crispness of a cold winter morning. There was no sign of the blizzard that had closed the village off, and as she looked down into the valley she could see the old works still standing tall. Glancing round the pub, she could see a clock on the wall but no sign of a calendar. Even so, she guessed she was something like three months before the creation of the bubble. Maybe even four.

She nodded to herself. That would explain the odd behaviour of the tunnel. As they stood at one end, they were closer to the collapsing bubble and everything had fallen apart. The more they moved through it, the closer they got to this point: moving back through time with every step until their inertia dragged the entrance back before the tunnel's creation. With a bit of work, Isabella imagined she could open the tunnel up again: one end here before it was created, the other there long after it was destroyed. The paradox would be pleasing, even if the tunnel itself was useless.

"So," said a voice from the shadows. "This is him?"

Isabella didn't jump. After all, she had known this particular visitor would be here.

Out of the shadows stepped a young girl, just about four months younger than Isabella herself. She was dressed in a long trenchcoat, and resting on top of her closely shaved head were a pair of dark aviator's goggles. The younger Isabella smiled a smile of innocent friendship, but her shadow peeled itself up from the floor and lurked behind her, claws bared. Isabella could feel her own shadow start to bristle, even in its weakened state. She tried to keep it in check, but it felt its territory being threatened: it sprang up from the darkness and bared its teeth.

The young girl smiled the kind of smile that made even Isabella want to hit her.

"Is he alive?" she asked, leaning down to touch James.

Isabella couldn't stop her shadow: it leapt forwards, claws flashing down for the young girl's fingers before they could make contact. Isabella had no idea if it would really have hurt her. Perhaps it would – this shadow seemed to have a will of its own, and Isabella could barely say she had it under control. But the young girl's shadow intercepted, its own claws blocking any attack on its owner. There was a sound like clashing metal, and then the two shadows drew back again to attack.

"Stop it!" both Isabellas snapped together.

The two shadows seemed to look at their respective owners sheepishly, but their claws stayed bared. They moved slowly around the room whilst the two women spoke, trying their hardest not to look like they were circling each other. The young Isabella just smiled that smile again, and went to brush James' hair from his face.

"Leave him alone," Isabella said, a little more sharply than she intended.

Her younger self raised an eyebrow.

"It's the other one you need," Isabella said, as if it explained everything.

Cobden was still lying unmoving on the floor, but at least the pool of blood around him had stopped expanding. Perhaps the machines in his blood were preparing to rebuild him. Most likely they weren't: the quantum conjoined were an odd breed, and their biology expected what happened to one to happen to the other. With CobdenBright being both dead and alive, the poor machines were probably confused about whether he needed saving or not. It was bad news for Cobden, but it did make him perfect for Isabella's purposes.

The young Isabella just wrinkled her nose at him.

"He doesn't look like something I need," she sniffed, prodding him gently with a toe.

"It works," Isabella answered firmly. "He's quantum entangled with a dead man: Baron Samedi will be all over him. But he's destined for Spinning Jenny – her taint is running through his bio-data already. Perform the ritual, and neither of them will be able to resist. Neither of them will be able to back down. They'll fight to the death, and spacetime will be the first casualty."

"How many bubbles do they create?"

"We're only interested in one."

"So are the Great Houses," the young girl sniped casually. "We keep their eyes on us, and all of this will be for nothing."

Isabella scowled, and tried not to think about Faction rituals. There might be high regard for a sibling who killed their younger self, but it didn't seem like the most sensible option when the massed ranks of Faction Paradox numbered just one. Instead, she released her grip on her shadow just a little, and hoped it might do something deniable.

"That's for me to worry about," she said, her arms folded.

The younger girl looked at her, as if deciding whether to say something. Isabella's shadow loomed again, and even the girl's shadow seemed to think twice. Isabella kept her stare blank. Her younger self tutted dismissively, and turned to make for the door. Behind her, her shadow made a great show of cleaning its claws before lifting Cobden up from the floor and carrying him after the girl. Just as she reached the doorway, the younger girl stopped and looked back over her shoulder.

"There's something …' she paused, rolling all the possible words around her mouth for a few seconds. "Something odd about your shadow."

It stayed impassive behind Isabella, claws sharp and clean.

"It isn't mine," Isabella answered glibly. "You'll find out."

And then she turned her back.

Death came as something of a surprise. She had lived with it for so long – learned how to use it as both a tool and a currency – that it was understandable that she had formed some picture of what it must be like. Nothing precise, nothing definite, but a vague understanding that whatever it was like, it wouldn't be anything like this. This was just the same thoughts and feelings, pulsing through what felt like the same tired old flesh. The same regrets and the unbearable burden of what she had lost.

Elizabeth tried opening her eyes. She blinked them hard, once, twice, three times. But still she could see nothing. Probably there was nothing to see. She lay unclaimed by any of the Loa, and was instead left to rot here in complete solitude and darkness. She wondered if this was where her Bill had ended up, whether he was still somewhere like this now, missing her. Or perhaps he had forgotten her by now. Certainly she would have to forget herself if she was going to spend eternity in this darkness.

For a moment, Elizabeth sat on the ground and did nothing. There was nothing to do, except sit and remember. In the darkness, she started to see shapes, faces she hadn't seen for decades. She recognised some as the others who had died in the fire with Bill. Bad enough that she hadn't been able to avenge his death or preserve his echo, but worse was that she had done nothing in the name of these poor wretches. They had been unremembered and unmourned, and the world had gone on quite happily without them. Even now, Elizabeth couldn't put faces to half of them.

She realised that her eyes were open only as she closed them.

"Well now Betty," she murmured to herself. "That's quite enough of that."

If this was the afterlife, then she was going to have a good long time in it. There might not be anything else to do here, but the very least Elizabeth could do was not drive herself to distraction with moping and self-pity. So she had done all she could in the name of her loss, in the name of her Bill. It was a shame that those others didn't have someone to love them that way, but there it was. As much as it had been to her when he was alive, her love of Bill hadn't made her life any happier when he was gone so perhaps they were better off without it anyway.

All she could do was what she had always done.

Just carry on, as best she could.

She was here, and here was a place. Which meant it was a place she could leave, and get back to wherever Spinning Jenny was. Elizabeth was old and unsuited to change, and she had learned her lesson well. No matter what a waste of her life revenge had been, it had been hers and it was what she knew. There was no reason she could see why she should let a little thing like being dead stop her when nothing else so far had. Besides which, she would never rest easy in an afterlife that didn't have her Bill in it.

So in the darkness, she reached out with her hands and tried to gauge the limits of her hell. It seemed that she was being kept inside a globe just tall enough for her to stand in and no more. But the strange thing was the way that her prison felt as she touched it: the inside of the globe was warm and yielding, giving under her touch and sometimes even moving. It also had a distinctly furry feel, as if her prison was an inside-out cat or dog. She recalled that in her pocket she had been carrying matches, and was pleased to discover that these had been transported with her to the afterlife. Perhaps they too had sinned, and needed to learn the error of their ways.

By touch alone, she took a match from the box and lit it.

The flame guttered for a second, and then took a weak hold of the stick. Even so, the light was bright enough to hurt after the complete darkness. Elizabeth had to blink hard to get her eyes working again, and as she did she saw the true nature of where she was being held. She reached out with the match, and saw the gently quivering body of one of the bat creatures in front of her, breathing in and out. She couldn't see its head or its wings, as these were tucked neatly underneath the body of another bat, which was tucked under another and so on and so on. There must have been a thousand of them, each clinging tight to another to form this perfect globe around her.

Either this punishment was an irony that escaped her, or Elizabeth wasn't dead. She was still in the bubble. Or at the very least a bubble. A bubble of bats. She shivered.

"Please put that match out, Mrs Howkins," said a voice.

The voice didn't seem to come from anywhere in particular, and even in the now dim light of the dying match Elizabeth could see she was entirely alone. It had sounded clear and unmuffled, but she still allowed herself to consider the possibility that it had come from the other side of the wall of bats around her. Perhaps there was a small hole somewhere that she hadn't found, letting the sound through the furry bodies without distortion. Elizabeth tried to spot it, even though she was fairly certain that the idea was ridiculous.

"It's for your own good," the voice said again, seemingly right by her ear now. "There isn't much air in here."

Elizabeth cocked her head, but there was still nobody there. She gave a languorous flick of her wrist, and the match went out. She doubted that the speaker could see her now that the darkness had rushed back into the cell, but she set her face into a look of mild disdain regardless.

"Thank you," the voice said, with something like a sigh. "I don't suppose you have very long, but I should try to keep you alive as long as I can. Of course, my orders were to arrest you. I wonder if this will do?"

There was something distinctly off-putting about talking to somebody she couldn't see, but who appeared to be so close to her. Of course, she wasn't going to let her discomfort show, but all the same. The very least the owner of the voice could do was to introduce themselves.

Arrest.

Elizabeth was a fool: they had already been introduced.

"And do you intend on arresting me, Sergeant?" Elizabeth asked the air.

There was a slight hesitation.

"I may not," the voice admitted.

The voice sounded nervous, as if expecting the direst consequences of such an admission. But then it probably was. Elizabeth had first become aware of Sergeant Brierly some years ago in India, under Major Webber's predecessor then but no less the consummate soldier. They had crossed paths more than once since then, and the young girl had acted strictly according to the letter of her commission and only on the strict execution of her orders. Elizabeth had been quite pleased when she noticed that Webber had brought the Sergeant with him again: she was exceedingly easy to predict, and hence very easy to accommodate for in any situation.

Except, of course, this situation. This was uncharted territory for both of them, and Elizabeth would have to tread very carefully. In the few moments of life she apparently had left to her.

"Where are you exactly, Sergeant Brierly?" Elizabeth asked.

More silence.

"That isn't an easy question to answer, Mrs Howkins," the Sergeant admitted. "I may stray into philosophical territories if I attempt it. Isn't there something else you would like to talk about, while we have this chance?"

"Nothing else particularly comes to mind," Elizabeth answered archly. "Perhaps we should risk philosophising?"

There was another pause. Elizabeth got the distinct impression that the Sergeant was asking someone else for permission to speak, or at the very least for advice on what words to choose. That might be all very well, but time was apparently at a premium and if Elizabeth was to discover any advantage to her situation, she would rather she did it before the air ran out.

"Of course I would hate to rush you," she said sharply.

"I'm sorry, Mrs Howkins," the Sergeant said, sounding genuinely apologetic. "I am still acclimatising ... this is not something I have done before, and it seems to take more concentration than I had hoped."

"Whereas I will apparently soon be asphyxiating," countered Elizabeth. "During which process I'm sure you will have ample opportunity to gather your thoughts. Please: don't let me interrupt them."

The bubble trembled for a moment, as if every one of the bats making it up gave a little shiver at the same time. Elizabeth's hands went out to balance herself automatically, but there was no solid ground. Everything was warm yielding fur, and she wobbled unsteady as a dipsomaniac before leaning her shoulders heavily against one wall. She could hear the flutter of the bats' heartbeats in her ear.

"How much do you know of my nature, Mrs Howkins?" the Sergeant asked.

"I know you aren't human," Elizabeth answered.

"Oh," the Sergeant sounded surprised. "You do?"

"Sergeant Brierly: the short answer," Elizabeth snapped. "Where are you?"

The bats fluttered again.

"I'm all around you," the Sergeant answered quickly. Elizabeth couldn't help looking around her, even though it was obvious what she meant. "I am the bran-puca. I am the bats."

Brierly did her best to concentrate, but it was difficult. There was always a brief moment of disorientation when she had to change hosts, but this was more than that. From one point of view, she had been in this host longer than she had been in any other – possibly longer than all the others combined. In many ways it was the perfect host for her: she could feel the cold empty sea of loaspace crashing against her apparently fragile body, but its strange currents did little more than ruffle her fur. The bubble was collapsing all around her, and with it went any semblance of the real world, but Brierly could feel little more than mild interest. Indeed, she was beginning to suspect that the body she now inhabited was practically invulnerable, which would make a lot of sense.

The problem was, however, the voices.

Not the normal hurly-burly of her ongoing internal debate. Quiet the contrary – there was something so very reassuring of having those many voices back with her, after losing them during the attack in the Sportsman's Arms. The constant rumble of the disagreements, the slow and gradual movement towards consensus, was as reassuring as a heartbeat echoing gently in her ear. No, it wasn't the voices inside her that were taxing her concentration. It was the echo.

"Sergeant?" Brierly managed to pick out Mrs Howkins' voice from the babble only with some difficulty. "Are you trying to tell me the creatures have consumed your mind? Are the others in there as well?"

Brierly thought of the Major with a sharp pang of guilt.

"No," she answered. "This isn't the bran-puca. This is me: my body was only ever a house for all the people I was. When I need a new one, I invite the owner to join me and ask them to allow me in."

"Would that we could all be so versatile," Mrs Howkins remarked, with something like sadness.

She said something else, but Brierly lost it on the swell of voices.

"I'm sorry," she said. "This takes so much concentration."

"I can imagine," Mrs Howkins said, speaking as if to a deaf acquaintance. "You are controlling each of these creatures? Do you split yourself between each body, or ... no: you have multiple personalities, yes. One in each body would seem to be the most elegant arrangement, am I right?"

"No, no," Brierly shook her head almost without thinking, and the echoes grew loud in disapproval. "There is only one bran-puca."

If she concentrated, Brierly could see Mrs Howkins' disdainful look around.

"Yes," she said. "I can see."

Brierly tried to focus. With every moment it was harder, but then at least she knew how this would end for her. For this individual, anyway: it was as inevitable as anything that had already happened. What that would mean for Mrs Howkins, Brierly didn't have the mathematics to understand. But none of the options felt as if they would be particularly appealing to the old woman.

"The bran-puca is engineered, Mrs Howkins," Brierly explained as simply as she could. "Designed by the Great Houses to be at an angle to normal spacetime. That is why they use them in situations like this. They only ever need one: it is remarkably efficient. This means nothing to you, does it?"

"Well at least there I can agree, Sergeant."

Yes, her mind was definitely getting clearer.

"The bubble, Mrs Howkins," Brierly tried to explain again. "It had its beginning and its end tied in a knot. It was a perfect closed loop of time. But the bran-puca moved differently within that loop to you or I. We didn't notice, just kept moving forward through our own time. But the bran-puca could move with it. Every time the bubble looped back to its beginning, the bran-puca went too. Within minutes there could be two, four, sixteen, two-hundred and fifty, sixty-five thousand. And still only ever one."

And yet with Brierly's keen ear for the multitude of voices within her, each iteration of the bran-puca brought another multitude of echoes to ignore. There were billions of iterations in the bubble now, each one giving a thousand voices to the babble. Each voice clamoured for Brierly's attention, making it all the harder to hear her own internal debate, let alone the voices of those outside her. Even though with every passing iteration a multitude of voices left, they were replaced by yet more. And so on and so on until Brierly's algebra failed her.

Mrs Howkins was pinching the base of her nose with two long fingers.

"So the bubble is gone?" Mrs Howkins asked after a sigh.

"Not yet," Brierly could feel it straining and tearing around her, but it was not gone yet. "But it will collapse. And before it does, I escape through the closing gateway to realspace. You have to understand – I've seen it happen. I'll have to go soon. Do you see?"

"Every moment, you increase by the square of yourself, minus one," Mrs Howkins answered calmly. "I'm afraid I don't have a head for mathematics. It sounds like you will still be here long after the bubble collapses, but I can't see how that could even be possible. Either I'll be trapped here forever, or the bubble will pop and so will I. Would that be the shape of it, Sergeant?"

"Or you will use up your air supply," Brierly added helpfully.

"Thank you," Mrs Howkins replied calmly. "You are right: we must always look on the bright side."

Brierly felt a tingle in what she could only assume was her belly, and knew that it was the flow of the strange energies that were released each time the bubble folded back impossibly on itself. She also knew that if she was going to do what she had always done, now was the time for her to flee through the closing gateway. There were some parts of herself that wanted to see what happened if she didn't go. Perhaps time itself would fracture and she would awake in her old body in the Strines snow, and warn the Major to leave well enough alone this time. But those voices were the minority, and she already had consensus on what she must do.

It was odd, leaving a conversation but remembering quite clearly how it would end. Parts of her wanted to make her farewells to Mrs Howkins: despite everything, Brierly had more than a little fondness for her. But she knew that would just confuse her, given that from her perception the conversation was still ongoing. So instead Brierly gracefully detached herself from the bubble of bran-puca, and sped unerringly to the narrowing gateway.

As she had always known she would, she made it through.

Elizabeth's head swam. It was something to have your life given back to you, only to have it snatched away again. When she had been in a dark afterlife, she had still had hope of a kind. Now she had uncertainty again, and the creeping feeling in the pit of her stomach. She had only ever dedicated her life to one thing. It was a worthless thing, a stupid pointless scream of frustration at a world that hadn't given her what she wanted for very long. She was ashamed of it, but it was hers. And she hadn't managed to achieve it anyway. She might as well have died with Bill for all the impact she had had.

And yet, underneath it all, there was something else. Her hand reached out almost unconsciously to touch the soft fur of the bats all around her. They trembled, and in the darkness she thought she could hear their squeaking breaths. And this was Sergeant Brierly, who had chased after Major Webber chasing after Elizabeth as blindly as Elizabeth had chased after her revenge. Elizabeth could hardly understand it, but she felt a little jealous of the Sergeant. The courage to change, even just a little: it was something Elizabeth knew she didn't have.

"How long do I have?" Elizabeth asked softly.

There was a pause, as if the Sergeant was struggling to remember where she had left the conversation. Which of these actual creatures was it talking to her, Elizabeth wondered. The voice seemed to come from all around her, and also from nowhere. But when the Sergeant spoke again, Elizabeth realised that was because she was hearing it directly inside her head.

"I don't know," Sergeant Brierly admitted.

Of course. Life was uncertainty.

"But it doesn't have to be that way, Mrs Howkins," the Sergeant added.

Elizabeth looked up.

"You can take me through the gateway?" she asked.

If it was possible, then she had a chance. She would need to plan, of course, and there was little enough time for that. But if she could get back before the Baron struck the final blow, if she could find a way to separate her Bill from Spinning Jenny, and if she couldn't do that then at least she could find a way to strike the killing blow herself. It was shameful and it was worthless, but it would be enough.

"In a way," the Sergeant said. Elizabeth recognised her tone. "There are a multitude of people inside me, Mrs Howkins. We could always welcome one more."

"You'd take my body?"

"No. I only move host when I need to. If I can be frank, Mrs Howkins, I'm quite enjoying this body: I don't think yours would offer much improvement. But that isn't the only way that people join me: I can bring them in as well. It means leaving your body behind, and you will have to play your part within the parliament. But you would survive. And you would be part of something bigger than yourself."

Elizabeth considered for a moment.

"I hate to bring this up, Sergeant," she said archly. "But your orders were to bring me in for trial and execution. How do I know this isn't just some last ditch attempt to perform your duty?"

Sergeant Brierly scoffed.

"You can't always do as you are told, Mrs Howkins," she said firmly. "Sometimes you have to do what is right."

Elizabeth closed her eyes, and tried not to let the words wash over her. She had never been one to follow orders, but she wasn't so deluded that she thought she was doing what she considered right either. The courage to change, even just a little. The chance was there. Perhaps just this once, Elizabeth could surprise herself.

"Are the Loa still out there?" she asked quietly.

The Sergeant paused, and Elizabeth imagined her poking a head up out of the ball of bats. How much of the bubble was there left to look outside of? Perhaps they were floating naked in space already, and the gateway slamming shut behind them.

"There are two still fighting," the Sergeant reported briskly. "But the collapsing bubble is stirring up currents that have attracted their attention. They are fighting a little closer to us than they were."

"Can I see them?"

Another pause.

"If I open any space, you'll lose your air all the quicker," the Sergeant warned.

Elizabeth laughed hollowly.

"In the circumstances, I'm not sure it matters," she said. 'Please. I would like to see her again, just this one last time."

Sergeant Brierly didn't respond. But Elizabeth could suddenly see light starting to fall on her body. It was coming from above, a thick purple light that made her think of the velvet lining of a coffin. Looking up, she could see that one of the bats had gone, and a hole had appeared. It was small, but still big enough for the air to start pulling out of it. Elizabeth started to take her last big gulps, but what was left was already thinning. But still she could see, out into the wild seas outside the bubble.

It felt like staring down into a deep well – that same vertiginous terror that she might somehow slip and fall. There were no stars, but as the waves crashed against each other they gave off a spume of sparks that lit the whole ocean. They twisted and danced like fireflies before disappearing back into the dark purple seas. And there, not so far away, were the loa. Two giant sea monsters, all mouths and barnacled skin. They twisted through one another, dancing like doomed lovers in their last tango. Mouths kissed skin, and thick black blood leaked into the sea, and still anyone who had a heart would feel it ache to see such alien beauty.

But all Elizabeth saw was what they had taken from her.

She was an old woman. Too old to change now.

Without another word, she tensed her legs and forced herself up through the sky. She could hear the Sergeant shouting at her, more than one voice echoing dully in her head but easy to ignore. Instead, she burst

141

her way through the small hole above, forcing the other bats out of her way and throwing them hither and thither as she tore through them. With the last of her strength, she made her feet make purchase on the outer skin of the Sergeant's protective shell. Then she pushed, and kicked off into that impossible sea.

With her last breath in her lungs, Elizabeth swam for the Loa.

Brierly felt each of the bran-puca lose its grip on the others, felt some spill out into the empty space beyond the bubble and then struggle to pull themselves back again. She could see Elizabeth getting further away, already too far for Brierly to reach her, and even if she could what good would it do? The old woman had made her decision, the same one that she had always made. Soon she was gone, hidden by the flapping of a multitude of leather wings.

The gateway was closing, and one by one each Brierly would escape.

The last of the air dissipated into that strange purple vacuum. It was the last part of the bubble to go, save the gateway itself. Those last few breaths of Strines were the final parts of the real world to falter and die out there. Save, of course, for Mrs Howkins herself. She would last a few seconds longer.

Brierly escaped, as she had always known she would.

There wasn't enough air. Her lungs were just too small. Or else her legs didn't have the power they needed. She tried to look up to see the loa ahead of her – how far away? But her eyes wouldn't open. They felt frosted over with ice, but possibly it was the eyes themselves that had frozen. Only her lungs burned, as she tried to keep hold of those last moments of air that would keep her alive until she reached Spinning Jenny. But she knew it was a dream – she would die, and float out here as a dessicated corpse for all eternity. If Elizabeth was going to get her revenge, she would have to start looking for it from the afterlife. So be it, then.

Then she heard a pop.

It was an incongruous sound to hear, and it caught her attention for two reasons. Firstly, she recognised it instantly: it was the pop of a cork being pulled from a bottle. But secondly, she noticed it because it was the only sound she had heard out there on those strange seas. Everything had been silence since she had left Sergeant Brierly and the air supply behind. Possibly she was mistaken. Perhaps what she was hearing was her eardrums bursting, or her lungs finally giving out. But then she felt a heavy weight suddenly land firmly on her back, and heard the scratch of a match being struck.

"Oh little sister," said a voice she couldn't quite place. "You are in a hell of a bad way."

Elizabeth found she could turn her head. She found she could breathe, and the ice fell from her eyes as she opened them. She expected to find herself back in the grey lands with Bill's echo looking disapproving. But as her eyes blink-blinked she could see she was still there, floating in the seas between the universes. She could see the loa, what looked like miles away in the distance and orbiting her slowly as she span uncontrollably. But even when she was completely upside down, the weight still pressed down on her back. Then two feet appeared, one either side of her hips. Elizabeth twisted her head to try to see who was sitting on her back.

"You know," remarked Major Webber conversationally as he lit a large cigar, "you is going to die."

Elizabeth blinked again. He took a long drag on the cigar, then leaned back to blow a series of smoke rings. The match was cast casually overboard, spinning end to end across the ocean. It still burned as it drifted away, until it got too far away for Elizabeth to distinguish from the sparking foam on the waves. Major Webber didn't look at it: he was taking a long swig from the bottle of brandy he was holding in his other hand. The cork was tucked into the breast pocket of his uniform jacket, but Elizabeth suspected it wouldn't be needed again.

Webber looked like he had seen better days. His skin was pale and taut, and his eyes had sunken deep into their sockets. But his jacket was pristine, as sharp and as bright as the day it had been taken out of the quartermaster's stores. It was his dress uniform that he wore, complete with bow tie and tails. It was dyed such a deep, dark black that he seemed to be a shadow against the rolling purple of the sea. He looked down at her and flashed his eyes, a broad grin spreading across his face. His teeth were perfect white and sparkled like stars.

"I rather suspect that is up to you, my lord," Elizabeth said. Her voice was crisp and clear, and echoed slightly as if she were in another bubble. "Please forgive me: I have nothing to offer you. This was all rather spur of the moment."

Webber snorted a giggle, smoke coming out of his nose.

"You got no brains, child," he laughed. It was strange to see Webber's face smiling so easily: Elizabeth had never seen it happen when he was alive, and if she'd thought about it would have suspected his face would crack. "How'd you think this would turn out for you, eh?"

"Well I hoped I would meet you, Lord Samedi," Elizabeth admitted. "Or that I would avoid you."

The Baron smiled and nodded like Elizabeth had said something truly wise, and took another swig of his brandy. Elizabeth vaguely wondered if Webber had ever drunk so much when he was alive. Drink, cigars, smiling: now that Baron Samedi was riding his corpse, he seemed to be having more fun than in his whole lifetime combined. Perhaps he was unhappy about that, wherever he was. But then again, who knew what arrangement he had made with the Baron in his last few moments?

"Well, little sister," the Baron said, suddenly solemn. "You done met me. What you gone do now?"

Elizabeth hesitated a moment. Talking with the Loa was much like the bubble she had just left: comforting and so familiar, but fraught with strange and unknown dangers. She had brought no offering to show her respect for the Baron, and besides which he knew her as well as any kind but authoritarian father. She could ask him any favour she desired, but he knew that ultimately she had only ever seen him as a means to an end. Dissembling would quickly use up whatever patience he had.

"I'm going to kill Spinning Jenny," Elizabeth said firmly.

She expected him to laugh, but instead the Baron just nodded sagely.

"Look over there," he said, waving vaguely into the distance with the brandy bottle. "Go on now: look."

Elizabeth turned away from Webber's body and looked. He was pointing her out across the seas, where the waves were getting fiercer and fire danced on the crest of each one. The Loa were closer now, twisting and whirling with a speed that seemed to increase the closer she got to them.

Chunks of flesh were being torn from each of them, flying out into the ether. The flesh of the Loa was strange stuff – wherever it landed, it would no doubt cause no end of trouble.

Elizabeth realised she couldn't tell which was which. Perhaps Baron Samedi would tell her if she asked him. But you asked questions of him warily: he had a reputation for giving you the plain simple truth when he answered. Once you'd heard it, there was no way to unhear it. Even after everything, Elizabeth wasn't sure she was ready for one of the Baron's answers.

"See?" Webber's voice came from behind her. "I'm gone kill Jenny."

Elizabeth didn't look back.

"Only if I don't get there first," she answered.

The Baron laughed at that, a single sharp burst like the cry of a crow. Elizabeth turned her head back round to him, and saw that he had his marketplace face on. He was willing to deal, then. The only question was what he was willing to offer: Elizabeth would pay any price required to get what she wanted, without hesitation.

"You know," he mused, tossing his cigar out into the rolling sea, "my wife, she like you. Mystery to me why she do, but she do. And she say you only doing what you doing cause you lost your man. All a man can hope for, have a woman love him like that."

Elizabeth resisted the urge to ask what Baron Samedi knew about what a man hoped for. Perhaps he knew better than most, anyway. It was the Baron who met them all, after all. It was the Baron who dug their graves for them, and welcomed them home. Man, woman and child, he met them all in time.

He took another swig of brandy and rolled it thoughtfully round his mouth.

"Here's what I'll do," he said eventually. "You stay out of my way, and I'll give you this knife. This knife here is all you want, you hear?"

Elizabeth saw him take the shadow of a knife, seemingly out of his own thigh.

"Will it kill Spinning Jenny?" she asked.

Baron Samedi smiled that toothy smile.

"Better than that," he said, and Webber's sunken eyes sparkled. "This knife? This knife cut your man right out of her belly. Him go free wherever the hell you want him to be, you use this knife."

The Baron held the knife out towards her, hilt first. She had seen shadow things before, of course. They always looked a touch insubstantial, as you would expect. But not this knife. It looked like it had been carved from the darkest ebony, something so black that light fell into it and couldn't escape again. Elizabeth couldn't help but reach out to it: her fingers brushed it gently, and the blade seemed to sing.

The Baron pulled it away, ever so slightly.

"We got a deal?" he asked.

The Loa had their own rules, Elizabeth knew that. They were so far divorced from the lives of even the most experienced human soul that it was impossible to attempt to judge them. All you could do was remember the simple truth of it: whatever they promised, whatever they gave you, it would never, ever work out the way that you hoped. It wasn't that they would trick you, that they were working to make everything worse. Just as many times they made things so much better, with just as little concern for what they had done. It was just that they were so distant from anything human that you couldn't hope to communicate. They might use words you thought you understood, but only the Loa knew their true meaning.

To ask a favour of the Loa was to risk everything. To accept their gift was foolish.

But Elizabeth had a simple choice. She had no illusions about why she had started her obsession, no grand hopes for what it might achieve. She focussed on her revenge because it was the only thing she had found that could stop her sitting alone in the dark and howling. She knew it wasn't what Bill would have wanted. It wasn't even what she would have wanted … wasn't even what she wanted now. It was just the only other thing she could do.

The knife wouldn't get her revenge. It probably wouldn't even get her Bill back. All it could offer was hope. Was there some small part of her left that was able to hope of living another life, even for a small amount of time? She had no illusions about who she had become, but if she took the knife then she would be admitting that she still had hope of being somebody else.

"We have a deal," Elizabeth said.

Baron Samedi smiled again.

"Good girl," he said approvingly, and drained the last of his brandy.

Elizabeth took the knife. It ached like pins and needles.

"You wake up from all this," the Baron said, discarding the empty bottle and standing between Elizabeth's shoulder blades. "You wake up from all this and you'll find the knife where you put it. Find some flowers too. Little blue flowers, growing where they damn well shouldn't. You gone need them: you get your fella out of Jenny, those flowers is all he'll be able to eat."

"And how do I get close enough to Bill to use the knife?" Elizabeth asked.

Baron Samedi smiled, and kicked away.

"Look up,'" he said, as he floated off into the purple sea.

Elizabeth looked up.

While the Baron had been talking, Elizabeth had been floating closer and closer to the Loa. Now she was right under their metaphorical feet: looking up, she could see the expanse of their bodies, rolling through the sea above her. She could see their tentacles and the rough sandpaper skin of their mouths. There were eyes there, many faceted eyes that made her feel sick and were close enough for her to reach up and touch. They screamed silently, and went about the steady business of tearing each other to pieces. Elizabeth felt the blood rain down on her.

Then one of the mouths moved languidly towards her.

In one bite, she was gone.

# 13. January 1854, Strines

It was early morning. Not so early that the sky was still dark, but that cusp of light and dark where the morning still felt like a night. When James stood in the tap room that early in the morning, he could see the whole expanse of the valley laid out beneath his windows. The trickling stream running across to the printworks, and the chimneys pulling his eyes up to the railway line disappearing into the trees. At that time of the morning, the sun hadn't managed to burn off the morning mist yet. Everything looked vague and half-formed, and the horizon gently bled into a pale grey sheen.

There had been a time when James had felt his soul lifted by those early morning views. But now the village in mist filled him with an unease that he couldn't articulate. And the clouds looked like they were getting ready for snow: that was something else that made him uneasy these days. Mist and snow: he couldn't explain it.

He wanted nothing more than to climb back into bed and get back up at a more reasonable hour, but there was work to be done if he wasn't going to have the regulars bashing his ear as soon as he stepped out of the front door. And first on the list was cleaning the ash of yesterday's fire out of the grate. Something else that gave him an unexpected case of the shivers these days.

A door opened behind him, and he glanced up.

"You here to help?" he asked.

Isabella smiled wanly, wrapped only in the shirt he'd been wearing yesterday.

"Water," she croaked, getting herself a glass and disappearing.

Yes, back to bed would be most appealing. But there was work to do.

He knelt in front of the fireplace.

It was a busy evening in the Sportsman. Most of the village had appeared in the pub as the day had worn on, and every one of them seemed to have been struck by an unquenchable thirst. Partly, he knew, it was down to Isabella: every since she had taken a room here, the pub had been busier. People wanted to catch a glimpse of her, and solidify the opinions they had already formed. She didn't spend much time in the bar, but when she passed through James could see the heads turn one by one by one.

"So how's she doing now, Jimmy?" one of the regulars asked, leaning forwards over the bar. "We still don't see much of her in the village."

That was a lie: they didn't see anything of her in the village. Anything she needed from outside, she relied on James to get for her. If she needed to take the air, she'd stick her head out of a window. She had been here nearly five months now, and James couldn't swear that she had ever left the building. If she had, she had snuck out in the dead of night when James and the village were sleeping.

"She's not been well, Job," James answered gently. "You know that."

Job grinned widely.

"Sure you've been tending to her, James."

James smiled thinly and nodded to acknowledge the hit. The idea of grasping Job by both lapels and pulling his face down hard onto the bar did occur to him. Possibly he had been spending too long in Isabella's company. But instead he finished pouring the young man's gin and handed it over. He had a business to run, and Job's ha'penny took priority over James' pride.

Job looked like he was about to add some other witticism, but he was distracted. Over at the other side of the room, there was an ominous rumble. There were two men in that corner that James had never seen before – possibly they had walked down from the Ridge, which was enough to make James wary. If a man couldn't find somewhere to drink close to his home, there was usually a good reason. But their pennies hadn't bent in James' teeth, so he was willing to give them a fair chance. Now it looked like he was about to pay the price for his lenience.

One of the men seemed to have offended his companion, since he was now on his feet and shouting into his face. The other man was unconcerned, and indeed had a smirk on his face that seemed designed to encourage someone to try to wipe it away. Neither of the men paid any attention to the room. James couldn't really blame them for that – there wasn't a man here that would risk a beating on the Sportsman's sake, no matter how much time they spent here. Even the police proved unwilling if they were nearby – the courts still seemed to think fisticuffs was part and parcel of the position, and it was a rare judge who took an attack against the police into account when sentencing.

Which of course meant that it came down to James. For the sake of his customers, James found himself stepping into each and every situation that he would rather sit out. The only consolation was that somebody would buy him a drink if he got knocked on his backside. Usually the cheapest beer going.

James rolled up his sleeves and started to move.

And then stopped.

The smirking man had been pulled to his feet by his lapels, and his companion was drawing his arm back as everybody else moved away. As the crowd parted, James saw Isabella standing there between them. She looked from one to the other calmly and impassively, and then James saw her lips move as she said something softly to both men. The reaction was instant: they both laughed, and turned back to their business. The smirking man kept smirking and his red-faced friend still intended to punch him.

Isabella reached up and placed a hand gently on the man's fist.

Again, he turned to her. This time, his face was darker, and James could see the other fist coming up to strike. Isabella didn't seem to have noticed, just stood there calmly looking up at him. James heard himself shout a warning, but she didn't seem to hear him either. The fist came up. It was a fist that could pound skulls to powder when it connected, and moved with the speed of a wild horse. Isabella looked very small and very helpless, standing underneath that fist as it came down.

But it didn't connect.

Instead, the man twisted suddenly and awkwardly, his feet kicking out and knocking over the table he'd been sitting at. Something had hold of his arm and was pulling it back with such force that he lost his footing completely and was dragged backwards towards the door. In the darkness, James couldn't see who Isabella's protector was, but he didn't need to. He knew that even if every candle in the pub was burning bright, he would still see the man dragged back on his arse by a vague and dark shape. As if he was being attacked by his own shadow, or someone else's.

Isabella said something else to the smirking man. The smirk disappeared, and a few moments later so did he. Isabella didn't look at any of the other people there, but none of them returned the favour. Every eye was on her as she paced solemnly across the floor, moving into space that suddenly opened up in front of her as she passed. As she came close to the bar, she glanced up at James and gave him one of those smiles. He couldn't help smiling back, even as his knees trembled beneath him.

"I'm feeling a lot better now," she said softly.

Then she disappeared behind the bar and back up to the rooms above.

James glanced across at Job, but he had nothing to say now.

"All right then," James couldn't help smirking. "Who's next?"

After that, it was clear that nobody was going to go home. They wanted to tell each other the story of what they'd all seen, spreading the few scraps that they knew about Isabella as thinly as possible. The braver and drunker of his patrons had the nerve to ask James directly, but he diverted their curiosity as best he could. It wasn't so much that he didn't want to tell them – although he didn't: he wanted to guard Isabella as jealously as he could from every one of those men in there because not one of them deserved her. Neither did he, he knew, which was of course the problem.

But it didn't matter: he didn't know much more than they did anyway. She had been in the village for five months, and in his bed for three, and he could still tell them little more than her name and that she wouldn't eat eggs. Perhaps even those small details would have been as voraciously consumed as the other scraps being passed hand to mouth.

James didn't think he would be able to bear their questions all night, but fortunately he had already arranged for Ann Yarwood to take over behind the bar. He had an errand to run that night, and probably his absence would only serve to loosen his customers' tongues and purses even more than if he'd stayed to give them Isabella's history. So he disappeared a little early and headed upstairs to his room.

He found Isabella there, staring out of the window as the first of the snow started to fall. She was wearing her long coat, and for the first time in as long as James could remember, the smoked-glass goggles were resting on her head. It looked as if she had recently shaved her head as well. She had done it close, practically down to the bone. She didn't turn around as he walked in behind her. He didn't feel that he could break the silence. He couldn't even touch her.

"The snow's here," she said, matter-of-factly.

It sounded to James as if she had been expecting it all her life.

"It won't be too bad," he tried to reassure her. "It won't settle."

Isabella didn't answer, but from the curve of her shoulder, he could tell she didn't agree. He took another step forward, reached out for her. Then he thought of her shadow and its razor-sharp claws. He thought better of it.

"Isabella?" he asked softly. "Is something wrong?"

She didn't answer immediately. He decided to risk losing a hand, and rested it gently on her shoulder. She shrugged it off with a shiver that made him think that she might have been crying. He had never seen her cry before. He wasn't entirely convinced that it was even possible.

"You can tell me," he told her.

"I haven't told you anything else," she replied sharply. "Are you sure?"

"I don't care about that."

"You don't?" she almost laughed. Almost.

"Isabella —"

She span around sharply, and her face was a becalmed ocean. If there were dangerous undercurrents there then he couldn't see them. But that was always the way with undercurrents: you never saw them until they had pulled you down. So perhaps he was going to drown here. He turned the idea over in his thoughts, and surprised himself with what he found. He had always thought his first concern would be for the business, for the pub and the till. But now the moment was here, he found that all he wanted was to show her that he wasn't afraid.

"It's time, James," she said coldly, and the air seemed to thicken behind her.

He wanted to show he wasn't afraid. Which would be hard, since he was.

There in that room, she terrified him.

Always had.

"Don't go," he begged softly.

There was a crack in the mask she had pulled on at that. Just a flicker of something human behind the bone. Then she set herself cold again, and looked back at him with a look that anyone might mistake for disdain.

"I'll tell you," she breathed softly. "Come with me."

James hesitated, damn him.

"Where?"

She blinked, just for a moment. And then she strode past him to the door.

"I'm going up to Mellor Moor," she said as she hovered in the doorway. She didn't turn to face him. "If you come with me, you'll find out about all of it. But you don't want to find out, James. Stay here."

"I can't," James told her. "There's a woman rented the spare room. She's coming on the train tonight: she won't pay if I'm not there to pick her up. Can't we ..."

But he was talking to himself.

By the time she got up to Mellor Moor, it was obvious that the snow wasn't going to stop. It was going to throw itself down at the ground, wave after wave after wave of it and it wouldn't stop until everything was snow. The path up to the moor crossed over the railway line, and then overlooked it all the way up to the crest of the valley: already most of the track had disappeared underneath thick snow, and anyone else would have doubted more trains would be able to pass. Of course, Isabella knew that there would be just one more. It was a wrinkle, but it couldn't be helped.

The moor stretched out across the very tip of the valley, and if she looked down to her left she could see Strines below her. Stone cottages and newer brick terraces, all with smoke pouring from their chimneys. No-one would be going out into the snow that evening. All the men in the Sportsman would relish the excuse to stay there the night through, even those that only lived just across the road. Looking over the crest of the hill ahead of her, she should be able to see all the way down into Manchester. But the snow and the cloud had it hidden: all she could see was rolling fields of grey.

"We're here!" came an exasperated cry from behind her. "Isabella, stop!"

But she kept on, each foot crunching deep into thick snow.

"Just a little further," she said, without looking.

She knew she was nearly there. Her shadow was practically screaming at her, and it was all she could do to stop it prowling off on its own. Now it had regained its full strength she didn't feel entirely confident that she could pull it back again if it went off too far: it knew its own mind far too well. The path bent just up ahead and doubled back on itself, rising up to the first patch of broken ground that marked the edge of the moor. That was where she was heading. The air seemed to glow there.

Down in the valley, the last train steamed by. She knew James would be watching it go, thinking of his wallet. But he surprised her by not saying anything, just stomping steadily along behind her to their destination. Part of her wanted to stop, to turn and tell him to go after the train. But in this weather it wasn't entirely certain that he would make it back down the valley safely anyway. He must have been thinking it – he had lived here too long and too cautiously not to be worried. But still, he said nothing.

She reached the edge of the moor, and stood on a stone.

This was the spot: she could feel time slipping.

"Here?" James gasped as he reached her feet.

"Here," Isabella confirmed sadly.

She watched him look around, taking in as much of the view as the cloud would let him see. She wondered if he had even been up this far before: perhaps he had lived his entire life down in that valley, never moving more than a mile in any given direction. It would be easy enough to find out – now he was here, his bio-data was starting to crackle and spark like an electric cable: she could take just a peek and see his whole history cascade out behind him. The years alone, and the last few months with her.

"James –" she started to say.

But he interrupted, didn't hear.

"Why here?" he asked.

He probably thought it was the safest question.

Isabella closed her eyes.

"There's a cross here," she told him, eyes still tightly shut. "The local churches paid for it to be built, and they even held services here, on occasion. It's a place of worship etched into the landscape, the history. There's a power here that can be used, if you know the proper rituals."

James looked around again.

"There isn't a cross, Isabella," he said.

"It was built in the nineteen-seventies," she told him. His face froze as he tried to hide his concern. "But it bleeds backwards and forwards through spacetime. Because of everything that happened here."

"Is ..." James' voice cracked, but he tried again. "Is that where you're from?"

Isabella couldn't help herself: she smiled.

"No ..." she stopped herself. "I'm from Strines."

He reached up to her, tried to take her hand.

She could let him reach for her, take his hand and wait the storm out up here. They had talked about it before, spending a night away from the pub and under the stars. He had seemed to think she didn't believe he would do it, but she knew he would given time. No, what she had known was that this moment would always come. It was written in their blood, scarred deep into the history of this place. She glanced up at the sky: behind it, she could see the shapes starting to gather. And even so it would be easy not to. He was an easy man to try and make smile, and the idea of having a little more time was as seductive as he was.

She didn't reach for him, and he couldn't quite get his hand to hers.

"Did I do something?" he asked, confused.

She wanted to tell him that he hadn't. But she didn't think it would help. How could she explain it? The two of them being happy just wasn't so important. Not when you set it against everything else. There were more lives involved in this than just theirs. They swamped her, overruled her. That was just the truth of it.

"There will be a bubble," she told him, knowing he wouldn't understand. "Part of this universe and at the same time completely not. It should vanish in an eye blink, but it won't. And the Great Houses will notice, and they will send people. They're so predictable it doesn't even matter how many iterations we go through: every time, they will send people. And every time they will need a tunnel: bio-data existing inside and outside the bubble at the same time that they can cast a line between. That bio-data is yours, James. You will be their tunnel: its waiting in your blood even now."

He looked up at her with heartbreaking trust.

"What can I do?" he asked. "Will it hurt?"

"When they get in the bubble, they will collapse it," Isabella ignored him. She had to close her eyes to do it. "I can't let them do that. So much depends on that bubble, James. But if they get inside, it will happen. Unless the tunnel collapses while they're inside, and the bubble vanishes. They will assume the bubble collapsed, and the only two people who might have investigated closer will be dead."

"Dead?" James echoed.

"And so will you be," Isabella breathed.

Her shadow leapt up from underneath James, dark as night against the blazing snow. With one arm clamped around James' neck, it held him still. It needn't have bothered: James didn't move. He just looked up at Isabella, still not understanding. Isabella could tell that he was remembering every day of the last three months, wondering what this meant for them. He didn't understand that she just had no choice. How could he? She couldn't explain. It sounded hollow: some things were just more important than two people.

The shadow sliced him open with a claw, and light bled out.

## 14. June 1931, Manchester

The work in the factory was repetitive but easy, and most of the women took the opportunity to chat to their colleagues rather than concentrate on the machines. But they had quickly learned not to try talking to her. She kept her machine running and ignored everything else around her, staring deep into the heart of the cogs and gears as they entwined. The only days she ever looked up were those when it was snowing. Even now, after all this time, she couldn't help but watch the snow. When it fell, it forced her to remember it all. As if she might scrape away the flakes from the city outside and find all that history still alive underneath.

When it snowed, Elizabeth couldn't help but remember.

Nothing had changed. Perhaps it never did.

Broken roads wound around grey hills, the air choked with a thick smog that didn't seem to really emanate from anywhere. The horizon was a forest of broken chimneys, each greying the sky with a pale, pitiful smoke. But all around her the buildings were ruins, bricks tumbling slowly down into rubble. The mill that had been there last time she was here was nothing but a broken wheel submerged in the water, claimed by a furry black mould that slowly ate it away to nothing.

Elizabeth hadn't woken here. As soon as the Loa's teeth had closed around her, she had found herself back. She supposed that it wasn't really a place, but then she supposed that she was no longer really a person. In some ways, she was just a frozen and desiccated corpse floating between the universes, but in others even that was an illusion. The first thing she had learned all those years ago was that reality was just a state of mind. Even so, she did wonder what would happen if she did find her Bill and managed to escape with him. What would they be escaping from and to?

Tucked into her belt, she could feel the heft of the Baron's knife.

"You came back, then?"

Elizabeth turned, and saw that she wasn't alone. The old man was still here, his tattered clothes only just clinging to him and the bloodstained scarf still wrapped around his throat. The wound beneath looked fresher, as if it had reopened recently. Perhaps it had – he was only ever a part of Spinning Jenny, after all, and she wasn't facing the brightest of futures. But as well as that, he was a man, and one that now she recognised: he had been one of the twins, and still bore the scar of the shadow's attack on his brother.

"I never found out your name," Elizabeth said conversationally.

He just smiled, confused.

"It's been so long ..." he tailed off in vague apology.

Elizabeth looked around again.

"How long since I was last here?" she asked.

Again the man shrugged.

There was a strange electricity in the air for a moment, a sensation that made Elizabeth shiver. In the distance, several of the chimneys trembled and then collapsed gracefully to the ground. She could see thick black smoke tumble up into the air, mixing with dark clouds and making it seem like the night was nearly on them. The feeling passed, but left in its wake a strong unease. Spinning Jenny did not have much time.

"It comes more frequently now," the old madman whispered at her side. Then he smiled, even though it was clear by now he could only half remember how. "But I imagine all that will be done with now that you're here again."

"It will?" Elizabeth was only half-listening.

"You have to save her," the old man said, as if it was obvious. "It's your responsibility."

The blade still touched her skin, a shard of concealed ice.

The world shook again, only this time the attack seemed closer, or stronger. That queasy electric feeling returned, so strong that Elizabeth found herself retching even as the ground shook under her feet. She could see the old man still where he was, still standing but frozen into place as if time had stopped. All the colour and definition in his body flickered for a moment, and then vanished. It left behind the shape of the man, filled with a darkness so complete that he seemed two-dimensional. Deep inside it – deeper than could even be, possibly – flecks of white fell.

Elizabeth felt her skin tightening, ice forming, and knew instinctively that her body was returning to the state it should be in, floating between the universes. Her heart seemed to freeze in her chest, holding on so tightly to its last beat that she felt it would have to burst. She had come close to death before, and had always managed to remain calm and plan her way through to the other side of it. But this came on so suddenly and took hold of her so completely that she couldn't help but be afraid. She was an old lady, and she had always secretly assumed that at the moment of her death all those years would give her peace and perspective. But here she was, terrified and desperate to cling to a life that seemed to be fast departing.

"I'm here, Betty," a quiet, calm voice said in her ear. She couldn't look – her eyes had frozen over again – but she knew who it was. "Don't worry. I'm here."

She felt a slight pressure on her hand, and she knew that Bill was holding it. Everything seemed to be compressing down into a dark, black tunnel. She had no idea whether it was just her sensation dying, or if the entire landscape was dying around her. She supposed it didn't matter. Instead, Elizabeth concentrated on making her cold dead fingers squeeze tight. She felt them close around Bill's hand, and just like that the fear seemed to pass.

Then everything went black.

And then it was all white.

Specks of white exploded out of that complete darkness, white diamonds burning with the heat of a thousand suns. They seemed to race up to her, and Elizabeth assumed that this was the final gasp of her life leaving her. But she could feel Bill holding her hand, and hear the rasp of her lungs as they pulled air into them. Her skin started to feel warm again, and her eyes popped open as the ice turned to water. All she could see was the blinding white light, but then it quickly faded to reveal the old landscape still there. No – not the old: a similar landscape, but smaller, dustier, greyer. The silhouette of the old madman was still in front of her, and then suddenly he was back, still smiling that half-remembered smile as if nothing had happened.

"That was a close one," he said, without any sense of urgency.

"You all right, Betty?" Bill asked.

Elizabeth knew that she wasn't. That she hadn't been for longer than she could remember. She hadn't died, but being so close and having Bill there to comfort her was almost too much to bear. She knew that when death came, that was how she wanted it to be. And she knew that Bill was gone, and that was impossible. She started to cry, but her eyes were still cold and dusted with ice. No tears would come.

The knife suddenly felt warm against her skin.

"I know you think this is bad, Betty," the shadow of Bill was saying to her urgently. "And it is. It would've been best for all of us if you could've stopped this on your first go round. But that's by the by now. Don't you be worrying about that. There's still time. We can drop you back again. But this time you have to do it. Betty, are you listening? You have to do it this time."

But she wasn't listening. She was deciding.

No, she was decided.

She pushed herself back to her feet, her hand slipping to the hilt of the blade at her back. Her other hand grabbed the ghost of Bill by his wrist, pulling him forwards so sharply that he stumbled down to his knees. He ended up staring at the black shadow blade. The madman saw it too, but his reaction wasn't as fast: the smile melted from his face as curiosity replaced it.

"Betty," Bill warned, sounding scared now. "Don't do this."

But she was too old to listen to Bill now. She'd grown stubborn as she'd grown older, and her mind was already set. As the blade slipped easily out of her trousers, she let its tip continue up in a tight arc. The blade flicked crisply through the air, barely even slowing as it met with the madman's belly. He reached for the wound, but the blade continued in its upwards sweep, and then all colour bleached from the madman again. Now the blade was just arching up through a snow-filled night, a snowstorm with the shape of a man.

"Betty –" Bill started to say.

"Quiet, Bill," Elizabeth snapped.

She pulled him firmly after her as she jumped into the snowstorm.

The manager came out of his office, his eye fixed on his pocket watch. At six precisely, he rang the bell that hung by the door, and then headed back into the office. He didn't look up at any of the women, and they didn't look at him once the bell had been rung. They were already on their feet and heading for the door, keen to get on with whatever the evening held for them. Elizabeth watched them go, and tried not to imagine fire licking at their heels.

She got up slowly and collected her things, unwilling to admit to herself that she was in no hurry to leave. She glanced back at the office, and saw the manager giving her a sympathetic look. Possibly he thought that she was just another young girl with nothing to go home to except hungry mouths and damp walls. He knew better than most the true state of the business, and even those who knew less weren't optimistic. He walked around with the air of a condemned man waiting for the axe to fall. The only job he had ever had was managing the girls on the factory floor, and if this place went under – when – there was nowhere left to go. Elizabeth had seen this city when the factories had bulged at the seams with workers and the canals were choked with narrowboats. Now this was the last factory on the street without its windows boarded, and the waterways were fast becoming choked with rats and weeds.

Elizabeth pulled her shawl tight around her head and set out into the night. If she was quick, she could catch the omnibus back to Stockport and miss the rain that was threatening. But if she was slow, she could delay preparing Bill's supper for maybe another hour. Any longer than that, and the neighbours would be sure to talk.

She looked down at her hands. They looked older than ever before, and they were starting to curl as arthritis got its teeth into her. She thought of the things those hands had done, the power they could pull from the fabric of the universe. It seemed more like a dream than a memory. She could barely recall the rituals she needed to reach the Loa, not that it mattered. The last time she had tried, Jenny's voice had been so weak as to be almost silent, and the only presence was that of the Baron. He had the city firm in his grip now, and Industry was so close to Death that she would be gone by now. Perhaps the last vestiges, just hanging on. When the factory closed, she would know for sure.

The rain started to fall, but Elizabeth didn't hurry.

The air felt warm and fresh, and it was only then that Elizabeth realised just how stale the air of that dying city had been. Above her were the stars, and under her the frosty grass. Her heart was pounding fit to burst and she could feel Bill's hand still in hers. She looked across at him, lying on the ground beside her and couldn't help but smile. It was hard to remember the last time she had, and she didn't want the moment to end.

"What have you done, Betty?" Bill asked reproachfully.

"No," she said softly. "Quiet."

And they lay there for a few minutes more. There would be time enough for the rest of it later. Time enough for both of them.

The house was an old back-to-back, so old that Elizabeth might have been able to watch it being built when the Loa first dragged her back through time. It wasn't much, but the windows were still intact and the walls didn't bow too much. She and Bill rented the back rooms from a family who lived less than ten miles away, and the other couples they shared the building with were quiet and kept to themselves. It wasn't their little terrace in Strines, but things could have been worse. Probably would have been by now, if they'd have stayed.

When they had finally pulled themselves from the ground that warm evening, Bill and Elizabeth had found that they were standing in the grounds of the old works. For a moment, Elizabeth had worried that they were back inside the bubble, but there were the chimneys and factories of the new works before them. Built from the bricks of the old, standing steady and firm until the fire ate them away. She had looked to Bill for some kind of reaction, but he was content to wait for her to take the lead. Elizabeth remembered that had made her feel a little awkward, not because she wasn't used to making her own decisions but because Bill had never seen her do it.

A few minutes walk later, and they had been hovering in the doorway of the Sportsman. It had looked unchanged from how she remembered it: not from her exile a hundred years in the past, but from all those nights with Bill and a small sherry after their shift at the factory. She could hear the noise of practically the whole village inside, thought that she could even recognise a voice or two amongst the babble. But that door was a razor blade that separated then from now: if she stepped through it, there would be no going back. She would know where she was, and what had happened, and she would have to adapt accordingly.

She remembered she had taken Bill's hand again, and felt it limp in hers like a dead fish. But he pulled her through the door like he knew exactly what he would find in there. And what they had found had been their old lives. The shock of it had been so great that they hadn't even realised the cruelty. Everybody had been in the pub that night, every friend and workmate that had died in the fire that had claimed Bill. They had smiled and welcomed her, and even though she could still see every line and wrinkle on her hands, they all acted as if it was the Betty and Bill of fifty years ago who had joined them after only a few hours absence.

It felt to Elizabeth like she had walked through the gates of Heaven. She had decided that night that they would have to leave. She knew she couldn't stay, waiting every day to see whether the fire would come as it had before.

She put her key in the door and leant her weight against it to free up the rusting mechanism. It strained for a moment and then burst open with that familiar creak. Mrs McAllister was in the kitchen, and glanced up guiltily at the noise: she was scraping the leftovers into a soup pan, and from the look on her face Elizabeth guessed that not every plate there had been hers. But she gave a grim smile, and her neighbour turned back to her cooking.

Elizabeth took each step upwards as slowly as she could. The paint was peeling on the walls, everything stained brown and soft. As she reached the top of the stairs, she stopped and pretended to examine it. Her door was just to the left on the landing. She could see it was closed, but all the same she put on her pantomime of a distracted woman. As she got closer, the unease grew.

"Sorry I'm late," she said, hanging her coat behind the door. "I missed the bus."

Bill didn't say anything. He had barely spoken for a week now, and hadn't seemed to move for two. When they had first moved in, he could at least make it down the stairs and even into the yard out back. In the old days, he might've been out there smoking, but she hadn't seem him touch a packet since she had freed him. When he was outside, he just looked up at the stars as if searching for something. Now, though, he lay on top of the bed and looked at her with sad, sunken eyes.

"Wasn't much of a day," she said, turning away. "But I don't imagine yours was much more exciting."

She caught a glimpse of herself in the mirror, saw the young girl that she used to be looking awkwardly out at her. The first few times she had seen her reflection, she had had to stop and check herself: every inch of skin she could see was old and wrinkled, and when she touched her face it was the loose-skinned face of an eighty-year-old woman. Somehow the mirrors and everybody else saw Bill and her as they should have looked in 1931. She imagined they would be most surprised when she died of old age in a few years, apparently still in her thirties. Now of course she was used to it, and she barely gave the stranger in the glass a second look.

She looked back at him, motionless on the bed except for the slow heavy rattle of his breathing. Sometimes, it just hit her. Like now. She had to sit, and rested herself carefully on the edge of the bed. She rested a hand in his lap, and he looked up at her without a hint of expression. They sat like that for a moment, neither speaking. They both knew: there wasn't much more to be said.

"Do you want your supper?" she asked softly.

He nodded, tried to smile.

She looked out of the window as she stood, and saw that the rain was well and truly coming down now. The sky was dark with cloud, and the cobbled streets outside had turned into a flowing riverbed. She realised how dark it was, and reached for the matches to light a candle. It guttered and danced, before straightening up to shed a little light around the room.

He chuckled grimly from the bed.

"What is it?" she asked, turning.

He shook his head, but she knew what it was. The room was filled with the candle's soft light now, and the shadows danced and rocked. But there was more light than there should have been. It had been Bill who had noticed it first, and when he had mentioned it Elizabeth had been surprised to discover she wasn't surprised. A few days had passed by then, and there were so many other things about their new lives that this was just one more. The light filled the room, passing straight through her as if she wasn't there: she had no shadow any more.

Later, she lay in bed and looked at the ceiling. The paint was just as damp-stained as the walls, and here and there the plaster bulged ominously. Everything was dark now: the cloud outside had blocked out any hint of the moon and the stars, and Elizabeth was embarrassed to admit that twice now she had checked that the house wasn't surrounded by a wall of ice. The rain still hammered down, pounding against the slates above her and dripping drops somewhere nearby: hopefully it was outside the house, but she couldn't be certain.

Underneath that, she could just make out Bill's rasping breaths.

He had fallen ill shortly after they found the house, but Elizabeth knew the two things weren't connected. He had been slowly fading ever since she had pulled him away from Jenny. Just as the rest of the city seemed to have been. They had seen doctors, of course, but they couldn't find anything physically wrong with him. But then nor could they see that Elizabeth was an eighty-year-old woman, so she gathered they might not be seeing things as they truly were. She had tried examining him herself, but her connection to the Loa had withered so much she could barely make out the faintest aura about him. All she could see was a grey smudge.

There was a sudden gust of wind, and the window rattled in its frame. Elizabeth glanced over, but it held and the rain and the wind stayed outside. Her eye was drawn to the radio that sat on the dresser, a small squat box with a dial poking out of the middle like a short stubby nose. She had bought it second-hand with her first week's wages, thinking that it might help Bill keep himself entertained when he had to take to his bed. He hadn't listened to it once as far as she could tell, but sometimes she turned it on when she got back from the factory and listened to the dance music.

She hadn't listened that night, but it was on nonetheless. The light behind the dial was flickering like candlelight, and now she realised it she could hear the static hissing just under cover of the rain. She wondered how long it had been on without her noticing, whether Bill had been listening to it while she was at work. She knew he hadn't, but the idea that it had turned itself on made her uneasy. All she had to do was get out of bed and turn it off, but still she lay there in the dark next to Bill. Silly old woman: everything she had seen in her life, only to be scared of this.

That snub-nosed dial began to turn, and the radio screeched and wailed at her. Odd snatches of songs and conversations rose up through the static only to fade away again and die. When the static sang, she could hardly bear it. She wanted to scream and throw the radio across the room, but then when the voices came she begged for the noise again. They sounded so strange, so inhuman, and their words were nothing but an urgent rumble. They gnawed at the edge of her understanding, only managing to impart their anxiety and none of their meaning.

"Elizabeth?" came a commanding male voice through the static.

Elizabeth didn't move. Her fingers wanted to draw some protection in the air, to carve a vevé into the bedsheets. But she held them still. That was all a long way behind her now, and besides the wench was dead. Instead she lay as still as she could, her eyes fixed on the glowing dial of the radio and her heart pounding steadily in her chest. Bill didn't move beside her: perhaps he was still asleep, or perhaps only she could hear the voice. Perhaps there was no voice to be heard.

"Elizabeth," the man's voice said, this time more sharply. "I don't have time for this."

Elizabeth tried to find her voice.

"Leave me alone," she said.

Her voice shook a little. She was out of practice with giving orders. Now she simply took them, and hoped that the pay they gave her at the end of the week would be enough to stretch to the next.

"Don't be ridiculous," the voice snapped back. It was growing louder. "It's taken me a hundred years to find a way to talk to you: I'm not going to stop before I've even started."

Elizabeth let her hand rest on Bill's chest almost without realising that she was doing it. A hundred years ago she had been in the bubble or inside the Loa. She wouldn't let them take Bill away from her. Despite everything, she wouldn't let them do that. She could only think of one person that would come for her across the centuries, to collect the debt that she owed. She would have expected the Loa to have more power, but perhaps even they were fading as the rest of this grey, desperate world ground itself deeper and deeper into decay.

"Please, Lord Samedi," Elizabeth pleaded, aware of how low she had fallen just by the tone of her voice. "Please leave us be."

The Baron just laughed.

"Elizabeth," he said. "It's Brierly."

Elizabeth breathed damp air for a moment.

"Brierly?" she echoed. "But you're a man."

"It's been a hundred years, Elizabeth," Brierly's voice sounded genuinely amused. "Things change. Internal politics, you know how it is."

Elizabeth had to admit that even with all the things she had seen in her life, she still had no idea how it was with Brierly. But despite the changes, now Elizabeth truly listened she could hear the Sergeant in there. Something in the tone, the timbre of the voice. The confidence he possessed on those occasions when he knew he spoke with the force of multitudes. It stirred old memories, old emotions. Elizabeth swung herself carefully out of bed and walked to the radio.

"Where are you?" Elizabeth asked it quietly.

"Exactly where I went when you left me," the voice replied. It still sounded jovial, but there was an edge hidden there. "I escaped the bubble into the Great Houses' tunnel. But I didn't manage to escape the tunnel. I'm still here. That's why it's taken so long for me to reach you."

"You want me to help you escape?"

"Do you know how?"

Elizabeth thought for a moment. She hadn't thought about anything for so long, not even recalling a treasured happy memory. She was afraid that anything from back then would be tarnished by the damp and the decay in the air now. So instead she had let her mind get rusty and cold.

"No," she said sadly.

"No," Brierly echoed. He hadn't expected anything more, clearly. "The last person who knew how to open the tunnel died fifty years ago. That isn't why I need you."

"What then?"

"Spinning Jenny," Brierly said.

There was no chair by the radio: they had no furniture except the bed and the chest of drawers the radio sat on. Elizabeth felt the old echoes of herself shimmer and disperse, like smoke in a gentle breeze. She folded to the floor, her legs crossed and her head in her hands. She could hear Bill's ragged breathing behind her. How had they ever thought that they could escape?

"The attack is still happening," Brierly went on. Elizabeth didn't know if he could even see the effect his words were having on her. "You have to understand: it's 1854 and it's now. None of it ever ends. There's still time to save her. We have to save her, Elizabeth."

Elizabeth felt the words catch in her throat, but she spat them out.

"Why would you want to do that?"

They lay there, frozen to the air and sharp as ice.

"Haven't you seen what's happened here?" Brierly's shock managed to transmit itself quite clearly over the airwaves. "Go to the window. Look at it. Have you even still got a job? Have you got any hope left at all? Because it will only get worse, Elizabeth. She is the Loa of Industry, and this is the world without her."

Elizabeth looked to the window, but everything outside was just a grey blur. It was dark, and the night was blurred by a fine downpour. There was nothing to see out there, and nothing that really mattered. She turned her head back to the bed. This was the world without Spinning Jenny, and she had survived it. She knew she could not survive again in a world without Bill.

"There's nothing I can do," Elizabeth answered.

"Elizabeth —"

"There's nothing I can do!" she shouted.

The room went silent for a moment. Even the hiss of static, the gentle pit-pat of the rain, stopped for that one moment. Elizabeth felt ashamed in a way she hadn't since she was a little girl. She was too old to feel like that again, but now every layer of her skin seemed to have been peeled back. It had thickened when Bill had died: it had had to or she wouldn't have survived. But ever since she had come back here it had all been washed away by the rain, blasted by the dust. She couldn't stop herself from feeling, and so in the end there was nothing else she could do.

"It's 1931, Brierly," Elizabeth said, trying to sound calm. "I couldn't get back to 1854 if I wanted to. I'm sorry."

There was silence for a moment more. Elizabeth rose.

"You can't get back?" the voice echoed suddenly. Suddenly confused. "Elizabeth, surely you know? You must."

Elizabeth didn't want to listen any more.

"Spinning Jenny isn't dying," Brierly told her.

But Elizabeth turned off the radio.

The factory closed the next week. There was no announcement, no arrangements or final apologies. Elizabeth and the rest of the women arrived at the door that Wednesday morning and found it locked. They all knew then, but most of them had nowhere else to be. They waited for most of the day, praying they would discover it had all been some kind of mistake. Then one by one those with any money left had disappeared to some pub or another. Elizabeth had money, but no desire to drink. Instead, she started the long walk home.

The road back to Stockport took her past the shadow of grand town houses built for the factory owners: those that were still inhabited now were full to bursting with the families of those few left with work. The owners, those with the money, had carried on their slow journey away from the smoke and the grime of the city and had now made it as far as Cheshire. As Manchester eased into Stockport, so the houses grew smaller and huddled together for protection. But the inhabitants remained the same: the working poor, pulled to the city with the promise of jobs that were slowly drying up.

The walk home took three hours of slow walking, but Elizabeth took every step. She could have taken the bus, but then her thoughts would have been swamped with everyone's idle chatter. This way she had three solid hours, with Brierly's words slowly making their way through her closed up mind, dusting down every cell and waking them from their enforced hibernation. Her thoughts were still nothing but Brierly and Spinning Jenny when she got back to her rooms.

Bill glanced up at her, still lying in bed.

"You're early, love," he wheezed at her.

"Factory's closed," she answered.

He didn't say anything: he'd already known. Why else would she be back?

"Would you like your tea?" Elizabeth asked, hanging her coat behind the door.

Bill considered carefully, as if his stomach had been blockaded and lines of communication were still precarious. He looked thin this morning, old. His hair was still the same dark black, but there was no fat left in his face. Dry skin hung on his bones, but only out of habit. He looked like he needed a good meal, but Elizabeth knew it had been a good long time since he'd had one of them. He couldn't keep going like this forever. Neither of them could.

"Alright," he sighed, as if doing her a favour.

Elizabeth took off her cardigan and let it drop to the floor. Her arms and her shoulders were bare, paper-thin skin hanging loose on the memory of tight muscles gone to seed. Bill didn't watch her, but she always found herself standing like this in front of him. Laying herself bare, ready for his gaze. She suspected she wanted to remind him just what she was going through to have him here again, but it didn't matter: he never looked, never gave any indication that he knew. Could he even see what he ate as she did, or did it seem to him just to be meat and two veg? She knew she would never ask, but still the question remained.

She held her arm out, palm up. Along the inside of her forearm, following the line of her veins, a small row of little purple flowers grew. They looked a little like miniature cornflowers, but their heart was a deep dark blackness. Where they grew from her veins, the skin puckered and reddened. Elizabeth tried to pick the least sore patch and pulled up a dozen of the little flowers: their roots came free as well, still dripping a little spray of her blood. She put the flowers on a plate and handed them to Bill, who smiled absently and started to pick at them. That was all he would be able to eat, Baron Samedi had told her, and the Loa hadn't lied.

Bill looked up at her, his face unreadable.

Elizabeth never knew what he was thinking these days: he would never tell her.

"Are you angry with me, Bill?" she asked him

He looked at her again, chewing slowly on a single bloom.

"Why would I be angry, Betty?"

"I don't know," she said. She felt completely naked, standing there with her arms exposed. The blood drying where the blooms had been plucked. "Because I saved you, I suppose."

He snorted, and for a second Elizabeth thought he was choking. But he wasn't: he was laughing. It was the first proper laugh she had seen from him since that night in Strines, and she knew it was filled with bitterness. Just look at him, bedridden and feeble when he was only thirty in body. He hadn't left the house in the last month, and might never leave it again. He didn't look like somebody who had been saved.

"Would you save your leg by amputating it?" he asked her.

Elizabeth didn't answer, and he went back to his dinner.

That night, the radio crackled again.

Elizabeth dropped it quietly out of the bedroom window, and let it say whatever it wanted to the rats at the bins. She shut the window more firmly than she had intended and went to lie next to Bill until the dawn finally came.

There were two more sleepless nights after that, lying in that bed next to Bill and feeling each of his ragged breaths. Part of her wished that they would just stop, that he would stop clinging on so tightly and just go. That part scared her, not because of what it wanted to happen to Bill but because it didn't seem to care what would happen to her. She had given everything to have these few moments back with Bill. Everything. If he was gone again, she knew there was only one thing left she could do. Certainly, she could never fight to have this again.

But Spinning Jenny wasn't dying.

That was what Brierly had been struggling to tell her for the last hundred years, four words that were so obviously untrue. Everywhere she looked, factories were closing and workers were getting left on the streets. There was no industry any more, just faded old drunks and hopeless children stealing what little they could get from other hopeless children.

The Baron was the only one winning this battle. There was nowhere you could look now where you wouldn't see death and decay.

But Spinning Jenny wasn't dying. Elizabeth knew it was true.

So on the morning of the third day, she slipped out of bed before Bill woke, before the sun came up. She knelt at the side of the bed and reached underneath, finding there a dark uniform covered in dust. She brushed it down as best she could and then dressed in silence. By the time he woke, Elizabeth had gone.

# 15. June 1931, Strines

The world was barely there anymore. If he squinted, he could just make out the sign across the tracks through the driving rain. He had his thickest coat on and a hat that pulled down over his ears, but still the water was getting through. He huddled as close to the bridge as he could, trying to use it for shelter as he looked down the line and waited for the train to arrive. He wouldn't have long to wait: he had learned the timetable by rote, and timed his journey up the hill accordingly.

Only a minute later, the train pulled into the station in a cloud of steam and boiling rain. The guard poked his head out of the window to see if anyone was going to be brave enough to leave their nice dry carriage, and then quickly pulled it back in again. The engine started to growl again, but one carriage door popped open. It was hard to see through the rain, but the alighting passenger seemed to be a little unsteady as she climbed down. She clung onto the door to steady herself far longer than would have been necessary, if she had been a little stronger on her feet.

He hurried over, lifting an umbrella over the old woman's head and offering an arm for her to take. She was still wearing that British Army uniform, dyed black, but the body underneath it didn't seem as solid as it had before. Here and there, the cloth flapped freely in the wind for want of any muscle to cling to. She looked up at him suspiciously, and he suspected that she was about to tell him what he could do with his offer of assistance. Then she recognised his face.

"Mr Braddock," said Mrs Howkins, with only a mild tone of surprise.

James smiled.

"You paid for a room, Mrs Howkins," he said, trying not to enjoy that for once he knew more than she did. "I wondered if perhaps you would care to use it tonight?"

Mrs Howkins hesitated. Perhaps she wondered just what he had planned for her, or perhaps it was just the natural surprise of seeing him here. He had aged, he was under no illusions about that. His waist had grown thicker and his jowls hung a little lower than they had the last time he had met her from the train. But despite that, he looked as if no more than ten years had passed since that first snowy night.

"Your bags are in the carriage?" he asked, delivering the second of the lines he had prepared. "Or should I wait to see if you are being followed?"

Mrs Howkins' eyes narrowed.

"Your manners haven't improved in the last hundred years, Mr Braddock," she said haughtily, pulling herself upright and stepping away from him with a poise that resembled the one he had first seen here. "Let us at least hope that your transportation has."

And she pulled away, heading towards the exit from the platform.

James followed with a smile.

Unfortunately, the transportation hadn't improved: James hadn't brought any, and instead they walked back to the pub through the rain. James let Mrs Howkins have the umbrella: he didn't mind getting wet, and would soon dry off again in front of the fire at the Sportsman. He had thought the walk would give Mrs Howkins the time to get answers to the questions she had about him before they got into the village, where the answers might cause some embarrassment. But instead she had spent the first leg of the journey looking at the towering chimney of the new works, lost in her own thoughts.

"It hasn't closed yet?" she asked him eventually.

"No," he told her. "Nobody's making their millions, but it should see another winter or two."

Mrs Howkins eyed him up and down.

"As should you, Mr Braddock."

James took that as his cue.

"I haven't died yet, Mrs Howkins," he said with a chuckle. "I can assure you that no-one is more surprised by that than me. If you wanted me to tell you why, I'm afraid you would be disappointed."

"And you've stayed here all these years?"

"This is my home, and I have the Sportsman to think of."

Mrs Howkins clicked her teeth in annoyance.

"That wasn't exactly what I was referring to," she snapped. James thought that she had lost much of her patience since he had last seen her. Or perhaps that he simply wasn't as scared of her. "No-one has said anything about your longevity?"

James shook his head.

"This is a small village, Mrs Howkins," he said with mock severity. "They wouldn't be so impolite."

That silenced her for a few more paces, and by the time she spoke again they had made it to the top of the hill that led up to Strines proper. The road that cut through the heart of the village stretched away to their left and their right: James took a second to catch his breath and then turned to the right. As Mrs Howkins followed, he realised that she too had been trying to catch her breath. He didn't know how long it had been for her since they had last spoken, but however long it had been had not been kind to her.

"How did you know I'd be here?" she asked as they passed the post office.

For the first time, James' amusement faded. It was the question that he was least looking forward to answering, because it was the one that he had asked himself more than once that day.

"I don't know," he said. "Some little voice inside … I don't know."

She nodded to herself, as if the answer confirmed something.

"I don't suppose you would know?" James asked hesitantly.

Mrs Howkins didn't answer, just walked on a step more.

"What happened in 1854?" she asked.

The last ounce of good humour that James possessed dissolved away in the rain. It trickled down onto the road, and was washed away to sea. It was the other question that he knew she would ask. What he couldn't be so sure about was how she would take the answer.

He looked up the road ahead and saw the lights of the Sportsman.

"Let me stand you a drink," he said.

As Elizabeth stepped over the threshold into the Sportsman's Arms, she felt her head starting to swim and her knees wobbling. The fire was raging in the hearth at the far end of the bar, but it wasn't just the blast of heat. It was being here again, without Bill at her side and with what had once been everyone she had known in the whole world waiting for her just inside.

After the fire, she had tried to go in three times before she had just given up and retired to her home. She could have lived with the way the others who had lost people tried to draw her in, might even have found some comfort there if she'd tried. But she couldn't get used to Bill not being there when she reached out her hand, nor having to go to the bar herself to get her glass of sherry.

She wondered about Bill now. She had been gone all day: was he wondering where she was, perhaps? Or would he already know? Perhaps he was already on his way here now, fully aware of what she was planning and determined to talk her out of it. Perhaps he was too weak to leave his bed. The flesh on her forearms ached.

"Come on," Mr Braddock said behind her, his voice not unkind. "Let's just go in."

As she stepped inside, the wave of nostalgia and terror grew stronger. They were all there, from the girl who sat next to her at her calico press to the foreman of the factory. They all glanced up as she entered, Mr Braddock steering her gently towards the bar. They each gave a polite smile or a little nod of recognition, then went back to their conversations. Elizabeth wondered what they thought, seeing her here without Bill beside her. But then perhaps they didn't care: they hadn't been here for the last six months, and not one of them came up to ask where she had been.

"I would be grateful for a drink, Mr Braddock," Elizabeth said, her voice shaking a little. "Preferably a strong one."

"Way ahead of you, Mrs Howkins," Mr Braddock said.

He left her to stand at the bar while he nipped behind it and took the brandy down from the shelf. He poured a large measure, and then as an afterthought poured another for himself before putting the bottle back. Elizabeth reached into her pocket for her purse, but he shook his head and pushed the glass towards her. She took a long sip and fought the urge to cough: despite everything she had done in her life, she had never learned to drink hard liquor.

Mr Braddock smiled wryly. Elizabeth looked around the room again, but everybody seemed to have decided that she wasn't there. Even the man standing beside her at the bar seemed content to be served by the barmaid, without even the most perfunctory attempt at small talk.

"What happened?" Elizabeth turned back to Mr Braddock, fixing him with her coldest look. "If I go back, what will I find in 1854, Mr Braddock?"

Mr Braddock would have made a good card player.

"Why would you think I could tell you that?" he asked.

Elizabeth set her drink down with a scowl.

"Because you were there."

"So were you, Mrs Howkins."

"Afterwards," she spat frostily. "Tell me what happened to you after I escaped."

Mr Braddock looked down at the bar and saw his drink as if for the first time. He picked it up and brought it up to his lips, before pausing for a moment, letting the glass rest halfway to being tasted. Then he set it back down again, untouched. The look in his eyes said that he had come to a decision.

"I could," he said, pushing the drink to one side. "But I don't think it would do any good. I could tell you what happened to me, yes. But what makes you think that the same things will happen if you go back again? Haven't you worked any of it out yet, Mrs Howkins? That isn't how this works."

She wanted to ask him how it did work, but he wouldn't be stopped now.

"And besides," he said grimly. "You're not here for what happened a hundred years ago. You're here for what happens tomorrow."

A shiver of ice ran down her body, and she had to put her glass back down on the bar in case she dropped it. All of this was impossible. He was impossible. But somehow the idea that he knew as well – that a few words from him now, here could stop it all – somehow that was just one thing too far. She closed her eyes just for a moment, and found that she could remember the words quite clearly of a chant intended to cut through a false reality. For a second, she faltered, suddenly terrified that she would open her eyes and find herself standing again in that grey dusty twilight. Then she chided herself, and let the words flow through her.

When she opened her eyes, the bar was still there, and Mr Braddock behind it.

"How can you do nothing?" Elizabeth asked, deflated.

"How can you be certain there's something to do?" Mr Braddock countered. He nodded over Elizabeth's shoulder, towards the bay window. "If you told them tonight what might happen tomorrow, do you think it would change anything that has happened to you? Do you think you would remember?"

Elizabeth turned to look where he was directing her. There was a table in the window, where people liked to sit because it offered a view of the entire valley. It was where Elizabeth and Bill had always sat whenever they had been here. Elizabeth's heart sank in her chest. It was where Elizabeth and Bill were sitting now, their hands not quite touching under the table as he sipped at a pint of stout and she left a glass of sherry to sit on the table.

She took a step towards them, two. Mr Braddock didn't stop her. It was them. It was her. She hardly recognised herself, but when had she ever seen herself both young and from outside? But Bill was unmistakable, dark hair and neatly pressed suit, that battered old cap he loved so much resting just inches from his fingertips. He sat, sipping his drink and staring out of the window in just that way she always remembered. It was only now, seeing it from a distance, that she realised he was looking at her, reflected in the dark glass.

Elizabeth desperately tried to remember this night, but it was no good. Tomorrow was too memorable, too bright: it had burned away every memory around it. Had this happened? Could she have looked up from her drink and seen herself, an old lonely woman standing at the end of the bar? She couldn't reach the memory, so tried instead for something similar: had James owned the Sportsman back when she was young? Even that was slippy, elusive. She felt sure that he hadn't, but the memory of who had wouldn't come.

She felt sick.

"Is this even real?" she turned on Braddock.

He held up his hands.

"How can anyone answer that?" he asked.

"Why are you doing this?" she spat instead.

He paused at that. Perhaps it was a question he had never asked himself. Or perhaps it was, and the answers were just too numerous to express. He seemed to come to another decision, and pushed the second brandy towards Elizabeth.

"You needed to know," he told her, "if you're going to make any kind of proper decision."

Elizabeth glanced back over at herself again.

"What does it matter now?" she asked bitterly. "If it changes nothing, then what does it matter which way I decide?"

"Mrs Howkins," Braddock said earnestly. "That's when it matters the most."

Elizabeth drained her glass.

She turned down the offer of a bed for the night, and instead relieved Braddock of the brandy bottle and set off walking. She told herself that she didn't know where she was going, but she wasn't surprised when she found herself cutting across a field to find the old works looming. The moon was bright above her, but she cast no shadow on the grass. The brandy still burned in her throat, and she knew that part of her had taken the drink because it had known she would need it. Not to steady her nerves, but to appease the Loa.

She hadn't so much as thought one of their names in months. Everything had been slowly shutting down around her, including her ability to see anything beyond the distorted and murky world her ageing eyes showed her. It wasn't that she had forgotten how – although she had – but that there was simply nothing there to reach. But tonight felt alive with electricity and potential. For the first time in months, Elizabeth felt she could reach out and shake the world into the shape she wanted it to be.

If only she knew what it was she wanted.

Midnight came and went, the time when she kept telling herself she would perform the ritual. It wouldn't make the damnedest bit of difference, but there was still something pleasingly traditional about it. Instead, she took the brandy glass she had borrowed from Braddock and poured herself another stiff measure. She told herself she would leave enough to be a suitable offering, but by 2am most of the bottle was gone. Perhaps she wouldn't need it: perhaps she would just march back up to that pub and take up Braddock's offer of a bed. Perhaps she would wait here until morning and warn everyone who came in to work to spend the day at home instead.

"You're pissed," a shrill voice sneered from the darkness.

Elizabeth looked up, but had trouble seeing anything.

"Pissed old bird," the voice sneered again, then belched. "S'disgraceful. You're setting a bad example."

The girl stepped out of the darkness and half-tumbled into a sitting position besides Elizabeth. She was dressed strangely, although Elizabeth did acknowledge there was a little hypocrisy in her thinking that. But Elizabeth's outfit was strange given her sex: it was hard to imagine the circumstances that the girl's outfit would be appropriate in. She had hair that was both long and cut close to the bone, depending on which part of her head you were looking at. Her eyes were heavily shadowed with purple kohl and her dark trousers were slit here and there with holes. The jacket she wore exploded with black cock feathers.

Elizabeth fought the urge to protest her sobriety.

"I didn't ask you to join me," Elizabeth said instead, keeping her tone polite and her voice precise. The girl just smirked. "I am honoured. And ashamed: I have nothing to offer you except my company."

The girl cocked her head and fixed Elizabeth with a stare.

"S'alright," she said, breaking into a grin and producing a bottle. "I brought my own. You're a bad influence: now I've gotta catch up."

And the girl tipped the bottle back and poured half of the sweet-smelling liquid down her throat. She barely even seemed to swallow, and wiped her mouth with a sleeve when she was finished. Elizabeth said nothing, but the girl smiled and passed her the bottle anyway. Elizabeth thanked her and took a smaller swig.

"So what now?" the girl asked.

Indeed: what now?

"I don't know, Mama," Elizabeth said sadly to the little girl. "I just don't know."

The girl tutted loudly.

"Ah child," she took a swig of her drink. "Don't tell me that. I got to like you when you just went out and did it. Who cares what anyone else thinks, eh? Someone took my husband from me, I'd give 'em just the same colour of hell you did. No point trying to step back now, girl. You in."

Elizabeth looked up at the moon. He gazed back with blank dark eyes.

"Your husband," she told the child, "gave my Bill back."

The girl didn't look at her. She just kicked her feet into the earth and took another swig of her bottle. She looked no more than ten or eleven, but Elizabeth doubted that anybody would have been fooled by that. The Loa could ride any body they wanted to, and only a fool wouldn't recognise all that power forced into such a small container. The little girl was so full of spirit that she was practically bursting at the seams. Perhaps there was no-one else in the village who would recognise Maman Brigitte, but even the most ignorant of them would know to treat this girl with respect.

"Whoop," the girl said, expressionless. "You got your man back."

"Except, of course, that I didn't," Elizabeth said.

That was the first time she had said the words out loud. Somehow it made them more real, more definite. She half-expected to see them drop heavily onto the grass in front of her, burning and turning the grass to soot. But they didn't. Once they were out, they were just words after all.

"Ha!" the girl laughed coarsely. "You should complain: least you came out of this with one shadow, eh?"

Elizabeth tutted.

"I think I would prefer that the other shadow was fighting too."

"You think your shadow's gone off fighting? You're a good girl, Lizzie. I got time for you. But you ain't got the will for a fighting shadow. It'd eat you alive. Better off without it. Stick with that shadow husband you got."

The girl nudged Elizabeth with a shoulder, and passed over her bottle. Elizabeth took a swig. The drink burned her throat. It was strong enough to take the paint from a wall, but it was rich with spices too. Elizabeth couldn't say that she actually liked it, but she was more than grateful to the Loa for sharing it with her.

"Christ, child," the girl spat. "Don't you wanna be happy?"

And that of course was the question.

After the fire, Elizabeth had known she would never be happy again. She had never admitted it, but the path she had ended up on had never been about making Spinning Jenny pay for what she had done. You might as well try to revenge yourself on a tidal wave or a hurricane. She could see it now for what it was: the anger of a damaged child, striking back at the world that had hurt it. It had never been about Bill, only ever about herself. And now she had what she wanted, and he was back. What did it matter what happened to the rest of the world? She had him back.

She had decided long ago that she would sacrifice anything to get her revenge. And now she had. All she had to do was to learn to live with that.

"Maman Brigitte," Elizabeth croaked to the child. There were tears in her eyes. "Please. I don't know what to do."

The girl rested a hand on her knee.

"I know, child," she said, sadly. "But I ain't gonna help with that."

Elizabeth closed her eyes.

"With all respect, Maman," she said quietly, "I think you are."

The girl withdrew her hand and rose to her feet. Her face darkened, and the brandy bottle in her hand began to look more like a weapon. She hissed angrily, and despite her size and her age she seemed suddenly very dangerous to Elizabeth. She was very dangerous: she was a god, and she had destroyed the lives of others who had shown much more respect than Elizabeth.

Elizabeth felt a spark of something catch inside her.

"Your husband cheated me," she said.

"Cheated?" echoed the girl in disbelief.

"Cheated," Elizabeth repeated. She stood, dusting down her uniform before turning her attention back to the Loa's vessel. "I would do nothing to stand in his way, and he would give me my husband back. That was the deal that he brokered. I have kept my side of it. Did he think I wouldn't work out about the flowers?"

The child glared darkly. Behind her eyes, fire spat.

"You want to call my man a liar again?" she spat.

Elizabeth felt her heart beating again. It felt good.

"I didn't call him a liar, Maman," she answered calmly. "I called him a cheat. My Bill is still part of Spinning Jenny. And those flowers are part of the Baron. He used me to poison her. He used me to take my Bill away from me again. And he used me to take her away from the world."

"You think he can't do just whatever the hell he wants?"

Elizabeth held her ground.

"I know he can," she said. "But I think it invalidates our agreement."

The child's eyes bore deep into Elizabeth's. The bottle was thrown angrily to one side, smashing against the base of the chimney. Glass and alcohol anointed the smoky brickwork. The air seemed to darken around them, everything growing faded and indistinct save for the dark-eyed Loa.

Elizabeth held her ground.

The girl smiled.

"Good to have you back, girl," she said.

The sun had come up by the time Elizabeth had finished drawing the vevé. She had placed five of them at points across the site, carefully spaced and – for the moment – impossible to see. Drawing them had left her drained in a way that she could not recall ever having been before. But then she had never attempted a dedication on this scale before: there was bound to be some sort of toll on her health. The idea that she might not even survive the process occurred to her, but it didn't trouble her. In fact, there was something oddly comforting about it. If she did die here, doing this, then it would only give the ritual more power, and at least she would leave behind something beautifully symmetrical.

As the last line was scratched into the belly of one of the giant presses, Elizabeth heard the voices of the workers outside. They were getting ready to start their day, laughing and joking about some small embarrassment remembered from the pub the night before. They sounded happy, and it struck Elizabeth as strange that she had never really thought about them that way. It was hard for her to remember anything from before the fire without the way things were after draining into it. All the colour was gone, stained black by the smoke.

She knew it wasn't too late.

Even now, she could step out from her hiding place and start the shout of fire. The panic would spread long before the flames, and she couldn't imagine that anybody would be left inside. The air was throbbing with it: the build up of expectant power was so heavy in the air that Elizabeth struggled to breathe through it. But was it that expectation that made the fire inevitable, or was it that the world knew the fire was coming and was preparing itself for the heat? Elizabeth knew she could tell herself that it was all destined, and there was nothing she could do to prevent it. But that didn't make it true.

There was a choice. She could hear her own voice coming from the room next door, and knew that Bill would be there settling her at her machine before he went off to the foreman's office. They could still be together, could still be happy. Elizabeth could barely imagine who she would be without the loss of Bill to derail her life. The children, the grandchildren, the quiet comfortable life. All she had to do was step out and take it. All she had to do was nothing. Probably Braddock was right and nothing would change for her, but there would still be an Elizabeth Howkins out there somewhere who grew old and happy with her darling Bill.

In a moment, the presses would start and then it would be too late. No-one would hear a shout. There would be no time to warn them all. Elizabeth stood and looked at the vevé she had carved. Her hand trembled. None of this was predestined: she still had a choice.

But she knew what that choice would ultimately bring. She and Bill would be together for the rest of their lives, she had no doubt about that. But there would be no Spinning Jenny. This fire, these deaths, had been dedicated to her. Elizabeth had always known they had. They gave her the strength she needed to grow. Without it ... Elizabeth had seen what the world was without her. It was time for Spinning Jenny. It was time for change. And nothing ever changed without sacrifice.

The presses started up, and the air was filled with noise.

There was no more time.

Except she could still find Bill, still make him understand. All she needed was to catch his eye and she could sign him a warning that would save both their lives. The fire was needed, she had no doubt about that. But was Bill really needed to be in it? Of course he wasn't: despite everything, he was nothing to the universe. Just one more death fed to the new god of industry. Elizabeth could feel tears on her cheeks. She had no choice: how could she force everyone else to sacrifice their happiness, and not offer her own to the altar as well?

"Last chance," Maman Brigitte's voice echoed in her ears.

But that moment was already long gone.

The noise of the machines grew in pitch, until the air trembled with it. Power was in the air around her. It was a simple matter for Elizabeth to reach out her hand and let a small ball of it coalesce around her fingers. She held it there for a moment, seeing how it made her fingers impossible to see, just black sticks filled with dancing specks of white. She whispered the dedication to Spinning Jenny under her breath, and let the energy drip through her fingers.

The fire spread in an instant.

Elizabeth saw Maman Brigitte through the smoke. Her aspect had changed, and the young girl had gone somewhere else. Now she was a fat old woman dressed in a deep purple ball gown, striding through the smoke and the crowd drinking dark stout from a champagne flute. She was clearly enjoying herself, and every corner she turned she seemed to find something else that tickled her well-padded ribs. The fire danced around her like a kitten with its mother, but never got so close as to singe the tip of a single hair on her head. Amongst the fire and the screaming, Maman Brigitte was humming to herself. Elizabeth remembered the tune, and felt sick.

As the fire burned, it earthed that arcing potential in the room. Pulled it down, back into the machinery it had sprung from. The altar of a new god, prayed over every day from dawn until dusk. As she passed, Maman brushed a hand against the machines, and the energy changed again. It sank into the centre of the room, building into the heart of a dark star that crackled and popped with white fire. Larger and larger it grew, and Elizabeth took a cautious step towards it. She recognised it, of course. She had spent most of her life trying to kill it.

She looked deep into the heart of the Loa in silence.

"Spinning Jenny," she whispered quietly to herself, "please accept my prayer."

Elizabeth heard Maman Brigitte laugh heartily behind her, and turned to see her smash the glass onto the floor. The alcohol burned fiercely, belching out thick grey smoke. When it cleared, Maman Brigitte had stepped out of this universe. On the ground where she stood, the vevé burned in liquid fire, the vevé that Elizabeth had seen this day and remembered forever. It was the mark of Spinning Jenny, dripping with the raw power granted by every soul that had ever died on the factory floor.

The black hole crackled with energy again, pulsing like a beating heart. Suddenly it exploded into a single jet of energy that raced towards Elizabeth. She felt the urge to protect herself, but willed her arms to stay by her side. The fire, the energy, seemed to take on the form of a giant snake and raced around the factory floor. Elizabeth could see something like a mouth there now, sharp teeth being bared with a terrifying hiss. She wondered if anyone else in the village would hear it.

"Thank you," Elizabeth told it softly.

Then the mouth bit, and Elizabeth disappeared.

## 16. January 1854, Strines

He hung on the cross that wasn't there, and time poured from a wound cut down his entire torso. Isabella couldn't imagine the pain that he was in. But he didn't writhe and he didn't scream. He just looked at her with those eyes of his, and watched. He didn't even look accusing, nor even surprised. He looked for all the world as if he worried what this was doing to her and wished there was something he could do to stop it. But whatever she did now, those weeks she lived happily in James' pub were over now. Nothing would bring them back. Everything had its time. Perhaps all you did by trying to fight that was make things painful, make them worse.

Her shadow was at her side. It didn't speak, didn't move. But it didn't need to. Its very presence spoke of the importance of what she was doing here. She stared deep into James' guts. Through the blood, she could hear his bio-data singing to her. The tunnel had been born. Its two ends were rushing through the dark places to meet each other and touch. She could feel the oily vibration of it, feel the subtle change in pitch as one end opened for just the briefest moment. Then she felt it pucker shut again.

"The agents have been dispatched," Isabella said. She didn't know if she was telling James or her shadow. "They're in the tunnel now."

The shadow raised its claws, but Isabella stepped forward. She didn't expect him to appreciate it, but she knew that the least she could do was finish this herself. She had precious little else to give him: she could at least give him this. She reached to the small of her back and pulled a white bone knife from its sheath there. The knife melted any snow that tried to settle on it, and looked like ice in the pale blue moonlight. James glanced down at it, then back to her.

"Please don't," he whispered to her.

"I won't let it hurt," she promised.

It sounded so hollow.

The sky above her was darkening now, the falling snow seeming little more than static on a giant screen. The Loa were there, circling each other like cornered animals, energies of every kind sparking from them. Their numerous mouths snaked towards each other, taking chunks of flesh away that must have been roughly the same size as the village. It was impossible not to be in awe of them, impossible not to lose yourself looking up. They were so powerful, universes shook when they stirred. Watching them was a once in millennia event that Isabella had seen three times now.

"Please, Isabella," James croaked. "I know you don't want to do this."

A tear was moving down her cheek. She barely even felt it.

"What makes you think that matters?" she asked.

The knife was raised.

And then pulled from her hands.

No, not pulled: thrown. There it went, tumbling through the night like a falling star. She might have been the rawest recruit to Faction Paradox, but she knew enough to recognise outside control when she felt it.

She turned, and saw Elizabeth Howkins.

The old woman was standing knee deep in the snowfall, that ridiculous black uniform she wore flecked with snow and singed by fire. In her hand she held a small doll that looked like it had been thrown together in something of a hurry. It barely had limbs, and its head was little more than a large knot tied in the fabric. It had no facial features at all that Isabella could see, but it was sporting a rather impressive head of grey hair. Howkins was holding the doll's right hand between two fingers. Isabella could almost feel the pressure of them on her own wrist.

This just wasn't fair.

"How did you even make that?" Isabella snapped, her hand going up unconsciously to her own shaved head.

There was no look of triumph from Howkins.

"I believe I did tell you that I knew who you are," she replied.

Isabella let out a cry of frustration and launched herself at the old woman. She moved impressively quickly to protect her weak spots, but Isabella wasn't going for any of them. Her sights were set on the doll. Without it, experience had shown that killing Howkins wouldn't be that much of a struggle. Even with it, she thought that youthful enthusiasm probably still had the edge over bitter experience.

Isabella clattered into Howkins and grabbed for the doll, but even as she tumbled to the floor, Howkins managed to give a flick of her finger that saw Isabella's left arm suddenly bend back double on itself. Isabella let out a scream born more from frustration than pain, and kicked out savagely. Her boot embedded itself so deep in Howkins' torso that a kidney probably popped out the other side. The old woman gave a cry, but rolled out of harm's way without any other signs of discomfort.

"I can't say I know exactly what you are doing, young lady," Howkins said as she caught her breath. "But I do know the consequences of it and you need to know that I will not let that happen."

Isabella just spat and launched forwards again.

The old woman was lying on the ground, something dark dripping onto the snow from the side that Isabella had kicked. She was definitely not a day under a thousand years old, whilst Isabella had every advantage that youth and knowing exactly what the hell was going on could give a person. But despite all that, Howkins still managed to snap the arm of the little doll before Isabella reached her. The crack of bone breaking echoed across the valley.

Isabella tried to be stoic, but the pain had other ideas.

For a moment, she didn't know anything. It was almost a relief. She could feel the numbing chill of the night air, and the warm blanket of snow snuggling close around her. Above her in the sky, the Loa still fought, but now it had the air of an elaborate firework show that had been laid on solely for her. The moon was there too, but he turned away from them. It was a moment that was almost worth the pain just to have lived in. Then Howkins' face appeared above her, looking imperiously down.

"I am sorry," she said, but the sentiment didn't reach her eyes. "Stay there, and this can be the end of it."

Isabella made to move, and Howkins held the doll out warningly.

"You've forgotten something," Isabella breathed.

The doll jerked up out of Howkins' grasp, floating in the night sky just a few inches away from her hand. Howkins tried to snatch it back, but it jumped up and then held there. The old woman gave Isabella a look of such frustrated confusion that she couldn't stop herself laughing. It was like seeing the face of a dog, moments after it realised the ball it thought you had thrown was still held in your hand.

The snow started to stick to the doll. And to something else. As the flakes fell fast from the sky, a shape started to emerge. An outstretched arm, piano-player's fingers with slender claws extended far above them. The doll rested almost gently on two of those outstretched claws, suspended in space.

"Just kill her already," Isabella told the shadow.

What else could it do but oblige?

Elizabeth had to admit, she had forgotten the shadow. Not completely, but for long enough that it was going to prove a problem. It had been only six months since she had last done anything like this, but it was fast dawning on her that those months might as well be decades. When it came to bargaining with Loa and fighting misguided, homicidal children, it turned out that practice made perfect. She was out of practice and far, far from perfect.

It came to something when travelling back in time nearly a hundred years turned out to be the easy part. Admittedly, Brierly had tried to help her with that, but Elizabeth had already started to work it out for herself. Spinning Jenny wasn't dying: it was the only thing that made sense once you started to think about it. How else had the Loa managed to drag her with it back to the nineteenth century that first time? Once you entertained the possibility, it seemed remarkably simple. It wasn't dying, it was being born. Born in the crucible of the fire, and living its life backwards through history until it reached the dawn of the Industrial Revolution and was killed by Baron Samedi. A short span of years where industry blossomed out of nowhere and then disappeared again, just not in the order that anyone would usually associate with history.

And so the second time around she had been caught up again, only this time deliberately. Clinging on in the Loa's wake as it sped back down the years. Sometimes, she had to admit that the life she had lived wasn't all bad.

The shadow casually tossed the doll aside. It wasn't stupid enough to throw it with any force, and it arced gently through the air before coming to rest in a deep drift of snow. Isabella might feel a slight chill around her before the soft blanket of snow snuggled her up and kept her warm.

If she could reach that doll, Elizabeth would snap her neck just to be done with all of this.

The shadow drew its claws slowly through the air. If she could have seen its face, Elizabeth knew she would have seen a smile.

"It's not too late to stop this," Elizabeth said.

"Really?" Isabella snorted in disbelief. "Do you even know what this is?"

The shadow darted at her.

She knew it was coming for her, but it was still almost too fast to avoid. Elizabeth threw herself backwards, and saw the razor claws snip through a lock of errant hair. It floated gracefully to the ground as Elizabeth landed heavily on her back and started to roll down the hill. The shadow lashed at her with each roll, its claws only just missing her by fractions. She knew it was toying with her now, but there really wasn't much she could do to stop it. Behind it, she could see Isabella bending in the snow, her eyes fixed on the young Braddock as she reached for the dropped blade.

"Mr Braddock," Elizabeth hissed as she rolled. His head lolled loosely. "Mr Braddock!"

A blade slipped in close enough to graze the skin of her cheek. Elizabeth wasn't entirely sure that she still had an ear, but she kicked up hard with both feet and was rather surprised to make contact. The shadow rolled backwards like an acrobat in the circus, landing neatly on its feet again with claws brandished. Despite being made of shadow, they seemed to glint in the moonlight.

Isabella glanced over at them, the bone knife raised.

"Stop pissing about!" she snapped at her shadow. "Kill her."

Somehow, the shadow looked chastened.

"Wait!" Elizabeth shouted, holding up a hand.

And for some reason, the shadow waited.

"Really?" Isabella snapped again. "Just give up, old lady. You won't defeat my shadow."

The shadow still waited. Elizabeth's brow furrowed. She was developing something of a headache, but she didn't take her eyes from the creature. She still couldn't see its face, but somehow she doubted it was smiling now.

"Your shadow?" Elizabeth echoed, trying to keep the strain from her voice. "Is that whose it is?"

Isabella's eyes widened.

"You stole it from me," Elizabeth spat each word. "I'm taking it back."

And the shadow turned.

Time was of the essence, ironically. She could feel the agents of the Great Houses making their way down the tunnel: soon they would be inside the bubble and things would carry on as they had before. There was no time to indulge the old woman. As impressive as it was that she could have any influence at all over her shadow now that Isabella had claimed it, there had to be an end to it.

Isabella turned away from James and faced Howkins.

"Oy!" she shouted at her shadow. It visibly jumped. "Snap out of it!"

And that was that.

The shadow drew itself up again, its darkness blotting out most of the old woman's tiny frame, and moved forwards again. Isabella found that she wanted to see the fatal blow, but she was disappointed: the arm came up and then froze in mid-air. The shadow trembled as if shivering, but the deadly claws hovered over Howkins' head. There was blood coming from the old woman's ears, but Isabella knew that was a self-inflicted injury. She could feel the concentration coming from her in waves.

She really didn't have time for this.

She focussed her mind in a way that she hadn't had to since she first began practising negotiation with her shadow. The shadow wasn't just dumb muscle – it had its own desires and allegiances, but on the whole it would defer to the will of the family member who had first cast it. She didn't plead and she didn't beg. She just firmly and directly reminded it of what was at stake, and why they had both agreed this was the only way.

Unfortunately, Isabella could almost hear Howkins' counter-argument, one that relied mostly on sentiment and nostalgia but nevertheless was effective. For a moment, the shadow was caught between them. Its claws were raised, but it no longer had any idea of just who it should bring them down on. The shadow was hit by a solid wave of contradictory appeals, and in the end it found what was admittedly a rather simple solution. There was a loud tearing sound and the shadow split in two.

For a moment, the shadow looked at itself, radiating surprise. Then one of the dark creatures launched itself, claws slashing down across the face of the other. It ducked under the blow and brought its own claws up into its twin's chest, only to watch as it twisted away and sent a foot thundering into its jaw. They each dived at the other, fighting without quarter: one for Isabella, and one for Howkins, but there was no way of knowing which was which.

Isabella turned back to James, but a boot landed firmly in the small of her back and she buckled. She was on her feet in an instant, and launched herself at Howkins. Isabella's fingers clamped deep into the old woman's throat, and they both tumbled into the snow. Howkins was coughing and choking, but still had the strength to deliver a fairly substantial head-butt. Isabella's fingers lost their grip for just a second.

Howkins glanced up at James.

"Mr Braddock, can't you recognise a feint when you see one?" she gasped in frustration. "I can't keep this up forever. You have to let her out."

What? No!

Isabella pushed Howkins away as hard as she could, but it was too late. Her eyes met James', and for just an instant he looked unsure. But something he saw in her eyes decided him. He gave her a look of apology, and then threw his head back and screamed. The wound that had him opened from groin to neck pulsated a disturbing purple colour, and then burst outwards. A wind blew up from somewhere deep inside him and the snow whipped around them like flails. The light was so bright, Isabella could feel her skin starting to burn.

The gateway had ruptured.

It was open.

James could feel his skin blistering and tearing, but worse was the feeling of every second of his life slowing draining out of him one by one. The more the seconds drained away, the more disconnected he became from them, until the pain was practically something that had happened to a distant ancestor of his, the birth pains of the first mammal or the rasping breath of the first lungfish. Time was swimming all around him, and he could sense it sinking and coalescing into a black hole buried deep in his history. The sensation was not unlike drowning, except it was as if he had sunk to the bottom of the river and just pushed through into a new world underneath.

He could see the breach in the tunnel bleeding out of his chest, and feel the two ends of it linking across the possibilities of who he might be. For a moment he thought he might fall into himself and appear inside that little piece of Strines he could feel on the other side, only to fall again and arrive here. Round and round and again, until either he or the universe gave up.

Then he felt it coming.

It moved faster than time was falling into him. It didn't need to avoid any of the obstacles that littered the ruptured tunnel, just quietly ignored them as if they weren't really there. Or else it wasn't really there, or they were both somewhere else altogether. Then, with a flapping of leathery wings, the creature burst out through his chest and out into the snowy night.

"Brierly!" Mrs Howkins shouted up to it.

It looped once through the sky, and to James it seemed more solid and more real than anything else in that whole world. It gave a chitter of sound so high and piercing that James felt his eardrums burst, and then opened its wings and dived down to the ground where Isabella and Mrs Howkins still fought. They both looked up, Mrs Howkins with a look of relief and Isabella with something less positive. Despite everything, James felt a pang of guilt.

"Please –" Isabella started to say as Brierly bore down, teeth bared.

And then the bat creature struck Mrs Howkins clean in the chest, so hard that the old woman was knocked backwards and the audible crack of splintering ribs filled the air. The creature ate so fast and so furiously that within seconds it had vanished, burrowing deep into her flesh and her timeline. All that was left to show its wake was the pained look on the old woman's face as she tried to get air into her lungs. Even the shadow twins stopped their fighting and turned to look.

For a moment there was silence.

Isabella didn't know what to do.

She even found herself moving towards Howkins to help the old woman back up to her feet. But then she came to her senses. Whatever the hag had thought she was doing had clearly gone badly wrong. So that was the end of it. It was time. When it was done, she hoped she would be allowed to die quietly, having done more than her bit for the cause. She reached down for the bone knife, and stood in front of James.

"I'm sorry," she said.

She could tell from the look on his face that he knew she meant it.

Howkins started to chuckle.

"I'm sorry," the old woman said. "It tickles."

Isabella tried hard to ignore her. She raised the knife again.

"Young lady, when will you realise that you have lost?" Howkins snapped from behind her. "Haven't you got any idea what just happened here? You're done, and you don't even have the common decency to realise it."

Isabella spun, the knife pointing straight at Howkins' throat. And then she stopped: there was something strange about the old woman. She could see the slight indentation where her ribs had compressed inwards, moving dangerously close to her heart and lungs. As she watched it, the indentation blistered and vanished, as if someone had pushed it back out again from the inside. Howkins took a deep breath and rolled her shoulders to unknot them.

"That's better," she said.

"What have you done?" Isabella asked suspiciously.

The old woman giggled again, and then looked apologetic.

"I'm so sorry," she said. "Brierly is swimming upstream through my history: it's ... Wait! Ah ... that's better. She's out the other side."

Isabella just looked at her, her mind racing to try and understand what she was saying. The bran-puca was travelling through Howkins' bio-data? No, Brierly was moving through it: she must have claimed another voice for her collective whilst they were in the bubble. It was a smart move. But what was she planning now? Where was she trying to reach through Howkins?

A thought struck Isabella, and she looked up.

The Loa were no longer fighting.

"What did you do?" she asked again.

"Have you ever been claimed by a Loa?" Howkins asked, reaching forward to pluck the knife from Isabella's limp grasp. "Do you know anything of their make up? Every soul they ever devoured is there, enslaved to the Loa's will. Not unlike Brierly herself. Except she works things a little differently. Every soul with a free and equal voice in what the whole does. I think she's just explaining the system to the slaves now."

They both looked up at the sky, where the Loa swam.

"Do you think they'd find that tempting?" Howkins asked archly.

Isabella's mind raced. She looked back to James, still strung up on the cross. All for nothing. There was a chance that the breaching of the tunnel had done her work for her, but more likely with such a small tear the Great Houses had seen it coming and evacuated to one side or the other. And now the nature of the creature had been irrevocably destabilised, it would be impossible to use them as a distraction. Perhaps the attention of the Great Houses was already turning her way. If she managed to get out undetected, there was a chance she could try again, but …

"Young lady," Howkins said imperiously. "I know what you're thinking. But I think you may have forgotten one salient detail."

There was no time to waste. No time to say goodbye.

"Isabella," Howkins would not be ignored. "She knows it was you."

Isabella froze for a moment. She had never even considered that it wouldn't be safe for her to use the Loa in her manipulations. She was so far outside of their normal scale of vision that she could remain undetected.

Oh God, she needed to get away.

It was of course too late. All around the moor, silhouettes were appearing out of nowhere. If you didn't look closely, you might think that they were being obscured by the snowfall, but in reality their empty bodies were filled with endlessly tumbling stars. There were hundreds, thousand of them within a few seconds. Isabella tried to shout, but the closest to her grabbed at her with ice cold hands. She felt herself being dragged to the ground, disappearing under a sea of stars.

Then it all went black.

Elizabeth helped Braddock down as best she could, straining her eyes trying to see the imaginary nails pinning him to the cross that wasn't there. The light from his wound had faded, but it hadn't healed. He seemed pale and weak, barely able to keep his head from lolling into her shoulder. She struggled to keep him upright as his weight suddenly fell onto her, but after a few staggering steps planted her feet firmly in the snow. As she looked up, she saw the two shadows. They had stopped fighting and were looking to her expectantly.

"If you are looking for a fight," Elizabeth said dryly, "I rather have my hands full."

They didn't move.

"This is your fault," Elizabeth snapped at them. "Why don't you do something to help instead of standing there?"

They both moved for her as one. Clearly whatever conflict they had felt had been resolved as soon as Isabella had gone. One had sheathed its claws, but the other was coming for her with the moonlight still glinting on them. She refused to be afraid: this was the end of a long series of things that had tried to bother her, and she just didn't have the energy for it any more. Then the shadow with its claws hidden put its hands under Braddock's shoulders and supported his weight, and Elizabeth realised she could almost hear a wave of intent coming from both of them. Her shadows. Of course.

Elizabeth let the shadow take Braddock's weight.

"Be gentle," she warned, gratified to feel slightly peevish understanding come from the dark shape. "He's had a tough night."

The second shadow didn't wait to be told, and dived into Braddock's chest with his claws. They clicked and clattered like knitting needles, and Elizabeth could see the gaping ends of the strange wound slowly coming back together. The shadows didn't look up, but she knew that they were both satisfied with the outcome. And a little impatient to find out what they would be attempting next. But that was a question Elizabeth didn't want to ask herself just at that moment.

Instead, she looked up through the sky and saw the two Loa. They were still wheeling and writhing around each other, but this time Elizabeth could see that one was neatly evading the other's probing teeth without returning the attack. It looked like some strange kind of stately dance, the object of which was to entwine as intricately as possible without ever touching. It was probably deeply symbolic of something or other, but just at that moment Elizabeth was overcome with just how beautiful it all looked.

They danced a little more, and then they were gone.

Such was life.

"Goodbye, Brierly," Elizabeth said softly.

## 17. December 1940, Strines

The village was in complete darkness that night, and almost complete silence. You might have thought that it was dead and deserted, a grey ghost village nestled in the crook of the valley's arms. But there were still plenty of people there. Over the ridge of the valley, there were occasional bass thumps and flashes of light, and every one caused a corresponding pounding in the chest of every villager. You might have mistaken it for thunder, if it hadn't been for the angry whine of engines in the air, and the occasionally golden arc of bullets spinning upwards in answer.

Inside the Sportsman, James Braddock had a candle and a bottle of brandy on the table in front of him. Thick curtains kept the light from escaping outside, but still he relied only on that single candle. He was old fashioned that way, he supposed. That way and many, many others.

"Mr Braddock," came a voice from the darkness.

His heart skipped, even though he knew.

"Isabella?"

The word escaped his lips before he could choke it back. Mrs Howkins stepped out into the candlelight with an unreadable look on her face. Neither of them needed to say anything. Instead she sat down opposite him and poured herself a small shot of brandy. A bomb dropped somewhere, out on Manchester, but neither of them looked.

"You know she's dead, don't you?" Mrs Howkins said eventually.

James was surprised: he had always assumed that she knew more than him, ever since he had first met her at the train station. That was the impression she liked to give, he assumed. It was almost disconcerting to discover there was something about which he knew more.

"She isn't dead."

Mrs Howkins cocked her head.

"I'm aware these matters begin to get a little metaphysical ..."

"She isn't dead," James grasped the brandy glass firmly, rapping it on the table once for emphasis. "She's part of the Loa. Can you really not see that?"

Mrs Howkins raised an eyebrow.

"She was taken by the Loa of vengeance. If she is still alive, I'm not sure any of us should see that as some kind of comfort, Mr Braddock."

"Vengeance?" James almost laughed. "You think Spinning Jenny became a spirit of vengeance?"

"Brierly gave power to every soul that the Loa had ever claimed. Don't you think they would have wanted to use that power? Isabella would have only been the first: she had tried to destroy the Loa, so it was only right it would have taken her first. But there would have been enough petty grievances there to alter her nature completely. You can't tell me you haven't felt her influence? She had hold of me even from before she was born. She has me even now."

James said nothing. It was ... it was too much. And yet just hearing the words made everything else click into place. Of course that was what the old woman thought. What other evidence did she have for how the world worked?

"Mrs Howkins," James said softly. "She was industry. She was the god of every factory, every machine that ever turned cog on cog. And then you forced her to change. Can't you see what you did? Every voice was given a voice. You made her a god of co-operation, and she has swam into the heart of this century. This isn't the age of vengeance, it is the age of democracy."

Outside, there was another dull thump as a bomb landed on Manchester. For a moment, the sky was cast in a sickly orange light. The moon shielded his eyes, and then looked down on the Earth again.

"So I see," Mrs Howkins replied drily.

James couldn't quite believe it.

"What do you think this is about if not democracy?" he asked.

Elizabeth wanted to answer, but even after eighty years she still hadn't learned the words to describe what she thought this was. She was here – she was at least willing to accept the evidence of her own eyes on that – but what that meant was open for debate. She had been in so many self-contradictory heres before that the word now had little meaning. Was this where her life was going? Was this history the one that was set out in stone from the steps she had taken so far? Even if it was, she had learned enough to know that meant very little.

"You don't know, do you?" Braddock asked, softly. "You've only just arrived. Have you come straight from 1854?"

Elizabeth didn't see the point in lying.

"I've been here a week," she told him, watching his face for a reaction. "When the Loa retreated, I was caught in the slipstream again. I must say, Mr Braddock, you seem to know a lot of events you were unconscious for. Who told you what happened. Who told you I would be visiting tonight?"

Braddock didn't answer, but his eyes flicked over her shoulder.

Elizabeth was still getting used to her shadows, and it was at moments like these that her inexperience showed: they leapt up from the floor, claws bared and spoiling for a fight. She could feel their excitement tainting her own thoughts, and it was only with the greatest of effort that she was able to stop herself setting them loose. They snarled and snapped at the edge of her control, straining like a pack of rabid dogs on the leash as the woman stepped out of the darkness towards them.

Then she gave them both a look, and they quickly shrank back into nothingness.

"I don't believe we've met," Elizabeth said crisply.

The woman smiled, as if she had only just remembered how.

"No. But your shadows know me, I think."

"You're who Isabella was working for."

"Isabella didn't know I was alive," the woman answered. "No-one does. You're the second person I've told. After Mr Braddock here. If you knew the right people to talk to, you could cause a lot of trouble for me."

"The right people?" Elizabeth said quietly. "You mean the Great Houses?"

The woman didn't give the slightest sign of surprise.

"Amongst others," she replied. "Faction Paradox enjoyed pricking the egos of the greater powers. Which is why they conspired to destroy us. Any one of many would gladly finish the job."

Elizabeth planted her feet firmly on the ground, and worked her way from her neck down, tensing and relaxing each muscle she found along the way. She was an old woman, but she wasn't senile just yet. She could tell when the wind changed and a fight was getting ready to blow in. Her shadows might be unwilling, but she had never had the luxury of assistance before anyway. She could and would fight her own battles if it came to it.

"I don't see how I come to figure in your revenge," Elizabeth growled.

The woman's eyes widened.

"Oh!" she said, with surprise that sounded genuine. "You don't. You don't figure in any of it. It was never about you. And nor was it about revenge. We lost our home. In her own youthful, simplistic way, Isabella was just trying to make a new one. Somewhere we could regroup and rebuild. Let me reassure you that it was entirely accidental that you were involved in any of it."

Somehow, Elizabeth didn't find that particularly reassuring.

"If this is your idea of an apology," Elizabeth said dryly, "it leaves something to be desired."

The woman smiled thinly.

"I'm not here to apologise, Mrs Howkins," she said. "I'm here to recruit."

If she expected Elizabeth to show any surprise, the stranger was to be disappointed. Elizabeth had lived long enough to come to the conclusion that there was nothing that somebody somewhere wouldn't have the sheer brass neck to ask you to do if they thought it would benefit them somehow.

"Isabella made many mistakes," the woman continued, perhaps taking her silence for consent, "but she was right about one thing. Faction Paradox need a new home. Isabella was young and inexperienced, but she nearly found one for us. You have a unique understanding of the situation: I'm sure you would be better placed to find an outcome that would be acceptable for all."

"What makes you think I would try?"

"You have already shown the ultimate dedication to paradox," the woman said with a shrug. "You already have a shadow weapon. And you have good reason to want to change the path that your history has taken. Why wouldn't I think you would try, Mrs Howkins?"

Elizabeth's shadows trembled in anticipation. She could feel their eagerness, their natural pull to obey this woman's commands. She had power, then: that much would have been obvious even without the shadows. And a power that she was not used to having to demonstrate – the stranger's shadow lay still and flat on the ground, despite the flickering candlelight. Elizabeth could tell it would fight just as fiercely as her own if it was required. She was, then, someone that it would be better not to have as an enemy.

And she was right, of course. What had she come out of this life with, in the end? Her Bill had still died, and to replace her revenge she had the knowledge that it had been herself that had been to blame. She had sacrificed him to the greater good, and now where was the good for her in any of this? The only thing she had now that she hadn't before was an understanding: history could change – history could be changed – and the world would still survive.

The stranger raised an eyebrow. She was young and powerful, and used to things happening the way she said they should. Yes, best not to have her as an enemy. But Elizabeth had never claimed to have lived her life for the best.

"No, thank you," Elizabeth answered as evenly as she could.

She felt her own shadows bristle, but they were young.

The woman's didn't move.

"No?" she echoed, as if not quite understanding the word.

"You change the course of history if you wish, madam," Elizabeth told her quite firmly. "You pick the shape of it that suits your greater good by all means. I've seen people try, and I've seen them fail. There is no greater good. Only that which the greatest number think is for the good. You can try to tell them how it should be if you want, but the voice of the many will always be louder than that of the one. Goodbye, madam: I have to go now. I need to find my way back to my husband."

Elizabeth didn't wait for the reaction.

"Mrs Howkins –" she heard Braddock say.

Elizabeth prodded her shadows into action and they leapt out beneath her. Obsidian claws flashed in the moonlight and cut a hole in the fabric of the wall ahead. Elizabeth stepped through it without ever looking back.

James watched as the hole in the wall of his pub closed up like water finding its level. After a second, it was impossible to tell there had ever been anything there except shadow. He looked to the woman beside him, but her face was unreadable as she stared across the room. Outside the window, he could still hear the bombs dropping. He had been told that none would land on Strines, but then who could say with any certainty that what had happened before would happen again?

"Does she make it back to him?" James asked.

The woman didn't answer.

"Well that went as well as could be expected," she said instead, dusting down the folds of her clothes as if preparing for a journey. "No matter when you talk to that woman, she always thinks she knows best."

"So there's no other option, then?" James asked.

His hand reached for the brandy on the table.

"The pocket universe was always a luxury, Mr Braddock," the woman answered, clapping her hands together. "The Faction will just have to make do with what we have. Now, Mr Braddock: open sesame."

And the tunnel to nowhere in James' bio-data burst open again.

The woman stepped inside and disappeared.